A Tasty Dish

An Everheart Brothers of Texas Romance

Kelly Cain

TULE
PUBLISHING

Dedication

To my sweet Yuiza Marie who loves to read
as much as her oma.

And to my daughters, Diamond and Kamryn, because
they're my everything.

Acknowledgements

As always, this writing journey wouldn't be the same or as enjoyable without my book besties. Special thanks to Amanda, Jamie, and Bianca for revision help. You keep me from turning in hot messes to my editor and I appreciate that so much.

Thank you, Kristin, for hosting ARWA writing sprints nearly every day during NaNoWriMo. You drug me over the finish line, and I didn't even notice until it was over. Well-played, you.

Many thanks to Tasha and the Wordmakers community for not only hosting sprints, but for all the love, learning, and support. This is a community like no other and I'm so proud to call it home.

So much image and branding help came from K. Stirling. She saved me from putting subpar graphics out there (Well mostly. Sometimes I posted without passing it by her and she didn't hesitate to point out my shortcomings in that area. I *think* I've learned my lesson). She is also a phenomenal author, and you should totally buy her books.

Ongoing appreciation to my phenomenal agent, Amy, who is my biggest cheerleader and I'm so lucky to have her in my corner.

The professionals at Tule makes it easy to work with them which in turn makes it so much easier for me to write. Special thanks to my intuitive editor, Sinclair.

Visit Kelly's website at kellycainauthor.com and connect with her on BookBub.

Join Kelly's newsletter for inside info and exclusive content – Between The Sheets.

CHAPTER ONE

When things were before.

THE CLUB IS dark and the music loud, the beat reverberating through my bones. Indieknot is on stage playing a vaguely familiar alternative pop/rock tune. It's not my normal music scene, but it's catchy so maybe I'll check it out later. Weed still isn't legal in Texas like back home, but I recognize the sticky, musky smell as soon as I step through the door. I guess anything goes during South by Southwest.

I crowd Joy's back as she weaves through the tightly packed throng toward the band on the center stage. This is absolutely the opposite of my idea of fun, but I'm not here for fun. I need financing for my next project and this is where the woman is who can give it to me. Sometimes you have to sacrifice.

We round the stage and Joy shows her backstage credentials when we're met with a wall of security in the form of a tall brick of a man. He scans it and lets her through, but when I try to follow, he stands in my way.

Joy backtracks. "She's with me."

"No such thing. Everyone needs a pass to get back here."

I cross my arms and give him my meanest stare, straightening my spine. It usually works for me because I have the

1

height and defined arms to back it up. This guy though? Nah, he's not phased. Not even a little bit. Matter of fact, his lips twitch begging off a smile.

"Everyone. And I mean every single one, needs a pass to get back here."

I frown and lean against the wall. This asshole.

Joy peaks around the security guy. "Stay there. I'll be right back."

"Yup." I mean, I guess I could leave but what would be the point? I'm beginning to run out of options. I only need one yes, but I have to be able to ask the question first.

I stand there a few more minutes when my phone buzzes in my back pocket. I wore jeans because South by Southwest is mostly casual and that's typically my wardrobe anyway. Either that or shorts or sweats depending on if I'm shooting or not. One of the things I love most about this film business is the casualness of it. When shooting, it's almost like the grubbier, the better. You're working long days and doing all sort of dirty tasks either on set or location, so it's better to be comfortable than not. That's even on a big production like the ones I worked on for my father. Definitely true on my little indie films. Or will be if I get this financing.

The text from Joy holds no joy for me. *She's not here but is expected soon.*

Okay. What should I do?

She responds right back. *Do you want to wait? I think she'll be able to get you back here, but I don't know anyone else.*

Yeah, I guess so. What choice do I have?

I'm sorry, Kasi.

I tap out: *NP.*

Going to my father isn't an option. Not after what happened last time. I'm not sure I'll ever talk to him again. Definitely won't ever trust him. Tariq said the loss of his investment wasn't a big deal, but letting down my friend since elementary, especially over some bullshit, hasn't set well with me. I need this next gig so he gets his back in spades, and I restore my reputation.

So, for now, I'll manage this musty club and see what's what. Because Joy has been loyal and earned my trust, I'll follow her anywhere. She dreamed of becoming a lawyer since forever. Tariq and I are lucky our best friend decided to become our agent too.

I scrub my hands across my face. I'm not wearing makeup tonight, so no need to worry about smearing anything thankfully. I look down at my worn Chuck Taylors and am grateful they're comfortable for standing. Not so much for walking long distances, but we took a rideshare from the hotel, and it dropped us off fairly close.

When I look back up, there's a guy staring at me. Pretty good-looking but also pretty full of himself. I can tell these things. I've had plenty of experience the way I grew up. This guy is dressed to impress. Who? I'm not sure. He's wearing an expensively cut light-beige shirt that screams tailoring just for him, and brown trousers fitting around his trim waist.

He walks right up to me, a cloudy brown drink in his hand. "Hey, what's up?"

Not the greatest opening as pick-up lines go. I've had plenty of experience with those too. I think the worst one was, "Here I am, baby. What were your other two wishes?" Yeah, okay, bruh. Hold on while I drop my panties. I give him a flat smile. "Hi. Nothing much."

Doesn't leave him a lot to work with. The truth is, he may be smoking hot, but I have other business to attend, and I don't have time for a one-night stand type of situation this trip. There's too much riding on me getting this funding.

"You here for South by or do you live here?" He takes a sip of his drink and his eyes take me all the way in now that he's moved closer. He's seeing a hazelnut-brown-skinned Black woman with long, auburn cornrows and intense brown eyes. If he dares to venture lower, he'll take in a curvy figure with plenty of top and bottom. I'm a stone-cold smokeshow and he need not apply. He's fine, but not fine enough to temp me away from by business. I have plenty of men barking up that particular tree, and I don't trust a one of them.

I look into his alarmingly blue eyes, the color of the salty depths of the ocean, even in this low-lit club. "I don't live here."

"I do."

I nod because what else is there for me to do? Does he want a gold star? Next, he'll ask where I'm from.

"You here for business or pleasure?"

Okay, got me on that one. "Business. All business." I offer a slight smile and raise my eyebrows.

He takes a sip of his drink. "Okay, I got the message. It was nice to meet you." His spine is straight, and his head held high when he turns away from me. He's not worried about finding someone else tonight. I like his confidence.

I open my mouth to say, "You too," when he pulls out his backstage credentials and takes a step toward my old friend, brick wall. Instead, I say, "Hey, not so fast. I'm sorry for being rude. What's your name?"

He looks around like I couldn't possibly be talking to him.

Yeah, I know. Complete one-eighty. I can't miss an opportunity though.

He blinks.

"I'm Kasi Blythewood." I hold out my hand.

"Declan Everheart." He moves his drink to his left hand and reaches out to take my hand in a strong shake. Yeah, this guy has confidence like nobody's business. And why shouldn't he? Taller than my five foot ten inches. I'd say around six one or two. Midnight-black hair, cut into an expensive disconnected undercut with a matching perfectly trimmed beard. Clear olive skin and those eyes. He's not wanting for dates, I'm sure.

"I'm an indie filmmaker in from LA." There, I saved him the need to ask.

"Cool. Are you related to Reggie Blythewood?"

"Um, yeah. He's my father." Dammit to hell. Is there nowhere I can go without that man following? Time to change the subject. "So, what do you do here in Austin, Declan? You in the business?"

He leans on the wall next to me and turns his whole body into me. There's a foot between us, but it's an intimate move. "No, not at all. I'm a chef at my father's restaurant. Everheart Bar and Fine Dining."

Now it's my turn to ask because I've heard of that restaurant. You can't be planning a documentary about food and not know about the Michelin-starred restaurants. "Your dad is Flynn Everheart."

"One and the same." He downs the rest of his drink like a champ, and smirks. Clearly, he's a lot prouder of his pedigree than I am of mine.

"That's a bit of a coincidence. My documentary is about global cuisine."

He quirks a perfectly shaped eyebrow.

I take a moment to ponder if he gets them threaded or waxed. Probably waxed.

"That is a coincidence. Can I get you a drink?"

"What are you having?"

He looks at his empty glass. "It was peach-mint kombucha. They brew it here locally."

"So, like kombucha and vodka?"

He smiles and shakes his head. "No, just kombucha."

I wonder if there's a story there. Plenty of my childhood friends are on the wagon, and they don't drink at all. If they do, they fall off. Then again, maybe he only wanted kombucha tonight. "If you're getting another one, I'll take one too. I'd love to taste locally brewed kombucha."

"Be right back."

He's gone maybe thirty seconds before Joy comes from behind the security guy. "Sorry, my stomach is not agreeing with me. What did we eat?"

Ha, what didn't we eat? There's a goddamn food truck on every corner down here. Multiple ones. "Maybe it was the Maine lobster truck. Or the Peruvian food. Perhaps the South Philly cheese steaks." The longing in my voice is obvious. That Peruvian food truck was everything. I intend to make Peru my first stop when we film.

"Don't remind me." She holds up one hand and presses

the other over her stomach. "Seriously. I don't want to remember."

I chuckle to myself. "I know, girl, it's hard to pass up all this deliciousness. Yolo, right?" I wince at the saying that I never use. What's gotten into me? "You ready to go home? I can try to meet Melissa another time." I need this meeting, but my friend means more to me.

"I don't want you to miss her, but I'm not sure I can stay too much longer without causing a scene. I've already spent way too much time in the restroom. I'd tell you to stay, but you won't be able to get back there without me talking to her first. Ugh." Joy bends over and takes several breaths.

"Don't worry about me. If you can make it back to the hotel by yourself, I think I may have an in."

"Are you sure, Kasi? I can stay if you need me."

"A hundred percent. I'll see you later. Text me if it gets worse."

She pecks me on the cheek then heads for the exit. I sure hope this Declan guy can do something for me. I know what Melissa looks like if I can just get back there.

As if I conjured him, the man himself returns carrying two capped bottles of the same cloudy liquid he had before plus large glasses. He hands one to me, and I pour it into one of the glasses. He then waits expectantly.

I take a sip. "Yeah, it's really good." It is, but no better than any I can get in LA. California is the produce capital of these here United States. You can't beat it. But this is good, and I take a deeper drink. Very sour, but somehow still smooth. "Thanks, by the way."

"You're welcome. I'm happy you like it."

"If you're a chef, what are you doing up here exactly? Are you a big Indieknot fan?" I point at the band walking back out to the stage for another set.

"I wouldn't say big, but they're cool. I really like their song, 'Mad to Cook.'" The twinkle in his eye brightens and he grins.

I try not to roll my eyes. "Ha, that's cute."

"I'm actually here with my dad. He's backstage talking business with some folks."

I take another taste of my drink and grimace a bit at the bite. "If you're both here, who's running the restaurant?"

A shadow passes over his face, but he recovers quickly. "My brother, Knox. He's in charge when Dad isn't there."

"Oh, well I hear older brothers can be a pain." I'm an only child so I have no idea.

"I'm actually the oldest so let's hope not. Knox is the youngest. Weston's my middle brother, and he's the pastry chef." He leans back against the wall and takes a long pull of his drink.

Silence sort of sits there between us. I have no idea what to say, but the fact that his baby brother is second in command has to be a sore spot. That explains the shadow earlier.

"It's not a big deal. Knox is the more talented chef. He's keen with business too, but that's my strong suit, which is why I'm here with Dad." He shrugs.

I'm not sure if he's trying to convince me or himself.

"I'm sure your father values your opinion which is why you're here instead of your brother."

He draws his lips into a thin line. "Look, I don't want you to get the wrong impression. My brothers mean everything to me. We're very close, and I always want the best for them. Matter of fact, Knox just got accepted into a cooking challenge. He needs me and Weston on his team and we're going out to San Francisco next month to compete."

"Oh cool. What's the competition? Maybe I've heard of it."

"It's called *Restaurant Family Feud*. It's a television show."

"Yes, I know. I love that show. I've binged both seasons. The presenters are the best. They make it really interesting plus I love seeing the chefs compete. I like the home cook shows too, but the professional chefs take it to another level. That's really awesome."

To say he's stunned would be an understatement. His eyes are like saucers and those beautiful full lips of his are parted into an *O* shape. He shakes himself to recover. "I had no idea. Although maybe I should have considering the prize. I probably need to watch it myself before the competition."

I can't help but sound slightly incredulous. "You've never watched? You were just going in blind?"

"Like I said, it's for my brother. He wants his own restaurant away from Dad, although my father doesn't realize that yet. It's complicated."

I nod because this sounds like the same family drama I've been dealing with. "Yeah, I know about complicated family stuff."

"Do you want to talk about it?"

I release a mirthful bark. "Not even a little bit."

"Okay, I understand. We just met like five minutes ago.

Doesn't matter that I poured my heart out to you." He flashes a toothless smile and bats his lush eyelashes.

I observe him another moment. "You're not as cute as you think you are." I take another sip.

He moves a little closer and looks down at me over my raised glass. "We both know that's not even a little true."

I can't do anything but laugh. This dude is tripping, but he's not wrong. "Whatever."

"You never said why you're hanging out against this wall."

"I'm supposed to be meeting a possible financier here, but this guy"—I shoot a thumb the big man's way—"won't let me back there."

"Why didn't you say so?" He takes his pass out and holds in it the hand with his drink, then reaches for my hand with his other.

"I don't think it'll work. My friend's…"

The guard moves aside and doesn't give me a second look.

"Okay, never mind. I guess you have more clout than my friend."

"It's not me, darling. But what I'm really wondering is why you weren't able to do the same thing. Given who your father is."

I purse my lips and think about how I want to answer. "I don't like to use Dad's name for anything. I plan to make it in this business on my own merits." Especially since he's already sabotaged me. Proving him wrong will be the ultimate revenge.

"Well, that's just—"

The look I give him freezes his mouth, mid-sentence. "Be very careful, Declan. You don't know me like that."

"You're right. I'm sure you have your reasons. Meanwhile, let's see if we can find your contact."

I'm glad he corrected himself. Even though I have no interest in him, it would have been a shame to cuss him out after I finally got back here.

CHAPTER TWO

When he was smitten.

S OMEHOW DECLAN CONVINCED me to have a midnight snack, and that's how we ended up here, standing outside the door of Everheart Bar and Fine Dining. The parking lot is packed even at this hour, but Declan pulled his car into a spot with his name on it. Convenient, that.

"I hope we can find a table."

Declan smirks and walks through the door being held open by an attendant. "Don't worry, I know someone." He grabs my hand and pulls me along.

His long frame moves through the space like he owns the place. Which, I guess technically, he kind of does. We pass a small bar near the front door where patrons probably imbibe while waiting for their tables. As we head the way of the open kitchen, I marvel at the rich leather and wood booths, and gold fixtures. This place screams, "Look at me, I'm rich." I've been in quite a few places like this with my parents back home and abroad, but it isn't my scene as an adult. I prefer the surprise hole-in-the-walls where real cuisine is born. Food is my thing, second only to filmmaking. My documentary will combine both. Think Anthony Bourdain meets *Full Tilt Boogie*.

The kitchen is nice with an open hearth that takes up an entire wall. That's what really sets this place apart. "That hearth is pretty cool."

"It was Knox's idea. One of his greatest." He pulls out a chair at a small table bordering the kitchen, the chef's table I assume. It isn't quite inside, but very close.

A woman dressed in black pants and shirt with a white apron comes over to greet us. "Hello, Chef. What can I get you?"

Declan turns to me. "Do you need a menu, or shall I order for us?"

"Just this once since it's your restaurant, but don't make this a habit."

He leans in, whispering in my ear, "Are you saying there will be other opportunities?"

His breath on my ear, cool and confident, does tingly things to my lower stomach. I move away in a hurry. "Let's not get ahead of ourselves. It depends on how good a job you do on this order."

He laughs and turns to the waitress. "Shay, let's start with farofa and sea scallops, and filet mignon with crispy polentas and asparagus for entrees." He rotates my way again. "Would you like something to drink?"

I shake my head. "Water's fine." Even though we are getting along well, this is still business for me. Declan has a way in to what I need. I want a clear head to keep it straight. Turns out Melissa never showed up, but Declan was perfectly willing to keep me company. We talked more about the competition coming up and the plans for my documentary. We also discussed his mother dying when he was young and how much he missed her. We didn't talk about my family at all, but we did loosely discuss my childhood and what it was like to grow up in the bright lights of Hollyweird. His nickname, not mine. It doesn't bother me because I really grew up in Laurel Canyon, and now I live in a cottage on the beach in Santa Monica. I understand his meaning though.

When it became obvious that Melissa wasn't coming, Declan offered to see me home. He introduced me to his father since he needed to let him know he'd have to get alternate transportation. Flynn didn't look put out in the least. He was holding court with several men and women and didn't look like his night would be ending soon. I had the impression that one or two of those people around him wouldn't mind taking him home. He was definitely a handsome older man but looked nothing like his son, other than in height. He was loud and gregarious, and completely in charge. And perhaps looking for an investment opportunity.

"Water for me too, Shay. Thanks."

A good sign he thanks the waitress. Even if his father may be willing to invest, I couldn't spend time with him if he mistreats the waitstaff. I'd seen my father do it enough growing up and it makes me cringe every time I think about it. There's no need. We get it. You're a famous film producer. Everyone should be bowing. Blah blah blah. Declan seems just about as arrogant, but at least he has manners going for him.

Before I can open my mouth to comment on our order, another tall, pretty Everheart comes our way. It's obvious this is one of Declan's brothers because they share most of their features. This brother is about two or three inches taller than Declan though.

"Hi, Dec. Who's this?" His smile is friendly, and there is a sweetness to his voice and manner. Especially for such a big man.

"Weston, this is Kasi Blythewood. Kasi, this is my brother."

I wave because his hands are covered in flour. "Nice to meet you, Weston. Your brother tells me you're the pastry chef here."

"My brother has told you the truth." His eyes twinkle and his mouth curves into a broad smile. "Can I make you something special for dessert?"

Declan looks at me with his own twinkling eyes. "What do you say?"

Oh, the pressure is on. "Sure, but why not surprise me?"

Weston claps and flour drifts into the air. "That's awesome. Any allergies?"

"None, that I'm aware of. And I love everything. I haven't met a morsel I didn't like."

"Challenge accepted." He smiles wider somehow and turns to go back to his station.

"Wow, what a nice brother you have. You two look alike, but night-and-day demeanors."

He slaps his hand over his heart. "You wound me, madame. I am the opposite of nice?"

My face heats because that's not what I meant. "You're fine. I just meant that he's very sweet and doesn't try to hide it."

He smiles and picks up the water Shay just set down.

"It's okay. You're not the first person to notice the difference. Weston has a kind disposition, something he inherited from our mother. I'm more like Dad, and Knox is a blend of the two. It's funny how genetics work, considering she didn't have a chance to be too much of an influence on us. If anything, since I had her the longest, you'd think I'd be the sweet one." He shivers as though that would be a bad thing. Perhaps for Declan, it is.

"I agree on the genetics front. I'm definitely more like my mom. She's all no-nonsense and blunt. I get my passion from my father though. Even though he gets out of hand with it sometimes. I hope to be much better."

"I can already tell you are."

I roll my eyes because what else is there to do? This dude has only known me five minutes and already telling me about myself. Men, it's a helluva drug. "You just met me."

"Sorry, I didn't mean it like that. I usually have a sense about people. That's all. But you're right, I don't know you. I hope that'll change though."

I smirk and shake my head. This guy has game written all over him. "I'll only be here the week."

"A week is a long time to get to know someone. Given the chance."

"Don't you have a restaurant to be in? You do actually work here, right?"

He chuckles. "Yeah, no doubt. But I'm not here all the time. Plus, my schedule can be flexible sometimes. A perk for working with Dad. Sometimes that's a curse too."

Shay brings out the farofa, but another Everheart trails her with our sea scallops and sets them on the table. "I thought you were with Dad." He favors his brothers, but his voice is surprisingly steely. I expected a pretty tone to go along with the face.

"I was. Now I'm not."

"I noticed."

I clear my throat and Declan swings his gaze my way. "If you haven't guessed by now, this is my baby brother, Knox. He's put out because he has to work so hard."

Knox's eye color changes in an instant. I've never seen anything like it. "I'm sorry my brother is so rude. I suppose you'll get used to it if you spend any time with him."

I laugh because their dynamic is ridiculous.

The corner of Knox's mouth quirks before he can help himself. "My rude brother forgot to introduce you."

"I'm Kasi. Declan and I met earlier today. And I'll only be here the week for South by Southwest so he'll have very limited time to show me his rudeness."

"Well, I hope you enjoy the city while you're here. I'd say stay away from Declan if you want to have fun, but I can't lie. He'll show you a good time and be an excellent guide." He winks at me and goes back the way he came. Do people really wink anymore? I can't help but laugh.

"That's our Knox. Always the charmer." His face is smooth, but there's a harshness to Declan's eyes. Does he love his brother? Or does he resent him? They were only together two minutes, so I shouldn't judge, but I am curious.

"You don't seem to like each other very much."

He huffs and straightens in his seat. "My, you are blunt. Thanks for the fair warning."

"Just an observation."

The smell of the sea wafts up to my nose, and my stomach grumbles. I can't believe I'm hungry after everything else I ate today. Speaking of which, I check my phone to make sure Joy hasn't texted me again. The message log is empty.

Declan turns my way and leans into me. "Knox has a complicated relationship with Dad. He has more pressure on him than me or Weston. I wouldn't mind more responsibility, but it's not my choice. I think Knox resents us for not having to deal with Dad on the same level. But make no mistake, I love my brothers more than life, and I would protect them at all costs."

"I really didn't mean anything by it. It's none of my business anyway." I have a nasty habit of stepping over boundaries. One of these days I'm going to do something about it. Apparently today is not that day. "Do you really think your brother would leave if your team wins the restaurant?"

He frowns and lifts his glass of water. "In a heartbeat."

CHAPTER THREE

When he shows her a good time.

J OY GROANS WHEN her phone pings and cracks her eyes
open just enough to read the text. "Melissa is still interested. She got held up last night and never made it to the club."
Joy is sprawled across her bed in our hotel room, looking
none the better even after a full night's sleep. She moans, and
turns over, facing me, her golden-brown skin ashen, and her
hazel eyes bleak.

"Are you sure I can't convince you to go to urgent care?"

"I'll be fine. I've never let a little food poisoning keep me
down."

I shake my head and look over at the dresser. It's covered
with every remedy I could think of. When I pulled myself
out of bed early this morning, I went upstairs and had some
breakfast, then walked the few blocks to the pharmacy. This
time change is messing with me like nobody's business. "I
can't make you go, but I can stay here today and monitor
you."

"Please no. I just want to sleep, Kas. You'll mother-hen
me all day and that won't be good for either one of us. Just
go." She sits up, does a bit of a heaving motion, then runs
into the bathroom.

Yuck. She's right. Me staying here will definitely not be good for either of us. "You okay in there?"

"Yes, just go."

"Fine." I check the mirror and make sure everything's covered. I've thrown on some blue sportswear—a performance tank and some leggings, plus trainers. We'll be disc golfing at the park this morning, and I've noticed these hills in Austin don't play. Plus, it's already in the high eighties, so I'm definitely dressed for comfort. I put some last-minute gel on my scalp between the braids and apply some sunscreen and a little lip gloss. Don't want to mess up all this fine skin down in this Texas heat. "I'm leaving, Joy. I'll check on you in an hour."

She groans through the door. "How about I text you if there's a problem? I hope to be blissfully asleep in an hour."

"Okay, whatever." We both know I'll ignore that request. "Bye."

The Austin humidity is a sorry bitch. Even early in the morning. Declan has us covered though. I reach in the cooler for a cold water nestled next to kombucha, grapes, and cheese, and take a deep swig, then look out over the huge park. There's plenty of shade here on the disc golf course but walking to the first hole from the parking lot was a sweaty chore. "Whew, how do you people live like this?"

Declan shrugs. He's dressed down a bit today although he is more casual chic to my just plain casual. He's wearing distressed jeans that probably cost an arm and a leg, and a plain mint-green T-shirt that's hugging his muscles in all the right places. There's a crown tattooed around his right forearm and other tattoos peeking out from underneath his short sleeves.

"It's hot already. And so humid. How do you stand it down here?"

"I've never lived anywhere else. You get used to it. But this is not humid. Maybe compared to LA, but you should drive three hours toward the coast. If you think this is humid, you wouldn't survive Houston."

"Yeah, remind me never to visit Houston. Although that would be a shame because I hear they have some great food down there. Very diverse." The swamps of Louisiana are also on my list to film, but I definitely won't venture there during the hot months.

Declan cocks an eyebrow. "We have great food right here, ma'am."

"You're right, you do. Your restaurant has some great traditional food."

"Ouch. On the scale of backhanded compliments, that's got to be a solid six."

"I'm sorry. Everything that came out of that kitchen was delicious. Really superb and I'm not complaining at all. I saw flashes of originality on my plate as well as some dishes passing me by, but not a lot. Weston's Canelés de Bordeaux. That was the highlight of the evening, but I bet it's not even on the menu, is it?"

"It is not, but crème brûlée is. Like every other steakhouse." His tone is slightly resentful.

He picks a driver out of the huge disc bag belonging to his brother. Weston must think he's a professional or something. I'm not gonna lie though—I have serious heart-eyes for a couple of them. More than a couple.

"Do you have input on the menu? Or is it all your father and Knox?"

"If it were up to Knox, all we'd serve is pasta. Dad won't even allow one dish."

"That's really sad."

"It's his restaurant. That's why Knox is trying to open his own. Dad will never change. However, the farofa was my idea. It took some serious convincing, but he finally let me add it. Plus, the gobi aloo, the broccoli with lemon almond butter, and the baked fennel."

I stop in my tracks. "Dude, you do have something going for yourself. Those were all the dishes I was thinking of. You don't want your own restaurant?"

He pauses before speaking, his eyes momentarily cloudy. "Not at all. I'm fully committed to Everheart. Dad is a brilliant chef and I'm lucky to learn from him."

I offer a small smile but that definitely isn't what I wanted to hear. I know too well how easy it is to get stuck in the shadow of a successful parent. To take what meager offerings they give you while they suck your talent dry. It's too bad because Declan has a good mind for originality, and it's being wasted in his father's restaurant.

Instead of giving him my much-earned advice, I simply nod and smile. I barely know this guy, and it is totally none of my business.

He leans the bag my way. "Anyway. Come back in July and see how you're feeling."

"No, thanks. LA in July is much nicer."

"Is that an invitation?"

"Don't you have a competition or something to win?"

He smiles and looks at the map on a big rock, then squints into the distance to find the basket. "Do you see it?"

I can't help myself and giggle my ass off. "It's right there." Hole number one is usually the easiest on the course. I lean into him so we have the same line-of-sight, and point. "See?" His skin is warm and dewy, and I pull back because that skin is doing some things to my system.

He leans in a bit more than the situation calls for, reconnecting our arm hair. "I told you this wasn't my game." He shrugs, then puts a hand out toward the line. "You want to show me how it's done?"

"Oh, I'll show you alright." This can go one of two ways. I'm not trying to pigeonhole men, but in my estimation, they don't take instruction well. If Declan really wants me to show him what's what, I'll be happy to. Otherwise, this could be a long morning because I'm about to show all the way out. I know no other speed. Winding up, I do a couple of skips and hops, then let that sucker go. "Shit, wide right."

To his credit, Declan doesn't smirk although he has every right considering how I've been pumping up my skills. "Those were some impressive moves though." He measures the distance with his eyes, then looks down at the disc. "I'm just gonna throw it, then you can tell me what I did wrong." He launches it, and the disc lands about five feet in front of us. He shrugs and looks back at me with puppy eyes.

Man, I love this dude's confidence. Too much. "You really want to know?"

"Of course. Weston has tried, but I don't play enough to remember from one time to the next."

I dig through the bag and pick another driver. This one

is a little lighter than the one he chose. Next, I stand behind him, putting as much distance as I can manage and still be able to direct him. "Okay, so look how I'm holding the disc. Most people usually hold it like a Frisbee, but that won't work out here. Not with these discs. Now you try." I hand him the disc.

God love him, he tries his best to mimic my finger placement, but it just looks wrong.

After taking a deep breath—because I know what's coming next and I need to get myself together, this man is just too fine—I adjust his hand on the disc. As anticipated, sweat breaks out on my forehead, and it's nothing to do with the heat this time. This is the moment of my undoing. I can feel it. I'm gonna need Mr. Everheart between my thighs before I go. It is what it is. "Now, throw it."

Declan launches the disc again, and this time it sails to the sky, but chomps up a good amount of distance before landing. He really put some muscle behind it. His is nowhere near the basket, but a valiant effort.

Mine is closer to the basket, but not as close as I'd like, so I don't pull my putter yet. Declan's carrying the monstrosity of a bag, so I blindly explore inside and pull out a nice mid-range disc. It should do the trick. We split apart because our discs are nowhere near each other. "Do you want to wait until I throw, then I can come help you?"

"Sure."

It's difficult to tell if he's enjoying himself or not. His expression is smooth, and his posture is as erect as usual, even with that heavy bag. I admire his muscles while I walk to my destination and nearly trip over a branch. *Get it together, Kasi.* He's fine, but not break-your-neck fine. Okay, maybe, but I got shit to do, and zero time for traction.

After throwing my disc right near the basket, I backtrack to where Declan's standing. He watches me the whole way, and I recognize the heat in his eyes. I'm not dressed in anything special, just more workout gear, but it's tight and accentuates my healthy curves in the most positive light.

"You ready?"

His lips pull up slightly, and he responds from under hooded eyes. "Past ready."

It's clear neither of us are talking about disc golf anymore.

"Okay, champ, let's see what you got."

This time Declan does smirk. He fiddles with the disc a few minutes, then finally holds it out for inspection.

"Better, but here." I adjust his thumb just so, and I promise, there should not be that much heat in just a thumb. Fuck me. If I make it through eighteen holes, it will be the second coming of Jesus, because it'll take more than a miracle.

He throws the disc. It lands somewhere behind a tree, and we move on. I'm carrying the mini cooler, so I reach in for another water because I need to cool down. There's so much I should be concentrating on, and jumping into bed with Declan Everheart really ought to be somewhere lower on the list. But here we are.

One more throw and his disc finally makes it near the basket. He walks over, grinning like he's not all the way over par, and sets the bag near my feet.

"Good job, buddy." I laugh and reach in and rummage

for the putters. Weston has the bag organized well, but there are so many, it's hard to pluck one out without really looking. I finally find a couple to get the job done, and hand one to Declan.

He studies it, and shrugs, then flips it into the basket.

Okay, so he's more a fine motor skills kind of guy. Good to know. I flush thinking about how I can put those skills to use, then toss my disc in the general direction of the basket. We're so close, it sails in easily. Thankfully because my mind was definitely not on that basket.

"My eyes are up here, Kasi." He grins and picks up the bag, but heat radiates off his body.

I bite my lip, redirecting my thoughts, because all I can think about is how I can pencil Declan Everheart in for a good screw before I go.

CHAPTER FOUR

When he realizes she don't play.

I HAVE JUST enough time to jump in the shower and get myself together. The hot water beats down on my shoulders and loosens the muscles I overworked this morning. If I'm feeling it, I know Declan has to be. I touch the shower cap to ensure my braids are still covered, then soap up the hand towel and get to work cleansing the dirt and sweat from this morning's adventure.

When I step out, I wrap a towel around me and go to the closet for clothes.

Joy is dressed and ready, eyes bright, and skin glowing again, no longer sick. "You have fifteen minutes to get it together or we'll be late."

"Dang, how long was I in the shower?"

"Seems like an hour, but however long, I can't use the mirrors to touch up my makeup. They're all fogged."

"My bad, girl. Let me see if I can wipe one down."

She puts up her hand to stop me. "You just get dressed. I'll figure out the mirror situation."

I turn back to the closet and parse out my wardrobe, separating bottoms from tops, hesitating. Maybe I should have at least brought a sundress. I finally select a pair of black trousers and a blue silk top. Blue makes up more than half my wardrobe so no surprise there. When I hold the blouse up to my skin, I'm reminded of Declan and those piercing eyes of his.

Shake it off, Kasi. Remember why you're here.

After slipping my clothes on, I apply a little mascara and lip gloss in the mirror behind the television. I don't know why Joy couldn't have used this one, even if it is a bit awkward. When I'm done, I go over to my messenger bag and look inside. I catalog my presentation consisting of my treatment and budget. Plus, stick my laptop inside in case Melissa needs more information.

Joy's at the door, holding it open. "Let's get a move on."

"Okay, bossy. I'm coming." I pull the strap over my shoulder and follow her down the hall to the elevators. "You're looking back to normal, thankfully."

"Thankfully is right. My pants are practically falling off me. Another day, and I would've needed a new wardrobe."

"I'm glad. You had me worried for a minute."

"Well, get used to it. Your time is coming."

"Pardon?" Does she know something I don't?

"When you get this money. And you will get this money. You'll be off around the world trying all kinds of cuisine. You may think you have an iron stomach, but I'm here to tell you, food poisoning is no joke."

My skin turns cold. "Don't even put that on me, Joy. Like seriously, don't let that shit out in the universe. Take it back."

She laughs her way into the elevator and pushes the button. "Okay, I take it back."

I wish I had a smudge stick right about now. "I feel like you just put some bad juju on me or something." I shudder.

"You been down here three days and already think you know something about juju. Girl, please."

"Hey, I saw some cool stuff on Sixth Street when Declan and I were sightseeing."

She purses her lips and pinches the bottom one between her fingers. I know the inquisition is about to start, but I'm ready for her. "Sooooooo, Declan, huh?"

I shrug, hoping it looks more casual than I feel. "What about him?"

"You tell me. I mean, I know I've been in a sickness haze the last couple nights, but you've been coming back at a decent hour soooooo..."

"You have a lot of *so-ing* going on. There's nothing to tell. He thinks his father may be interested in investing in my film. I want a backup if Melissa doesn't come through."

"I already know all that. What about the man though?"

"He's nice. He's doing me a solid." I shrug and step out of the elevator now that it's made it to the ground floor.

Joy's hot on my heels as we pass through the lobby. "That's it? I mean, you were with him a lot."

I sigh, and snicker. "You'd think the man never goes outside. He fumbled his way through eighteen holes but did allow me to show him how to throw." He didn't complain once, and that made me soften a little. Men can be so weird about sports sometimes.

"I don't know what your fascination is with disc golf anyway."

"It's fun. And his brother, Weston, had all the equipment we needed." I fell in love with a couple of his drivers and took pictures. I'll definitely want to see if I can buy them somewhere.

That's really all I want to say about that. The truth is, Declan's been growing on me, but I'm not made of relationship material. Trust isn't something that comes easily these days. I mean, if your own father will fuck you over, then we already know about the rest of these men out here. Plus, Declan's too far up his own dad's ass. He's not available for anything either. If all goes well with Melissa today, that may leave us a little time to get to know each other on a physical level before I go.

"Okay, girl. Whatever you say." She checks the rideshare app on her phone and nods outside. "Our ride is here."

I step out into the sweltering heat and say a little prayer that all goes well with this meeting.

ON THE RETURN trip, Declan's name pops up on my phone for the second time in the past hour. He's supposed to be working, so I wonder how he has time to call me so much. I'm just barely out of the meeting with Melissa and I have a lot to process, and some work to do. I'm so close to making a deal, but I need to update my budget.

Joy leans over from her side of the back seat of the rideshare. "For someone just being nice and 'doing you a solid,' he sure is blowing up your phone."

"He probably just wants to know how it went. I'll text him when we get back to the hotel." I look through my budget and review it closely. Melissa thinks I need to add to the above-the-line costs, but it seems like more trouble to bring in a bigger name to host. I already have a verbal commitment from a guy I went to film school with. He's had some smaller roles over the past few years since we graduated, but no break-out role yet. It's only a matter of time, but Melissa thinks I need someone to headline this. She also believes it would be a good idea to have a trained culinary artist to travel with us while shooting. Someone who can be both in front of the camera and behind giving me guidance on the food aspects. I tap a finger on top of my closed laptop and think. I suppose she has a point. I know about food because I've been exposed, but I don't really *know* about food. I'm not an expert. I'm not sure about needing star power though.

"This is exciting, right? Melissa all but said to revise your proposal and you'll have your check."

I nod, smiling. "She did. I'm not sure I agree with everything she asked for though. I need to think about it a little more."

"Like what, Kas?"

"Mostly the celebrity aspect of it. Even if I had someone in mind, which I don't, we'd have to pay a big amount for this type of job. I'm an indie filmmaker. At least that's what I aspire to be. I'm not sure how comfortable I'll be taking it to another level."

She purses her lips again. "You're worried about your father, right? You think if it gets too high-profile, he'll come along and snatch it out of your hands again."

I lie my head on the back of the seat and close my stinging eyes. "I suppose I am. I hadn't thought of that, but you're right. It's always in the back of my mind that he'll use his power to rip me off again."

"You definitely have every right to those feelings. He'd be stupid to do you like that after the fallout from before. You haven't even spoken to him in over a year."

I don't know, but I can't let my guard down. This is too important to me.

WHEN I STEP into the hotel restaurant on the thirteenth floor, he's right there waiting for me next to the host stand. His mouth turns up into a slick grin as his gaze rakes me over from head to toe. Well, more like from breasts to crotch.

My mood brightens. Maybe he's up for a little no-strings romp after all. Instead of the quick pat I normally greet him with, this time I step into his outstretched arms and squeeze him close, molding all my curves to his rock-hard muscles. He holds his breath, but there's definitely a stirring next to my stomach. I lean back and look up into his eyes. "Morning."

He sniggers. "Yes, a good morning indeed." Reluctantly, he opens his arms and I slide out. "Self-seating. You want a table by the window?"

"Sounds perfect." The restaurant is all windows, and the view of downtown Austin is spectacular. I take a moment to take in the sights before sitting down.

Declan is close at my back, his hot breath singeing my

neck.

Neither of us speak as my gaze rolls over the sights Austin has to offer. The huge Colorado River splits the city. "This can't be the same Colorado River that runs near Cali, right?" I think back to a vacation Mom and I took years ago to Scottsdale where we did white-water rafting. It was relaxing and fun. Mostly because we didn't have Dad to contend with.

"No, this one is different. Colorado means red in Spanish, and the river is red in places."

"I thought red was rojo in Spanish."

He steps next to me, staring down at the river below. "It is. I guess the proper translation would be closer to colored red."

"You sure know a lot of non-food stuff."

He shrugs, a slight pink tinging his perfect cheekbones. Those babies could cut all these glass windows to slivers. "I've always had an affinity for geography."

What an interesting subject to be embarrassed by. I simply shrug because I'm not trying to get in too deep with Declan. I'm still feeling him out if we can have a little physical fun without it going sideways.

He must agree because he turns from the window and has a seat at the nearest table, picking up the menu, and scrunching his eyebrows.

"See anything good?" I plop down beside him at the round table. It seats six, but so do all the others. The restaurant's not even half full so it's not an issue.

"Just your normal fare. I'm thinking a western omelet. How about you?"

I open the menu and scan through. He's right. Nothing special about this place which makes me wonder why he chose here instead of meeting at a nicer restaurant. "I guess some pancakes. You really can't mess those up, can you?"

He snorts—the most inelegant gesture I've seen from Declan since I met him. "You'd be surprised."

"I bet yours are perfection."

He turns a smoldering gaze on me. "Maybe you'll let me make some for you one day."

"Dec."

"What's the problem, Kasi? We're into each other. I know I'm not imagining that."

I release a puff of air, covering what I really want to say. How I want to just give in. "I'm here for business."

He leans in closer, a whisper away from my face. His breath brushes my lips as he speaks. "That may be why you're here, but I don't think you'd mind a little more." His stormy-blue eyes churn.

My lips tingle from his words, and my skin flushes from the look in his eyes before his lids close. I breathe into my movement, pulling me closer to Declan's lips.

"What can I get you two?"

We break apart as the oblivious waitress smiles down at us.

Declan clears his throat and gives her our order.

"Nothing to drink?"

He raises one of those spectacular eyebrows my way, but I shake my head, sipping from the water that came with the table.

The waitress's timing was shit, but prolly saved me from

doing something I'd regret. Declan and I need to have a clear understanding before we partake in any carnal activities.

My phones buzzes with a text, and when I flip it over and read the text from Joy, I groan.

"Something wrong?"

"Yeah. Everything."

He doesn't ask. Just waits for me to fill in the details.

"Bad news from Melissa. Joy says it's a no."

"I'm sorry. Did she say why?"

My face heats. Not only from the rejection I thought was a sure thing, but for the reason. "Creative differences."

He nods. "That's too bad."

It is, because while creative differences isn't a lie, it's more about my stubbornness. We don't need a celebrity for this project, and I refused to change the above-the-line like Melissa wanted. "Dammit."

Declan places a big hand over mine. "Dad's still very interested. This is a fascinating concept. He thought the 'chef-in-the-wild' premise was brilliant."

I'm so close to getting this movie made and recouping Tariq's losses, I can taste it. I'd feel bad if I lost a stranger's investment. Losing money from my best friend since elementary school is a hundred times worst. Proving Dad wrong will just be icing on the cake. "Thank God."

"Well, some may have called me that before, but I don't really think of myself as a deity exactly." The cocky smirk is back.

"Yes, thank you, Declan. And thanks to your father for his consideration."

His eyes dim a bit, but he only shrugs. "Let's hope all

goes well, and you get your yes."

"Fingers crossed." And I do cross my fingers plus toes because opportunities are getting scarce on the ground. I'm even happier we didn't kiss. Even though my body was calling to his hard, we need to figure out this business. Especially since I need it so much now. I thought Melissa was for sure, but now that she's off the table, I must concentrate on the task ahead. And not get distracted by some blue-eyed pretty boy.

My phone vibrates in my bag, and I fish it out. There's a missed call from Mom, and after I listen to the voicemail message, I fire off a text in response. *I'll be home day after tomorrow. Lunch is cool. Just us, right?*

She knows better, but I like to be clear about things so there's no misunderstandings.

Of course, doll. See you at one on Sunday.

CHAPTER FIVE

When he was just being used.

B Y ALL ACCOUNTS, Dec's father seems intense, but I can
work with that if he cuts the check. Dec says we should
hear tonight but he's almost a hundred percent sure it's a yes.
"I'm surprised he gave you the time off tonight." I'm glad
because it's my last night, and I'm ready to get a little
something something before I leave. "Oh, and what about all
of you going to San Francisco next month? He approved
that?"

Dec exits the freeway and turns onto a dark city street.
We're not too far from downtown, and even pass the
Everheart Bar and Fine Dining sign. Lots of people fill the
streets still, all walking in the direction of Sixth Street where
the majority of the music scene is. "He doesn't manage the
schedule. I doubt he knows we'll all be gone for that long."

"Who does manage it? Knox?"

He tenses, then turns on a blinker at the stoplight. He
rotates to me while we wait at the red light. "Knox does
plenty, but even he can't run the entire restaurant single-
handedly. We have a manager, Ryan. She keeps it all at the
high level we've become known for. She's really something."

"Sounds like Flynn's lucky to have her."

"We all are." Dec presses a button above his visor, and a garage door raises as we pull into a driveway. "And poor Weston has the biggest crush on her, but Dad would blow a gasket. He has a strict no-fraternization rule."

"That's too bad." It's dark out so hard to see details but it looks like a two-story brick house with hedges and flowers out front. "Do you live here alone?" I do mental calculations of what this place must cost, but then I realize I'm using SoCal prices instead of Texas where everything's bigger.

"I do." He pulls the car into the garage and cuts the engine. There are no tools on the wall or gardening equipment spread across the floor. Instead, a huge speed boat takes up two spaces of the three-car garage. I stare at it, then rotate to Declan with raised eyebrows.

He shrugs and opens his car door. "I rarely get to use it, but what's the point of living near the lake if you don't have a boat?"

"My dude, I live next to a whole ocean, but a boat hasn't been on my shopping list. Jet Skis, sure. I even own a couple paddle boards, but a real boat seems like too much commitment?"

"I leave the paddle boards to Weston." He gets out of the car, so I do too. It takes me a minute to wedge myself between the open door and the huge ship pushed up against the car. Declan drives his car like a bat out of hell. I'd hate to see what he could do with this thing out on the open water. I shake my head and follow him through the garage door.

We pass through a laundry room and into a hallway that brings us into the kitchen. I don't think anyone would mistake what kind of person lives here. There's a huge island in the middle with six chairs lined up on one side and a six-eye stove next to a grill on the other. I circle it and find three ovens built in. There are cabinets everywhere and not one, but two refrigerators. It's elegant and lavish and very Declan.

"Whoa, this is really nice. Why do you need such a big house?" I'm still marveling at my surroundings and don't notice that Dec's not in the room anymore.

When he comes from outside, his hands are wet. "Did you say something?"

I must really be in awe because I didn't even hear the door open. "I asked why you live alone."

His lips turn up on one side. "Do you?"

"Well, yeah, but I live in a two-bedroom cottage that would probably fit in your living room."

"What can I say, I like to be comfortable."

This is something I'd already peeped about him—high maintenance all the way. I'm glad this is only for the night because I don't do fussy. "What were you doing outside?"

"Turning on the Jacuzzi."

"Kinda hot for all that, huh?"

"It's never too hot for the Jacuzzi."

"Well, alrighty then." I can try the spa I guess. The temperature is still upward of eighty but this is his turf so he probably knows better than I do. Back home, I could definitely do a hot tub this time of year. But only at night. Here, it doesn't matter if it's day or night—the temperature's the same sweaty degrees.

"Do you want something to drink?"

"Sure. What do you have?"

The smirk is strong with this one. He opens a wine

fridge and pulls out a bottle of red. "Unless you want something a little stronger." He raises those pretty brows.

"Wine's good." I definitely want to be all the way present since we only have the one time.

While he uncorks the bottle, I stroll over to the window in the adjacent room. Maybe a living room because the furniture is snooty and unlived-in. Not in the way my parent's living room is—all French provincial furniture and lamps everywhere. You'd swear Mom was a hundred years old the way she decorates. Declan's furniture is as expensive but modern. A white leather sectional sitting on a glossy wooden base. I'm guessing Bocote which would make his couch worth more than my car.

The backyard is bathed in fairy lights, and the pool is lit up enough for me to see it pretty well. There's a beautiful rock waterfall surrounded by plenty of greenery. Now this does remind me of home. At least the one I grew up in. To the left of the pool is a connected Jacuzzi. The size of the thing can probably fit ten or more people comfortably.

A stemless glass presses against my shoulder. "You ready to get in?"

I take the glass from him and energize my sexiest grin. "Past ready." I'm not subtle about what I'm talking about. Time to get this party started.

"Let me get you something to change into."

I'm about to tell him that's unnecessary but he's off down the hallway in a flash. Times like these remind me how athletic Declan is. He's so big-headed and fashionable, it's easy to forget there's more to him than arrogance and clothes. Layers. Ones I won't be peeling. I huff at the self-reminder why I'm here, and take a sip of my wine, then close my eyes at the ambrosia dancing down my throat. "Glorious."

"Were you expecting anything less?"

I almost spill my drink from his stealthy reappearance. "Jeesh, what are you, part cat?"

A smirk creases his full lips. Lips I can't wait to suck on. "Will this do?" He hands me a small pile of folded clothes.

"Is this your underwear? And undershirt?"

He walks back into the kitchen and picks up his own glass of wine. "I don't have any spare bikinis lying around."

I look at the label and gasp. Balenciaga. That's gotta be a grip. "You want me to get chlorine on these expensive drawers?" And with Declan's narrow hips, I'll probably bust the seams out of these boxer briefs with my big ass.

"It's fine. I have plenty."

I'm not trying to judge because it's not like I don't have a whole trust fund I dip into from time to time, and Dec actually works for his, but I'm also not wasteful. Plain old Hanes are fine unless I'm trying to be sexy. Then it's Fenty Savage all the way. Still a long way from Balenciaga coin. "Okay, then. What are you going to wear?"

He takes a sip of his wine, then strolls over, and stops right in front of me. He's standing so close, when he exhales, his breath breezes across my forehead. "I was thinking we could be a matched set."

"But where—" Oh, he must mean the ones he's wearing. Okay, I can get with the program. I take a sip and lick my lips ever so slowly.

He raises a long finger and brushes it across my jawline.

"Why don't you get changed? I'll meet you outside."

Heat races through my veins faster than I'm ready for. The feeling is dizzying so I take a deep breath and let it out which puts me closer to his front. His hard front. Judging by the underwear he handed me, if his are the same, no way the monster will be contained. And that's just fine with me. "Okay."

Declan walks through the door to the covered patio, and I strip down right there in the living room, caressing my body as I go. Damn, I'm already hot and ready for him. I spare a thought to when I got some last, and it actually takes a minute to remember. I've been going so hard getting everything ready for the festival, I haven't stopped to charge my sexual batteries. It's been at least four or five months. Dang, no wonder my skin is on fire. Then again, Declan Everheart can definitely light a match. I'm hoping it's a long, firm, thick match.

As expected, his underwear slides up to my waist, trying its best to gain purchase. It only half covers my behind, and most of the fabric wedges in my crack. The undershirt doesn't fare any better. My breasts practically spill out of the band the shirt ends up being.

When I walk outside, Dec is already surrounded by frothing water, sipping his wine, and staring at me from under hooded eyes. He slides his free hand under the water, leaving no doubt what he's gripping.

"You started without me." I set my phone and glass on the lip of the tub, and dip a toe in the water, testing the temperature. It's warm but not the heat I was expecting. Hopefully we're about to change that.

"I'm a self-starter."

I slip into the water and reach back for my glass. The wine is so red, it's almost black. The taste is rich and bold with a hint of black currents. "What is this? So good."

"It's a Rothschild Bordeaux."

"Sounds expensive."

He shrugs. "This is a special occasion." The smoldering grin he releases has me practically throwing my glass back on the smooth stones bordering the tub, freeing my hands.

My phone buzzes, low and incessant, but I ignore it. If it was Joy, she'd text, not email. Everyone else can wait.

When I dip back in, Declan moves considerably closer, and my hip settles right next to his, our legs floating together, entangling in each other.

"Did I mention how good you look in my underwear?"

"Wait until you see how I look out of it."

The irritating device rings again, and I release a harsh breath, turning around to at least make sure it's not an emergency.

This time, Dec's phone buzzes too.

We share a puzzled stare, then I flip mine over to get a look at the screen, and when I see Flynn's email pop up, I mentally slap myself because I can't believe I'd been in a lust fog and forgotten I've been waiting to hear from the man.

"It's your dad."

Dec frowns. "Yeah, I got it too."

I quickly dry my hands on a nearby towel and read through the email.

Your project is absolutely perfect. I love everything about it. I was all ready to cut a check, but some news came to my attention. I didn't realize you're Reggie Blythewood's daughter.

I stop reading and take a breath. My stomach sinks because I know what's coming next. The water shifts considerably, and I look up as Declan raises himself to the stones.

I spoke with him because I figured who better to give a reference for your project. I was disappointed to find out that it's not as sound as I initially thought.

My heart races. I know when I've been beat. Especially when it comes at the hands of dear old Dad. This is an all-too-familiar feeling.

Thank you for your consideration. I wish you the best of luck.

I stare at the offending device wedged in my shaking hands. This can't be happening. I get why Dad stole my idea and passed it off as his own. He felt like he had the right because I was under his wing. But why intentionally sabotage me?

I forbid you to strike out on your own.

Why? Because you've run out of ideas and need me to steal from?

Steal? You're part of Blythewood Productions. This is a collaborative team, but ultimately, that's my name on the door.

Yeah, well Blythewood is my name too. And I'm taking it with me to someplace where I get actual credit for my work.

Kasi, the Blythewood name does not exist anywhere else. If you leave, I suggest you find another profession.

"I'm so sorry."

The phone falls out of my hand when I jump. I'd forgotten Dec was even there. I lift myself out of the water, the air suddenly oppressive. "I've got to go."

"Now?"

Theoretically, I know this isn't his fault, but Flynn was

Dec's idea. And this seemed like a done deal. Disappointment twists my gut. "Yes, now." I pick up my phone and rush to the door leading into the house. All I want is my own clothes back on, and to get out of here as quick as I can.

"Kasi, slow down."

I strip with Declan standing right there. There's no heat in his eyes now though. "The deal fell through. That's the end of it."

"I understand you being upset, but let's talk about it. We can figure something else out. I'll speak with Dad."

I release an exasperated sigh. "What good are you?"

"Excuse me?" Declan stands there in his underwear, leaving nothing to the imagination, dripping on his expensive tiled floor.

I slip my shirt over my head and look for my shoes.

"Kasi."

"Your dad didn't come through. Time for me to go."

His pretty features twist into a scowl. This isn't something I've seen from him the past week, but his face settles into the expression easily. Almost like this is his true form. He's still beautiful, but quite unhappy. "You were using me?"

"What? Why would you even ask me a stupid question like that? I never said anything but." I click open the rideshare app on my phone because this is going south really fast.

"I'm pretty sure I'd remember that."

"Really? Because I told you I was here on business. Strictly business."

"And tonight? This was business?" His face droops before

he carefully rearranges his mouth into a cruel sneer.

"Tonight I was hoping to have an orgasm or two. Five minutes ago, you had busting a nut on your mind, and that's all. Am I wrong?"

He huffs. "Very wrong."

Damn. I was afraid he was catching feelings. It's my fault for not being clear before we came here. I got caught up. "Okay, well I'm going. Have a nice life, Declan." I try to find the garage door we came through but end up down another hallway.

"I'll get dressed and drive you."

I glance at my phone. "No need. My ride will be here in two minutes."

He rotates and returns back down the hall.

I follow him to the front door and when he opens it, I slip through without a backward glance.

CHAPTER SIX

When she left with his heart the first time.

CANCELING ON MOM wasn't really an option, but I was sorely tempted. They say you can't pick your parents, and man, they ain't never lied. It's not like I have beef with her, other than marrying a jerk, but I really don't want to see anyone with the last name Blythewood right now. Including my own foul reflection. Regrets? Yeah, I have a few. Now that a couple days have passed, I can see where I wasn't very charitable with Declan. Did I give him the lay of the land from jump? Yes. Could I have treated him better when I knew good and damn well he was thinking of something more than physical with me? Absolutely. I was too far in my feelings to care. Which brings me right back to this bench in front of the restaurant, waiting for Mom, wallowing in my spiteful thoughts about Dad. At least I've learned my lesson. I won't take it out on her like I did Declan.

According to my phone, she's ten minutes late. No surprise there. Growing up, Dad and I would tell her something started an hour earlier and she'd still be late but only minutes instead of hours. It's a good thing she married well, money-wise, so she doesn't have to get to a job on time. It wasn't always like that though. She went to law school and everything, but as soon as Dad's career took off, she quit the studio and settled into her life of charitable events and luncheons. Sometimes I wonder if they're really my parents. Then again, there's no denying Reggie as my father. I for sure have his drive.

I lean back against the stone wall behind the bench I'm sitting on and sip my Moscow mule. It's a classic, but I like the bite of the ginger. The restaurant has an outdoor patio to enjoy drinks while waiting for a table. There's no sense asking for a table until Mom gets here though. I take a cleansing breath and look up at the sun. It's nice being back in normal weather, but I can't lie, I miss Austin. Well, I guess I mean I miss Declan. He got more under my skin than I care to admit. I glance at my phone again for the time and contemplate sending the man a text.

"Hello, dear."

"Hi, Mom." I stand and hug her, wading under her wide hat. She's a half foot shorter than me, so I practically throw out my back trying to straighten up. She isn't wearing heels today, and I wrestle with her true height. Her flats look good with her linen pants and blouse.

"Did you get us a table?"

It takes everything I have not to roll my eyes. As it is, I smirk. Something I picked up from Declan while in his company. Ugh, why do my thoughts keep drifting to him? "I was waiting on you, Mom."

She waves a hand and strolls to the hostess stand. "Mrs. Reggie Blythewood, party of two."

I take a deep breath because my stomach just turned over. Of course she'd use Dad's name to get us a table without waiting our turn. It works too. The hostess turns and leads us to prime seating near the bank of windows. I pick up the menu, but Mom only watches me. "What?"

"I'm having the chef's salad. It's really good here."

Now I do roll my eyes. In the land of unrealistic expectations of women's bodies, I'm definitely a standout. I embrace my curves, and as long as I'm fit and healthy, I'm quite happy with my body. Unfortunately, Mom drank the Kool-Aid and being around all these industry folks most of her life has given her a certain ideal. That's fine for her, but I don't let anyone regulate my body, most of all her. "Great for you, Mom. I'm going to need another minute."

The chef's salad does look good, but I don't order it on GP. Instead, I have the spinach and feta stuffed chicken.

When the waiter leaves us to our own devices after taking our order, Mom smooths the already smooth tablecloth in front of her and readjusts the silverware.

I brace myself for the onslaught and straighten my spine.

"How was your vacation?"

I release a heavy sigh even though it'll go unnoticed. "I wasn't on vacation, and you know that."

She levels a gaze at me that would make lesser daughters whither. I'm not here for it. Not after what Dad did. "Careful, honey."

"You know I'm your flesh and blood, right? Technically, you're not related to Dad. You should have my back."

"This feud has gone on long enough, Kasi. It's time for you to rejoin the business."

So clearly she's lost her entire—I cut off that thought because I need to remember she has a unique perspective.

She came up a different way in a traditional time. Honestly, it's time to move into this century at least. "I'm not sure why you think that would ever be an option. Did Dad tell you he just killed financing for my project? I practically had the check in my hand."

She purses her lips and gazes at me. "You really believe that, don't you?"

"I was told that, Mom. The investor said those words." I take a sip of my ice water before speaking. I need to quell the heat rising up in my throat. "And you know this isn't the first time."

She pulls her lips into her mouth and takes a deep breath, closing her eyes. When she releases the breath, and opens her eyes, she seems ready to engage in this hard conversation. The thing is, it isn't her responsibility. Maybe she props up his choices, but she's not the one making them. "Dear, your father has your best interests at heart. The production company is your legacy. You only need to learn at your father's side, and the world will be your oyster. Exercise a little patience."

"Let's see here. Graduated from UCLA film school. Check. Master's in producing from the AFI. Check. Worked on film sets for six years starting as a production assistant working my way up through practically every job to assistant producer. Check. Check. Check. Then I manifest a treatment of epic proportions, secure some of the investment which Dad somehow absorbed without payback, and get cut out completely. Not even a producer credit. But Dad goes on to win a PGA award." I drink the rest of my water and pick up hers too. "Patience? Sure, that sounds like what's been missing from our relationship."

"Listen, honey. I'm obviously not going to be able to change your mind, but this not talking to your father thing is getting old."

"Okay. Then how's about you tell him to quit sabotaging my career and I'll be happy to come over and have a nice sit-down. Maybe we can watch Tariq in a football game some Sunday." It still amazes me how Dad could stiff someone he's known forever. Since Tariq was a little boy. I shake my head and frown.

She winces but doesn't acknowledge my pettiness. "I'll pass along the message."

The waiter sets our food in front of us, and Mom reaches across the table to hold my hand and bless the food.

Her salad is calling my name, and I bite the inside of my cheek in punishment for not just getting the damn thing. My chicken is fine, but dang that salad is loaded.

She takes a bite, and nods. "Really good. So, tell me about your trip. How was Austin?"

Another painful memory rises up before I can tamp it down. The chicken in my mouth suddenly tastes like concrete. "It was…" I shrug and look out the window. "It was a nice place to visit. You should go sometime."

"Who's the guy?"

I close my eyes a long minute. No surprise she would sniff that out right away. She always did have a nose for it. I couldn't sneak a guy in during high school because she would immediately find us. I only tried it a couple of times before I realized the deal. Even after moving out, if I dated someone for more than a few months, she was right on top of it before I could even figure out if I was in a relationship or not. The last few years, I've been hyper-focused so there's been no need for her particular brand of Spidey-sense. "Just a guy. No big deal."

"Tell me about him."

Resistance is futile so I launch into the whole story.

She narrows her gaze when I mention leaving him with his dick practically out. At least Mom's always been sex-positive; I don't feel the need to hide anything from her. Especially since I've been grown. "Do you plan on contacting him again?"

"I'm not sure. I probably owe him an apology."

She smiles and releases a sigh.

"Okay, I do owe him an apology. I'm not sure he'll want to hear it though. But I also don't think I was totally in the wrong. I gave him fair warning what I was looking for."

She nods and takes another bite of her salad.

I continue hate-eating my rolled chicken. It's good, but not what I really wanted.

"It's always good to set expectations, but you could have gone about it with a bit more grace."

"I know, Mom. I was just so pissed about—"

"Language, honey."

Ugh. "I was upset and took it out on him. He tried to help me, but it wasn't his fault everything fell through. We know whose fault—"

"Do you really feel the need to head down that road again?"

I huff and sit back in my seat. She's right, because there's nothing I can say to her to make Dad a better person. Plus, she'll defend him at every turn anyway so what's the point? "No, you're right."

She gives me a sad smile, then continues eating her lunch.

I eat as much as I can, but this situation with Declan is weighing on my soul. I nod to myself. I'll reach out as soon as I have time.

I WAIT ON my porch swing, expecting Joy and Tariq any moment. The breeze from the ocean sways the fronds from the miniature palm trees planted in my front yard. The small space is enclosed, which keeps the tourists out—a big draw for me when I went house shopping. I ended up having to do a lot of renovations to modernize the little bungalow, but I knew that going in. Houses built in the early 1900s are bound to need a little TLC. I kept the original white paint but changed the trim to blue. It fits in with the surroundings perfectly.

I sigh contentedly. It's good to be home.

Someone reaches a muscled arm over the gate and unlocks it from within.

"Alright now. Don't get shot."

A smiling Tariq walks through the opening, with Joy trailing behind. "Looks like someone spent a little too much time in Texas. Going all Wild West on us."

"Come here, big head, and give me a hug."

He does as asked, then sits gingerly next to me on the swing.

"It's sturdy."

"Just making sure. I don't want to break my leg then be out for training camp."

Joy hugs me and sits on the top step. "I know it's not time for training camp already, is it?"

"Nah, we still have a couple months before we head to Arizona."

"Where are you two coming from? Where's Ashley?"

I don't miss the quick glance Joy and Tariq share.

Tariq shifts uncomfortably on the bench, and we sway back and forth a couple times. "She took the kids to Stockton to visit her parents."

"You didn't go?"

"Nope."

I cross my arms over my chest, waiting for an additional explanation. None comes though so I turn to Joy. "Hi, girl."

"Hi. We just came from Tariq's friend's house. His name is Jeremy and turns out it was a setup."

The swing moves again. I try not to laugh, but I can't help myself. "Boy, you know better."

"That's what I said." Joy scowls at Tariq.

The man holds his hands up in the air, fending off the two-prong attack. "It was not a setup. I was only introducing one of my best friends to a teammate. You always have to take everything to the next level."

I smile and move closer under him. "But why did you feel the need to introduce them? And why wasn't I invited?"

"I hear you already have a man."

My mouth pops open audibly. "I do not have a man." I rotate to Joy and give her my best death stare.

It's pretty impressive, and she wilts under the pressure. "I didn't exactly say he was your man. Just that you met a guy in Austin."

"Right, a guy who lives in Austin." I put extra emphasis on "lives." "Besides, you already know what happened with that."

Joy rallies and straightens up as much as she can considering she's sitting on a porch step. "Okay, but I know you. Probably better than you know yourself."

I puff up, but she holds up a hand. "I haven't seen you that into a dude since Gregory."

Tariq flinches and turns away, suddenly interested in the windowpane behind us.

I narrow my gaze at Joy. "You know that name isn't allowed up in this house." Gregory, a producer under Dad's wing at Blythewood Productions, is dead to me. When Dad was screwing me over, Gregory was in on it the whole time. Given a choice between sucking up to my father and being loyal to me, he didn't even blink.

"Okay, sorry, but you really like Declan. I can tell."

"Purely physical."

She lifts herself off the porch and shakes her head. "Argue with your mama. I'm not here for it. What you got to drink?" She opens the front door and glides through without looking back.

"You're awfully quiet."

Tariq rotates back so he can look at me. "I know better than to step off in between that mess." He shrugs.

I hit his arm but don't have the energy to put too much force in the tap. Not that it would matter considering his arm is bigger than my whole thigh. "It's not like that. I just don't like talking about him. Now tell me what's going on with you and Ashley." I've never had much of a liking for Tariq's wife. She always struck me as a bit of a gold digger but it wasn't my place to say. I respect people's relationships, and Tariq is a grown man.

He leans back and sighs, scrubbing his hands across his face. "She's tripping."

"Okay. Care to elaborate?"

"She's just never home, and it's not like she works. Or even does charity like your moms."

"What about the kids?"

"You know I like to spend as much time with them as I can during the off-season so I've had them mostly. We have that nanny too, Mrs. Tingle. She's great with the kids."

"Did you ask her what's up?"

"Sure did. Several times. She always says I'm making something out of nothing."

I twist my lips to the side, but quickly straighten my expression back. I'm not trying to get in between husband-and-wife business. Especially since he didn't ask. "Let me know if you need anything."

He nods, a grim expression creasing his otherwise smooth face. "Joy told me about your dad."

Now it's my turn to screw my features into a frown. I put plenty of effort into it. "He's such a bastard. And somehow thinks he's doing me a favor."

"Maybe he is."

"How can you, of all people, say something like that? When he screwed me over, he messed with your money too. And I'm determined to make good on that investment."

"I've already told you don't worry about that."

I face him, looking him straight in the eyes. "That was a lot of money."

"It was, but it's not like I couldn't afford it. I wrote it off as a loss."

"Sure, but no way you could write that much money off."

"Listen, I don't know how many times I need to tell you it wasn't your fault and I'm not worried about that money. After my rookie contract, I signed a really nice one, and I'm five years into it, so I don't even need to worry that much about the money that wasn't guaranteed."

"Right, five years into a six-year contract. It's time for you to start negotiating another."

"True that, but I'm still not worried about it. Ashley spends it as fast as I make it anyway."

No way I'm touching that statement with a ten-foot pole.

Joy comes back outside, sipping from a tall glass of lemonade. "What I miss?"

Tariq and I exchange a glance, then I turn to Joy. "Girl, nothing new. You guys want to go to the beach?"

"Yup yup." Tariq stands, and I practically roll off the bench swing after his weight unbalances it. "My bad, Kas."

"Don't worry about it." I chuckle and walk over to the door. "Give me five minutes and I'll be ready."

When I walk into my living room, the cool breeze goose bumps my skin, and I walk over to the thermostat and lower it. I think about what Tariq said, and I know in my soul he means it, but I'm more determined than ever to get his money back.

CHAPTER SEVEN

When it becomes a business venture.

"OKAY, WELL I guess you're not going to answer your phone." This is my second time calling and I can take a hint. "I'd hope to apologize to you live, but I guess I'll just leave this on your machine." I take a deep, cleansing breath. "I'm really sorry about how I reacted when your dad pulled out of the deal. Obviously, it wasn't your fault at all. It was completely on my father. Okay, just wanted to say I'm sorry." I move to press the end icon, but I have something else to say. I'm not sure I want to, but I guess it won't kill me. "Hi, also, I wasn't using you. I mean, *just* using you. I was straight with you about what I wanted, but before the week was over, I was feeling you too. Okay, bye."

When I hang up the phone, I immediately regret the last part. He's not even taking my calls so I could have just kept that to myself. The main thing is he needed to understand I know I was a jerk.

I turn over in my bed and stare at the beams crossing the ceiling, contemplating my life choices. My next move is to get back out there and hustle. I'm just not certain who to go to next. I still can't believe South by Southwest was a bust. My phone heats in my hand. Or maybe it was my imagination because it's reminding me what a complete and total bust it actually was, in more ways than one.

I tap out a text message to my agent. *Do you want to meet for lunch?*

Joy responds right away even though she's back at work today. Her law office is in Santa Monica proper, so we meet up for lunch often. Sometimes with Tariq too since she represents him as well. *Sure. I think I can swing a half hour around one.*

Okay, but I need you in your agent hat, and I don't want to go to your office.

In that case, I can spare an hour. She adds a smiley face for good measure.

Since I have four hours before I meet Joy, I roll out of bed to fix a small breakfast. Ugh, that reminds me of Declan offering to make me pancakes one day. I guess that day will never come.

All I feel like making is scrambled eggs so that's what I do, plus some Earl Grey tea, and take it out on my back patio. The weather is milder here than in Texas, so I don't mind eating outside this time of year. I shudder. It's still unbelievable how humid it was down there in the middle of March. The salty air whirls in and lifts my hair off my shoulders. I took my cornrows down as soon as I got home so my scalp could breathe for a minute. I'm thinking about box braids or maybe a twist-out next. It depends on what I have coming up, which as it stands right now, is a whole lotta nothing.

I check my phone just to see if anyone has given me some love—an investor, my family…Declan—anyone at all. Not even a spam call, so I run some bath water and relax with a bath bomb, and turn on some old school R&B.

After bathing and reordering my bookshelf and the clothes in my closet and drawers, I've killed enough time to take the short walk to meet Joy for lunch.

She's already seated when I pass through the door. "Hi."

"Hi. What's wrong?"

"Dang. I haven't even sat down yet." I sit and peruse the menu. When I look up, she has an uncharacteristic smirk on her face. "Nothing's wrong. I just need to know our next steps."

"Did you call Declan?"

"This is a business meeting."

"Okay, so that's a no."

I set down my menu and cross my arms. "I called him. He didn't answer."

"Oh. Sorry."

"Don't be. I deserve it."

The waitress takes our order. Fish sandwich for me, soup and salad for Joy.

I take a sip of my water. "So anyway. I'm restless. I need something to do. Point me in the direction of someone I can ask for money."

"We've only been home a couple days. Why not relax your mind and recharge."

I level my signature stare at her.

She raises her hands in surrender. "Okay, I know better. I'll need a few days to line someone else up. I do have other clients, you know?"

"Yes, I'm aware. And I know you just took a whole week to focus on me. I appreciate it, honestly. What about Melissa?"

"What about Melissa?"

"Do you think she might reconsider? You know, if I change the budget."

Joy is shaking her head before I can finish the thought. "No. Part of her ask was seeing if you could be flexible. Or if you're one of those *artistic types*. Clearly it's the latter."

After I close my eyes a moment and take a deep breath, I stare at her. "That was mean."

"And true."

"And true, but still mean."

"You can miss me with that. I'm your best friend and I know you. You're stubborn. Have been ever since we were on the playground in elementary and Sherri tried to get you to draw the hopscotch grid different."

I shake my head. "What a bloodbath."

"Exactly."

"Okay, well do you have anyone else in mind?"

"There's plenty of people, but I have to find someone without ties to your dad. That's not easy in this town."

My face heats from anger. I shouldn't have to fight this hard to make my own way. I'm not asking anyone for special favors, just to give me a chance to present my package. It's really good and I have the credentials. "Yeah, I understand. Just let me know if you can get a meeting with someone. Anyone."

"I will, babe. In the meantime, what are you going to do with yourself?"

I shrug because I really hadn't thought about it. I've already put together everything I need for my film, other than the money, of course. I could do some prep work, but that would require me to dip into my savings which, in turn, maybe dips into my trust fund depending how much this will cost me. That's dirty money, and I try not to indulge unless absolutely necessary. Plus, there's plenty of restrictions and rules. Maybe I've reached that point though. "I guess I'll do some traveling. Some location scouting."

Joy claps her hands. "That sounds like an excellent idea. I wish I could go with you."

"Me too."

She raises her glass of water in salute. "Here's to plans and making it happen."

I frown but clink my glass to hers. "Cheers."

MY PLANE LANDED over two hours ago, and I'm just now driving out of the airport. I've flown to three different countries the past month and can't nobody tell me nothing about other countries being below par. LAX is the worst.

I barely keep my eyes open as I head north up the 405 toward home. Not for the first time, I question my lack of foresight about leaving my car at the airport. A twenty-dollar rideshare would have been so much easier. And probably safer too because the sun is setting, and it'll be right in my eyes the last few minutes of this ride. Twenty minutes later, I finally pull up to my garage. Unlike Declan, I have to get out, unlock the garage door, and pull it up before I can drive inside.

There I go again. All thoughts lead back to that delicious ice-cream cone I missed out on. I clearly pissed him off real good because he never did return my call. Thankfully, I've been too busy making my dreams come true. And figuring out how to regain Tariq's investment.

After I close the garage and roll my luggage down the alley that runs the length behind all our cottages, I reach over the gate to open it, but it's already unlatched. WTF? My fight or flight instincts kick in. Should I ease it open or turn and run?

"Hey, Kasi," Tariq calls from inside my yard.

"Boy, you almost got—" The rest of that sentence dies in my mouth when I see him. Well, not him, but who's sitting on the porch swing. My porch swing on my porch. "What's he doing here?"

Tariq frowns from his seat on the steps leading up to the porch. He looks to Declan. "I thought you said she wanted to see you."

Declan, his face smooth, not giving anything away, only looks to me.

Okay, maybe that was a little harsh. Especially considering my skin is prickling with excitement now that I've gotten over the initial shock. "I do want to see him. I'm just not sure what's going on here. Why are you two together? Yanno, on my porch."

Declan finally stands, and I notice the roller next to the front door. "Tariq was nice enough to meet me over here. I didn't want you to think I'm stalking you."

I huff, then walk closer. "I'm pretty sure ghosting someone for over a month doesn't meet the definition of stalking."

Neither of us makes an effort to reach for the other. Plus,

Tariq is a pretty large obstacle between us.

After a few minutes of uncomfortable silence, Tariq finally releases a sigh. "So, should I go or nah?"

He's looking at me, but Declan is the one who answers. "Thanks, man. I appreciate you meeting me over here. Unless Kasi needs me, I'll see you tomorrow for that hike."

My face tightens and I imagine my eyebrows have flown up somewhere into my curls. "You two know each other?" I don't ask anyone in particular. An answer post haste from either will do because I'm thoroughly confused.

Tariq chuckles and daps up Declan. "She's all yours, man." When Tariq passes me on his way to the gate, he bumps my shoulder, nearly sending me to the ground, with his big ass.

But I recover before I make too big a fool of myself and grab my roller, making my way to the porch. "I don't understand what's happening."

"If you let me in, I'll explain." He picks up his suitcase and waits expectantly at the front door.

I unlock the door and flip the light switch just inside, bathing the living room in soft light. I take a quick walk-through making sure everything is as I left it before depositing my suitcase in the bedroom. While in there, I take several deep breaths, my mind racing. I haven't heard from Declan since I left him at his front door in Austin. In his underwear. I called him to apologize but no response. Not even a text. Then a month later, he just shows up on my porch. Why is he here?

As if he read my mind, he calls from the other room. "If you come back, I'll tell you why I'm here."

I roll my eyes, then go into my bathroom and splash some water on my face. The mirror is not kind right now. The image staring back is of someone who looks like they just got off a sixteen-hour flight from the Sacred Valley in Peru by way of Miami, then navigated LAX customs for a couple hours. I look a hot mess. And I probably smell like plane.

"You look beautiful, Kas. As always."

He thinks he knows me so well. I turn off the water and stroll into the living room.

Declan has made himself at home, spread across my couch, legs casually crossed, and arms slung above his head. He's comfortable and confident in that way only Declan Everheart can be.

I ease onto the love seat. When I examine the room through his eyes, I can only imagine he finds it lacking. My furniture isn't worth tens of thousands of dollars. Nor is it fashionable and sleek. It's tasteful though and made of good quality. And it's good enough for me.

"Why are you scowling?"

Am I? I rub my cheeks and admit they are a little tight. "I was just thinking you look comfortable despite this place not being up to your usual standards."

He sits up, his brows drawn together. "Are you kidding? Your place is super cool." He rotates until he's staring directly behind him. "I love that cutout to the dining room. I can't wait to see the kitchen."

My face heats from his praise, and I immediately shake myself. I don't need anyone's permission or acceptance. Especially not his. "It's just a kitchen, but thanks.

So…you're here."

"Do you think I could get a drink of water? Or do you want to go get something to eat? You must be famished?"

"Did you just get here?"

He nods. "About an hour ago."

"Honestly, I'm too tired to go anywhere." I stand and amble to the kitchen. "Let's see if I have anything besides water." I haven't been home in a minute and have no idea what I left here. Push comes to shove, I can order a pizza or something. Although that'll be a far cry from the vibrant cuisine I enjoyed recently.

"Water's fine, for now."

"Sparkling or flat?" I was in Italy before Peru so now I expect the choice everywhere I go.

"Do you have Topo?"

"I'm not sure we can even get it out here."

"I'll just take a regular bottle of water if you have it. Tap is fine at this point."

I take the filtered pitcher from the fridge and pray I filled it before I left. Yes, pay dirt. Then I pour him a glass of filtered tap water. I hand it to him and dare him to comment on it.

He takes a long pull, then a breath, and downs the rest. "Thanks so much. I really needed that."

"Do you want another?"

"If you don't mind."

This time, Declan follows me into the kitchen. Although I'm not a chef, I do love to cook. My kitchen is well stocked with stainless steel appliances and a gas stove. I wish I had a little more space, but I'm lucky to have this much square footage this close to the beach.

"This is an interesting shade of green. I like it. Very unusual."

"The house was built in 1910. I've renovated a ton but tried to keep a lot of the original wood and stone. Even though those counters have been repainted, that was near the original color. Same with the brick backsplash. All original."

He fingers the brick, and my stomach clinches as his long digits slide across the rough surface.

Fuck, I need to get laid.

It's not just me either. Flames heat Declan's eyes when he turns to me and lets out a long, slow breath. "Business first."

Business? What?

I'VE SET DECLAN up in the spare bedroom slash office. There's a comfortable daybed in there along with my desk and camera equipment everywhere. He'll have to use the bathroom in the hallway, but it's not like he was invited so that'll have to do. He should just be glad the sheets are clean.

We ended up ordering from a local Italian place not too far from here, and I'm stuffed and sleepy, but couldn't sleep now if I tried.

I clear away all the remnants of our meal from the dining room table as Declan comes in with his messenger bag. He was mostly quiet during dinner but smirking the entire time. He has something exciting brewing just under the surface and clearly wants to build that excitement in me by making me wait.

It's working.

"Do you want something else to drink? Like some wine? I don't have anything near as good as what you served me, but there should be something decent."

His smirk is back. "Let's go through this proposal first, then think about celebrating."

Something pricks the back of my eyes and I blink several times. If this is what I think it is, I'm probably going to lose it. Right here in front of Declan. Damn him. "Celebrating?"

"You'll see." He removes a bound stack of papers, a glossy page on top. I can just make out the Everheart name before he turns it over.

"What's going on, Dec? Why are you here after cutting me off?"

The smirk dissolves, and the corners of his mouth turn down. "Listen, I'm not great with *feelings* and all that."

The quote is loud and clear which almost makes me giggle because who says that out loud? Outwardly, I only nod.

He adjusts the collar on his button-down shirt. It's a subtle gray and really makes his eyes pop. "The way you left wasn't cool. I get it, but taking it out on me was just wrong."

"I know. That's why I called to apologize."

"Yeah."

"Yeah?"

"I mean, I accept your apology, but I needed a little time first. We were really busy too, preparing for the competition."

I flip over my phone and check the date. "Oh wow. That's soon, right?"

He nods. "In two days. I'm on my way now."

The frown that pulls at the corner of my mouth hits me too fast to stop.

"Is something wrong?"

I can't admit that I'm salty over him only being here two days and already making plans with Tariq. "No, nothing."

The smirk is back, cocky bastard. "Want me to cancel my plans tomorrow?"

"It depends on what's in that binder."

The light overhead dims, then brightens again. I'm not superstitious, but that's pretty ominous. "What's going on?"

"You probably need a new bulb."

"Bro, if you don't hurry up and tell me why you're here…I swear to God."

His shoulders shake ever so slightly, giving away his light spirit. This better be good news. He flips the packet over, revealing the front. The biggest font at the top reads *Everheart Investments*. Lower, there's another line.

My stomach clinches. "What's happening?"

He slides the packet over to me. There are two lines instead of the one I initially saw in my haze of excitement. *Kasi Blythewood. Unmapped Cuisine, working title.*

"Holy Jesus."

"No, just me."

I blink back the tears as I thumb through the pages. My proposal is mirrored back at me. Everything is in line with what I shared with Flynn when I was in Austin. Until I get to a page with Declan's name and a big fat stop sign underneath. Producer. "Oh, hell no."

"I expected that reaction."

"Then why didn't you leave that page out? Just had to

try or something?"

"No, it's for real. You want the investment, you get me with it. That was the only way I could convince him."

I get up and pace the small dining room, wiping the wetness from my cheeks. This entitled motherfucker right here. "What do you know about producing?"

"You'll teach me."

"I most certainly will not."

"I come with the money, Kasi. May as well wrap your head around it. After what your dad told my dad, he wants his investment protected and he expects me to do it."

My skin prickles all over, and tightens so much, I want to jump out of it. I can't be this close to finally getting what I need to be thwarted so handily. This is my show, and I can't have Declan fucking it up. "No."

"No?"

I walk over to him and slam the packet on the table in front of him. "You heard me."

"Kasi, this is—"

"I said no, Declan. I do this on my terms."

He lifts his shoulders and lets them drop, then blows out a rough breath. "Fine then." He takes the packet and sticks it back in his bag, then stands. "I'm turning in. I'm jet-lagged. If it's still okay for me to stay."

"Of course it is. Listen, I—"

"No, you gave your answer. I'm done." He storms out of the dining room and turns right instead of left.

My place isn't that big so when he takes a couple of steps in the wrong direction, he reverses and passes the dining room without a glance inside.

I take a deep breath and hold it a long minute before letting it out. "What a clusterfuck." I decide to open that bottle of wine anyway, even though there's no celebration, and pour myself a glass, then take it into my bedroom.

My house is built pretty solid, but the pipes complain a little when you turn on the water. Declan is in the hall bathroom, probably about to take a shower. I can't believe he's this close and we're sleeping in separate rooms. I'm so conflicted on his whole offer—not the offer itself because that's a hell no—but how he kept working for me even after I went left on him the last time we were together. Just because we can't be in business together doesn't mean we can't be something else. Right? I don't even know anymore.

I take a long sip of my wine, listening to the water rush through the pipes. Maybe Joy can help me decide how to proceed with Declan. Clearly he's pissed because I turned him down, but I didn't miss the heat in his eyes when he stared at me. We still have the physical thing going for us if nothing else. I pick up my phone and call her instead of texting.

It almost goes to voicemail before she answers. "I thought you'd be knee-deep in Declan right about now. Or at least celebrating."

I sigh and look up at the ceiling. "You knew about it?"

"Obviously. I am your agent, you know. I arranged everything."

"And you didn't think to tell me because..."

"Because you were out of the country and rarely had service. When I tried to call, it would only go to voicemail. After a while, I figured it was the film gods telling us to surprise you. Were you not happy? You've been moping about him for over a month."

"Have not."

She snorts. "Okay, girl. Between 'why won't he call me back' and 'I'm never getting this investment,' you've been a mopey mess. This is a perfect opportunity—two birds, one stone."

"So you looked at the proposal?"

"Duh. I'm your agent."

"And you didn't see anything wrong?"

She releases an audible sigh and lets it linger for a minute. "I knew you wouldn't like it, but I figured you'd be reasonable, considering."

"Considering, what?"

"Considering someone was willing to invest without running it by Reggie Blythewood. That considering. What does it matter that Declan gets a producer credit?"

My shoulders tighten and raise up somewhere around my ears. "It's not just a credit. He wants to be an active producer. Travel around. Decide on locations and what we film. That's my job."

"What did you tell him?"

"No, of course."

"Of course."

"What's that supposed to mean?"

"It means that you're so desperate to get this film made, and recoup Tariq's money, but you won't compromise in any way. Just like with Melissa."

Ouch. Okay, that one stings. "That's different."

"Hmmm."

I know it's not different, and she has a point, but it's too much control to just turn over to someone. "This is how Dad fucked me over."

"Oh, honey. It's not the same thing. You worked for your dad then. Now, you work for yourself. And you have me watching your back this time."

I lean back against the headboard and take another pull of my wine. I hate this. I don't need someone else to help me produce. I definitely don't want it. And if he does, then sex is all the way off the table. I don't mix business and physical satisfaction like that. That's a hard line I won't cross. "We'd need some contracts drawn up."

"Already did."

"Joy, I trust you with my life. You're my oldest and dearest friend, ever since kindergarten. If you tell me this is the right move, I'll agree."

She doesn't even take a breath. "It's the right move."

I take several breaths before responding. "Okay."

CHAPTER EIGHT

When there was an agreement.

THE PIPES STOP creaking, and after a few minutes, the door to the hall bathroom opens. I opened my door so I could hear when Declan finished up.

I stand and finish off my liquid courage before taking off down the hallway and stop just outside the closed door to the spare bedroom. Should I knock? That seems weird in my own house. "Declan."

There's a small crash. "Shit." The door creaks open with fine-ass Declan visible through the crack, a towel wrapped around his waist. His olive-toned skin glistens from the moisture of his shower. His hair is slicked back, and his beard trimmed. He looks refreshed. His eyes tell a different story. They're weary. "Sorry about the noise. Something spilled out of my suitcase."

"Yes."

He narrows his gaze at me and widens the door another inch. "Yes what, Kasi?"

"Yes to the investment. To you being a producer."

One side of his mouth turns up in a half grin. "I... Really?"

"Yes, but a producer under me. Not by my side. I want

that in writing."

He leans that beautiful body against the door frame, allowing the door to swing open. "I can live with that."

"You've already seen Joy's contracts, haven't you?"

That glorious smirk is on display. He only chuckles and moves his hand near the knot of his towel.

Of course my gaze follows. My heart speeds up. And my palms get clammy, so I place them under my armpits. "Business only, Everheart."

"Kas."

"No. That's a hard line. I won't cross it. Let's get this movie made."

A line forms between his eyebrows, but his eyes sparkle.

"I'm serious, Dec. Strictly business."

He releases a puff of air. "Sure, okay."

"You think I'll change my mind, but I won't. I've learned some lessons in this business the hard way. Let's get on the other side and see what happens."

"But this could take months." Doubt flickers in his blue eyes.

"Now, see. You haven't even read the schedule or you'd know exactly how many months it'll take. We're in the middle of prep work so you're already behind." I reach for the handle of the door and slowly pull it toward me.

Declan jumps back out of the way, and the towel slides down nearly exposing him before he grips it again.

"I suggest you take tonight to familiarize yourself with everything in that packet, and we'll regroup in the morning." I shut the door in his surprised face.

He thinks I'm fucking with him, but he'll learn.

I stroll back to my room, smiling. We're really doing this. Instead of showering and falling into bed and sleeping off all those airplane miles like I have some sense, I pick my laptop up off my dresser and settle into a chair in the corner near the window. It's dark out, but the bedside lamp is on, giving me plenty enough light to find the keys.

First, I bring up the list of possible locations. There's ten, and I've only hit three. We'll have to pick up the travel schedule now. I didn't budget for a full location scout, only half. Declan and I will need to fill in the gaps. I blink. I forgot to ask if he's taking time off from the restaurant. He'll have to if he wants to be a producer. Will his dad allow that? And what about this cooking competition? Surely he'll need to drop out of that even if his brother needs him. Not for the first time, I exhale a sigh of relief I don't have any siblings.

I set my laptop on the floor and stand. No, I better not. If I go back to his room tonight, he'll think I'm playing games. I only have my mind on one thing right now, so I need to maintain some distance. Maybe a shower first will help clear my head. Just the thought of the hot stream raining down on me has my limbs loosening.

My phone lights up before I make it to the bathroom. A text from Declan. *Sweet dreams.*

Ha, he's really trying it. I respond, but keep it short, not trusting myself yet. *Night.*

This is going to be a long nine months.

AN UNUSUAL SMELL permeates my dreams, and I pop up in

bed. What the hell? I take a deeper breath. It's definitely coming from inside the house. I grab the bat I keep under the bed, and creep into the hallway. There's a quiet whoosh like the refrigerator just closed. Shit, I should have brought my phone. My pulse races as I creep toward the kitchen, bat raised high, and listen as hard as I can. There's no sound other than the heartbeat inside my ears, but the smell is louder. Unless I'm so jet-lagged, I'm imagining it. I peek around the corner and... "Aaaah!" Thankfully, I drop the bat mid-swing when I realize it's Declan. My heart gallops, and I know my blood pressure has raised fifty points. I can hardly breathe as I clutch my chest.

"What is wrong with you?"

As I come down from my adrenaline rush, my knees go weak and I drag myself over to the breakfast nook. My hands shake while I pick up the glass of water Declan put in front of me. He places his hands over mine to help me lift it and take a long swallow. "Thanks."

He sets a plate in front of me stacked high with pancakes. "Honey, jam, or maple syrup?"

I blink.

"Are you okay?"

"I forgot you were here."

"Clearly."

"I'm sorry I almost beat you up."

His early morning smirk is glorious. He also looks damn good in jeans barely hanging on his hips and no shirt, flipping pancakes in a pan I've never seen before. "You're forgiven."

Wait, back up. Jeans? "How much did those pants cost?"

He actually smiles, and his cheeks darken ever so much. "It's not polite to ask."

"That's what I figured."

"Kasi, what do you want with your pancakes?"

I know I didn't have anything in this house close enough to even resemble pancake ingredients. "Uh, syrup, I guess. Where did all this stuff come from?"

"I had it delivered."

"This early in the morning?"

He sits down next to me with his own plate of pancakes. "It's noon, Kas."

My eyes stretch out of my head, then I look around and really pay attention. The sun is shining high in the sky, and there's a bustle of people passing on the outside of my fence that faces the beach. I look down and gasp. "Shit."

Declan takes a long look from my shoulders to my thighs. "You always sleep in that?"

By *that*, he means a see-through nightie that barely covers my crotch. It certainly leaves nothing to the imagination. "No. I usually don't sleep in anything at all, but I knew I had company when I went to bed. This morning, not so much." I adjust my arms to at least hide my nipples while I eat. Normally this wouldn't be a big deal, but I'm supposed to not be encouraging Declan. "We need to meet Joy to sign some stuff."

"Yeah, at one."

"How do you know?"

He picks up the phone next to his plate. *Hi, Declan. I texted Kasi, but no reply. Make sure you both get here by one this afternoon to sign the contracts. See attached.*

"So you've already looked at the contracts?"

"Sure have. Hours ago."

I extend my glare to the ceiling after delivering it to him a good few seconds. "You do know I was in Peru yesterday, right? Excuse me for oversleeping."

He raises his hands in mock surrender. "I didn't say a word."

"You implied."

"If you say so."

"I do say so."

"Do you always have to get the last word?"

"Do you?"

"Yes."

I cock my head to the side, sizing him up. I just know he's going to be a hot mess throughout this whole endeavor. A thorn in my side. An arrogant temptation I'll have to expend way too much energy fighting off.

Declan just sits there, spine straight under my scrutiny. This man shouldn't be this comfortable in his own skin. No matter how gorgeous that skin is. Yet he holds my gaze with ease, waiting for me to try and snatch the last word.

I sigh and pick up my fork. I won't give him the satisfaction of playing his game. I do let my arms slip into a comfortable position. It's not my fault that means my nipples are exposed. All he has to do is lean back, and he'll see a lot more exposed from the rear.

He chuckles and eats his own pancakes.

When I can't eat another delicious bite, I put down my fork in surrender. "That was incredible, Dec. Thank you so much for breakfast. For everything."

"I hadn't forgotten I promised to make pancakes for you."

I smile because I hadn't either. It's the first thing I thought of when I calmed down after almost assaulting him.

He looks at me with those beautiful eyes and bites the corner of his sexy mouth. His muscles flex and squeeze as he crosses his arms.

I squeeze the tingle ghosting between my legs. "Um, we better get dressed so we can go." Time to get this back on track. I stand and grab our plates and place them in the sink. Anything to get away from the glorious view.

"Kasi, why fight it when you know we'll give in eventually?"

I rotate around and place my hand on my hip. "If you don't think you can respect my wishes, maybe we should reconsider before we go sign these contracts."

He lets loose a sly grin, running his gaze over my exposed body.

I look down and shake my head. It's hard to be taken seriously in a lace and net nightie. "I mean it, Dec."

He shrugs. "Anything you say." Then leaves and walks down the hall to the guest room. Hopefully to get a shirt.

Meanwhile, I'm standing here in little more than my birthday suit while I have the nerve to be salty about him looking so fine early in the morning. Or mid-day or whatever.

Declan calls from down the hall. "How far is Joy's office?"

"It's a ten-minute walk." I walk down the hallway, speeding toward my room, suddenly self-conscious. When I get there, I poke my head back out the door. "Are you still meeting Tariq?"

"No, I'll have to catch him next time."

"Next time? How did you two become such fast buddies?"

"He's a cool guy. We had to talk about something while we waited and since I never had time growing up for team sports like football, the conversation veered toward hiking."

"You know, we're going to be pretty busy so I'm not sure when you'll have time to meet up with him. Are you planning to move out here the next nine months?"

He draws his eyebrows together and purses his lips. "What do you mean move?"

"If you're going to produce, we have a thousand things to coordinate. The main one being prep work—location scouting, talent auditions, crew."

He screws his face into a frown and crosses his arms over his chest.

My stomach sinks because we may not be on the same page, and we haven't even got off the blocks yet.

"I'm not moving, Kas. I still have to work."

"You're kidding."

"Afraid not. I'll have time off when you need me, but some of those items on your list will have to be handled remotely. It's the twenty-first century after all."

I run my fingers through my curls, scraping my scalp in frustration. I want to feel my nails digging into my skull, relieving some of the pressure building there. "You can't half-ass this."

"I can assure you I will put all the energy into this project as required. I don't *half-ass* anything."

"Well, you're not still going to San Francisco, right?"

"Of course. I was always on my way there. This is a stop-over." He leans against the door, crossing his feet to mirror his arms.

"This isn't going to work."

"Have you always been this negative? Or is this LA Kasi? Because Austin Kasi was bold and confident. Where'd she go?"

My skin prickles from the slight. Mostly because he's right. This isn't me but he brings something out in me I don't recognize. "Fine. Have it your way, Everheart. But if shit goes south, you'll be the one on the hook." I close the door, then yank it back open. "And it better not go south." I slam it this time.

THE SUN SLOWLY sets over the pier and the air cools considerably. A great reason to live in LA is the night chill all year round. My fire pit in the backyard crackles and pops as Declan adds another log. All the contracts have been signed, and the check deposited in a business account that requires two signatures. I frown down at my laptop despite all that money floating in front of my face on the bank's website.

"You could have warned me about all the stipulations before we got to Joy's office."

He eases himself onto the bench next to me. "You'll recall I gave you an entire packet of information, right?"

Ugh, right. Then I'd promptly gone off on him and never read through the entire binder. Joy could have warned a sister though. "Hmmph."

"Your agent cum lawyer is very intimate with the terms. And you took your time and read through the contracts before signing so what's the issue now?"

I hate he makes me sound like a petulant child. It's time to anchor myself. "No issue. Where's your laptop? We need to get some work done since you're leaving so early tomorrow."

He reaches under the bench to the wooden slat below. "You know I have to meet my brothers. I synced my flight to meet up with theirs."

"I'm not complaining, Dec. Just stating facts." I open the budget. "Let's look at the below-the-line entries on the top sheet.

He leans near me, almost touching my shoulder with this chin.

"This is on our new drive. You can look on your laptop, you know?"

His breath ghosts over the shell of my ear when he exhales. "What would be the fun in that?"

Aaaaannnnnddddd now my clit's tingling.

He knows how he just affected me because the smirk is back.

I readjust, putting the slightest pressure on that swelling nub, and think about kittens. "We're not here to have fun, remember?"

He shrugs and leans back but doesn't put any distance between our thighs. "How could I forget when you keep reminding me?"

The laptop heats on my thighs, or maybe it's my imagination, but I set it on the slat under the bench and turn to Declan, giving him my full attention. "When I was in Austin, I was ready to fuck you to within an inch of your life."

He sucks in a breath, and it barely makes a sound, but I'm watching his lips when I say it.

"Obviously, we were physically attracted to each other. That goes without saying. I mean, look at us." I sweep my hand back and forth between our beautiful selves.

"There she is."

"Shut up." After rolling my eyes, I take a breath because my skin is heating in the best possible way, and that's the opposite of what I want right now. What we need right now. I put up a finger. "But, thinking about anything other than sexing you up wasn't on my agenda. More than anything, I want to get this documentary made."

He nods gravely, but there's a twinkle in those pretty blue eyes. "I'm sensing another *but* coming."

"Okay, sure. *But* I do like you, Dec. That doesn't change that my film is my top priority." I reach under the bench and pick up my laptop, settling it back on my thighs. "So, let's get this thing in the can, then we'll see if there's still interest there. Okay?"

After shrugging, he turns his laptop on. "Okay."

"Seriously, no more flirting. Alright?"

"I already said okay, Kas."

"Just putting it all on the table." He doesn't realize it, but that's more for me than him. Reminding myself of everything I just told Declan is the only way I'll make it through tonight, let alone the next few months. "So, let's copy the entries from the budget over to a spreadsheet and start figuring out how we're going to make this happen."

By the time we get through the production staff and background talent, Declan's already drooping. Filmmaking is not for the weak of heart. "Hey, pay attention. Let's talk camera package."

"I am paying attention. Why did you skip DP? And what's a DP?"

Flynn Everheart is my new favorite enemy. Yes, he's given me a shit-ton of money, but he's also saddled me with a producer who doesn't know anything about producing. Because of Flynn, I have my money, but he's stymied my freedom and put a good piece of ass just out of my reach to boot. I take a deep breath and try not to release it to where it sounds frustrated to Declan's ears. He helped me. I know that deep in my heart. I wouldn't have this money if it weren't for him convincing his father. Plus, Flynn is the one who insisted he still work and watch his investment. I need to be more charitable to Declan.

"It's the director of photography. Some call it a cinematographer."

"Oh, okay. I know what that is. They make sure the shot looks good, right?"

I smile at him because although the DP does a whole lot, that's pretty much what it boils down to. "Exactly right, Dec. And I skipped him because I already have my DP. His name is Neal, and I went to the AFI with him."

Declan nods, but when I look back at my laptop for the next line item, my peripheral catches him putting AFI in his phone search engine.

I chuckle to myself but shake my head and rotate to look at him. "You can ask me anything, okay? I know you're learning all this at once, but if you don't know something, I won't mind you asking."

"I appreciate that."

I smile and turn back to the business at hand. "Okay, lighting and equipment." We review for another couple of hours, and I allow Declan to look over my shoulder instead of staring at his own screen. He seems to perk up the more we collaborate and actually gives some good advice, especially when we discuss locations and activities we can do while there. This isn't going to be just a cooking-on-location type show. The talent has to be active and meet the ingredients where they are.

"Who's the talent by the way? I can't believe I haven't asked."

"His name is Josh. Another guy I went to film school with."

"Have I seen him in anything?"

"Maybe if you watched television. He's been in some national commercials and a ton of guest spots. Oh, have you seen the commercial with the dog dressed as a baby?"

"I've seen the memes going around."

"Well, that's him with the dog." I fish out my phone from the pocket of my jeans and scroll through until I pull up a picture of me, him, and Neal on the set of our student film. Seems like a lifetime ago. "See, that's Josh on the right."

"Okay, yes, I definitely remember him now. Does he

cook?"

I'm getting Melissa-vibes now, and I don't think I like where this is going, but I'm determined to keep my cool. "He's not a chef like you, but that's where you'll come in handy, won't it?"

He smirks, but not the sexy, cool smirk that sets me on fire. This is the smug, wiseass smirk that tells me he's about to say something I won't like. "He's got a great look, but don't you want someone with a little more...gravitas and cooking experience?"

"You have someone in mind?"

"I'd say my brother, Knox, but he'd never be interested."

That catches me off guard. I thought maybe he was talking about himself. The dynamic between the brothers is interesting. Too bad I'm not a psychoanalyst. "Josh will be fine, plus he's available and fits nicely with our budget."

He shrugs. "Seems to be a missed opportunity."

"At least meet the guy before you disparage him. Jeesh."

"It's your call, obviously."

Music to my ears. "Thank you. Now let's move on to extras. We'll use locals, of course. No airfare or hotel, but will still need to figure in meals, mileage, fringe, and—"

"What the hell is fringe?"

I laugh and pat his leg. This is going to be a long night.

CHAPTER NINE

When maybe there's a softening.

WHEN THE PLANE lands in Houston, and I walk through the jetway, the familiar heat wraps me up before I can take more than two or three steps. But it's ten times more potent than in Austin just two months ago. I can't get enough air—it's like breathing soup. How do people live like this? By the time I make it to the next gate for the flight to Peru, I'm drenched like I stepped out the shower.

Declan takes one look at me and laughs out loud. I'm momentarily stunned because I don't think I've ever heard a real laugh from him.

"I'm happy to entertain you." I set my backpack on the floor next to my feet and pull the wet blouse from my chest.

He moves in for a hug, but I scrunch my face. "I'm sticky." He envelopes me anyway and I sink into his touch. Even though we're in constant communication through video chats, I haven't actually seen him in three weeks. As it is, we only have a few days in Peru, then he's headed back to San Francisco for the second round of competition. They made it through the first one handily which didn't surprise me at all.

When he pulls back, a small grin plays at his lips, and he doesn't exactly let go. "It's nice to see you." He steps back and picks up my backpack. "We better get in line."

I don't say anything because his touch is stuck to my skin and that's all I can think about. The past three weeks have been nice. We've been kicking ass through our to-do list, and Declan's been much more of an asset than I thought he'd be. Once he got the industry lingo down and learned some things, he stepped up his game. I finally saw what he probably displays in the restaurant when his father gives him some room to shine.

And now we're headed to Peru together and I'm not sure how much longer I can keep this strictly professional.

The airplane is comfortable enough, and it's nice having a companion this time. "Did you say you've never been to Peru before?"

"No, never. I've been to La Paz which is right across the border."

"Oh, neat. Then you have an idea of the terrain and food."

He nods. "There's some cuisine I can't wait to try. And the Sacred Valley is prime for climbing."

"I'm happy you feel that way because that's kinda the purpose of this trip. When I came before, it was just to check out if it would fit my grand plan. Now we need to get into the nuts and bolts of the thing before we bring the crew and Josh."

"A dry run, I think you said."

I tap my nose. "Exactly that."

"You're still sold on Josh, huh?"

"Why wouldn't I be?" This is not the first time he's brought up our talent. Everyone we've hired so far, he's been on board with. Neal—he said a no-brainer. Declan video-chatted with our DP only because, as producer, I made him. One meeting with Kristin, and he was sold on her location management talents. But he's virtually met Josh twice and remains a skeptic. Yet he refuses to tell me what his issue is.

He sighs and puts on the eye mask the flight attendant just handed out. "Just reaffirming."

"Are you tired? We're just getting started."

"Late night at the restaurant. I just need an hour and I'll be ready to go."

"Your dad's a dick."

He sits up and removes the mask. "Actually, what he is, is your investor. You may want to remember that."

"How can I forget. But hey, if you don't mind him running you into the ground, who am I to care?"

"Well, you—"

"I know I phrased that as a question, but it was completely rhetorical. You do you, Dec."

He closes his eyes but doesn't put the mask on. Just when I think he's about to doze, he says, "You don't understand, Kas. He pits us against each other, but none of us want that. And everything's falling apart." He lets out a harsh breath, then opens his eyes, and puts that soulful gaze on me. "Knox is leaving."

"I don't understand what that means. Leaving where?"

"The restaurant."

"You're that confident you'll win? You still have two more rounds, right?"

He nods and pulls his window covering down as we take off. There are only two seats here in first class. We argued over the travel arrangements, but in the end, Declan refused to compromise on this. He's used to a life of luxury, and he's not even a little ashamed of it. When I traveled to Peru last time, I flew coach.

I grab hold of my armrests as the elevation tugs at my stomach, and hold my breath.

Declan rests his hand over mine, and squeezes, then leans into me. "Breathe, Kas." He puts both hands on either side of my face and applies the slightest of pressure.

"What are you doing?"

He smiles and drops his hands. "I thought you needed help. Sorry, it's habit from traveling with Knox."

"Knox doesn't like to fly?"

"He was young when our mother died. She's from Berkeley. Well, she was born in Italy but mostly grew up in Berkeley. That's where her family is, including my grandparents. They wanted her buried there. That was his first time flying and there was so much turbulence. I guess it left a long-lasting impression."

"That's, uh, really sad, Dec."

He puts his hand back on mine, and this time I turn it over and twine my fingers through his. "It was. Knox barely got any time with her."

"Do you miss her?"

"Every day."

"Really?"

"You seem surprised."

I purse my lips and think a moment. "It's not that I'm

surprised you miss your mother. It's more that you seem really close to your father."

"The three of us all have a tattoo in Italian. Roughly translated, it means 'A mother's love has no limits' so while I am close to Dad, he can't replace Mom."

"No, of course not. Is that the one on your chest?" For some reason, my face heats.

He lifts one of those perfect brows. "You were staring at my chest, huh?"

"I was…" I chuckle. "There's no sense denying it. I was definitely staring at your chest."

"Kas, what's the point of keeping up this sham?"

"You gave your word, Dec."

He raises his hands in surrender, then pulls his mask down over his eyes.

I stare at him while his eyes are covered and get my fill. At least for now.

We stand at the bottom of a thirteen-hundred-foot cliff, everyone looking up.

Declan turns to me and claps his hands, the biggest smile on his face I've ever seen. "This is going to be incredible."

"If you say so." When I came before, I walked the Sacred Valley but stayed on the floor of the valley between the mountains. The view down here is incredible, and the altitude is tolerable. Because this area is known as the Peruvian Highlands, we've chosen to film in Scotland too, for purposes of contrasting and comparing. I've not been to

Scotland, but I can't imagine it being as beautiful as here.

"I don't know why you won't climb with us."

I bark a laugh and finish loading the RC quadcopter with the cameras. "Because I've never hiked the side of a mountain before, that's why. My whole exercise routine consists of yoga on the beach and the free weights in the guest bedroom with some occasional disc golf thrown in for pleasure."

He does the thing where he scans my entire body unashamedly. "As cut as you are, those free weights must be bearing the brunt of your workout."

"You can't even see me." Even though it's May, the winter season is upon us down here south of the equator. Which is perfect because the mid-sixties temperature in the day with no rain expected makes for ideal filming conditions. It'll be helpful for their climbing too. I'd hate for Declan to fall off a cliff from a slippery handhold. The insurance company would be livid.

"I've seen plenty of you." He follows that up with his sexy smirk.

And dammit, for the life of me I can't keep myself from physically reacting. My nipples pebble. Just once, I'd like to be on the receiving end of that grin and shrug it off. At least my windbreaker covers the evidence.

I direct my attention back up to Renzo on the top of the hill. When we first video-chatted with Renzo to hire him for the shoot, Declan was friendly enough to him—as friendly as Declan gets—but kept switching his gaze to me. I can't bet that's what he was doing for sure, but to me, that's what it looked like. When I asked him about it later, he said I was flirting. Renzo lives up to the Peruvian meaning of his name, masculinity, but I certainly was not flirting. And even if I was, which would be highly unprofessional, it's not like it's Declan's business. Renzo fits our needs with his talent, but more importantly, all that brawn is coming in handy to get the shots we need.

I look over at the discarded crane and frown. Waste of money because trying to put a tripod on it didn't do anything to capture the angles we need. Instead, we put a sling on one end and Renzo is balancing it against his hip. When Declan climbs, he'll swing it out over him and get the good shots. I'll use the drone I'm outfitting to get aerials from another slant.

"Are you sure your harness it tight enough?" I nearly giggle but catch the sound right before it leaves my mouth. The local climbers stand next to Declan in their equally tight harnesses. It's not really an issue for Brigida, but for Declan and the other man, Ignacio, the gear basically puts their junk all on display.

Declan moves closer to me and pretends to help me with the drone. "Like what you see?"

"I've already seen it, Dec. The Jacuzzi didn't leave room for doubt about what you're packing." I thump his blue climbing helmet. "Cute hat though." He's been complaining about it since he put it on.

"I hate it, but I also don't want you to run that thing into my head."

"This is a very intelligent aircraft, Dec. And your helmet is in case you slip and take a nosedive into the ground."

"If that happens, this won't do me any good." He knocks

against the hard plastic.

A panicked breath lodges in my throat. "Wait, could that happen?"

He shrugs and strides back to the others, readying themselves to step on the first rung of the ladder.

No, it couldn't happen. They're all strung together, then attached to the mountain. Even if one of them slips, they're anchored to the rock.

Before I launch the drone, I review the video screen and start recording, aiming my shot right at Declan's dick. If he knows what I'm doing, he doesn't give it away. Instead, he rotates that firm ass my way, and steps onto the ladder, making me think he knew exactly what I was filming.

"You're supposed to wait until I yell *action*."

He waves his hand in dismissal, and climbs.

I signal Renzo on the walkie, and he responds that he's ready. He'll get the static shot from above as they climb until they get closer, then swing the tripod.

The others follow Declan, and I launch the aircraft, concentrating on getting great shots.

Declan doesn't miss a beat and climbs just as well as the professionals. When they're about halfway up though, the thin, high-altitude air messes with him. "Fuck, it's hard to breathe."

I wish I could offer him words of encouragement, but he's too high up to hear me. If I didn't have cameras on him, I wouldn't be able to tell there's even a problem from down here.

He stops and puts his hands on his waist, and takes some breaths. "Fuck."

I'm not sure I've heard Declan cuss before. That's twice in five minutes so this must really be a slog for him after all. The whole reason we're here is because the altitude concentrates the tastes and flavors of the food. But that also means that you know, it's high up. I chuckle to myself.

"Fuuuuuuuck, it's thin up here."

They're nearly at the top when Renzo's camera comes flying out of nowhere. It makes a perfect arc before retreating, then repeating until Declan and crew are almost at the top.

When they do make it up there, Declan raises his arms in triumph, then fist bumps both Brigida and Ignacio. It's funny because that's a lot of enthusiasm from Declan. But also because he towers over both of his crewmates and the fist-bumping just looks comical.

He whoops and shouts into the atmosphere. "The views are incredible." Then he puts his hands on his hips again and bends over.

Looks like the momentary euphoria made him forget he can't breathe.

I call Renzo on the walkie. "Shots okay?"

"Perfect. Uploading now."

When the recording comes through, I gasp with delight, then give Renzo a thumbs-up. I'll review in more detail when we get back to the hotel, but the quick look I've already given them makes me think one thing.

Declan's a star.

"THIS REMINDS ME a little of Italy."

We sit next to one of the pools at our boutique hotel surrounded by rolling hills layered with buildings in shades of brown. Others are sprinkled here and there nearby, but the pool is empty. I glance up to where his gaze has landed, and although the buildings of Italy are colorful, I get what he means. "I can see that. Was your mom from the Amalfi Coast though?"

"No, nowhere close, but we've traveled all through her home country over the years."

"I stayed in a place much like this. Although this is a converted convent and that was a converted monastery. Thirteenth century, I believe. It was gorgeous."

"Hmmm, sounds expensive."

I roll my eyes and change the subject with a swiftness. "Why haven't you looked at the footage yet?"

He turns on his cushioned lounge chair, and leans his upper body against it, but doesn't swing his legs up. "Honestly? I'm tired."

"Well, you climbed a rather large mountain in the thinnest of air. I think you're allowed a little relaxation." I smile. "I've never heard you cuss so much."

"I—" He looks up and laughs. "It was intense. For a moment there, I wondered if I'd ever get enough air."

"Well, thankfully our suite has enriched oxygen. You're looking better."

He rotates my way, and the smirk appears. "Which is why I don't regret insisting on staying here."

I shake my head and lie back on my lounge chair. Most logistics he left up to me, but where his comfort was concerned, he fought me tooth and nail. First-class flight, luxury hotel, and a hired car to get us everywhere.

"We should change and get in the pool. It's heated, you know. That would really relax my aching muscles."

I turn and look at him with a sharp stare, hoping to cut this conversation in the bud. "I didn't bring my suit."

He returns my stare, his gaze smoldering. "That didn't stop you before." He lifts a brow in challenge. "I have plenty of underwear with me."

So my glare didn't work. I should have known. "No flirting, Dec."

He releases a small puff of air and relaxes back on the chair. "Right."

"When you've caught your breath, we should go back to our suite."

He lolls his head my way, ever so slowly, a sly grin touching the corners of his mouth. "Didn't you just say—"

"To look at footage. Oh my gosh, one-track mind."

He sits up suddenly. "Okay, but then we eat. I'm starved."

"You mean the alpaca jerky wasn't filling?"

After lifting himself off the lounge, he stretches his long body, arms extended high above his head, exposing a strip of toned abs. He's still wearing the thin long-sleeved T-shirt he hiked in. The material hugs every single one of his muscles.

I swallow the excess saliva that's accumulated in my mouth.

When he glances down at me, I've fixed my face to an uninterested glance. "You have a glass face. Just so you know."

"Do not." I do, and my mother has told me that my entire life. If I'm thinking something, you know what it is just by taking a quick peek at my face. "Maybe stop setting thirst traps."

He chuckles so hard his shoulders shake. "You said don't flirt. No mention of being my usual striking self." He has the nerve to wink, something I've never seen him do. "And no, the jerky was mouth-watering, but wore off a while ago. You should have eaten some."

I scrunch my face. "But they're cute alpacas. I'll wear a pair of socks made from their wool, but that's as far as I'll go."

He reaches over to pull me up. "You're doing a documentary on off-the-beaten-path cuisine. I think you'll probably run into some food that will not be your usual."

"I get that, but alpaca?" I shudder as I follow him to the stairs that will lead us up to our shared suite. We have individual bedrooms at least. "Besides, the documentary is more about the adventure than the food. You already know that."

He skips up the stairs like he didn't just climb a whole mountain. I keep up, but I didn't exert myself nearly as much as he did.

When we reach the room, I rush inside to the equipment and set up the view screen. I bounce on my toes waiting for him to get settled onto a living room barstool bordering the table with the equipment.

I roll the footage, and bite my lip, shifting the entire time. Unable to sit still.

In complete opposition, Declan is a statue. No emotion

crosses his beautiful face.

When the entire video has played, I rotate to a quiet Declan. He's sitting perfectly still. "Do you see?"

He breathes hard a few times with closed eyes. When he opens them, he stares at me, then nods.

"Okay, so first we'll need to call Josh. I can do that." I dig around through the various cameras, cords, and other electronics until I find my phone.

Declan puts a hand on mine and offers a slight smile, tinged with sadness. "It's not that simple."

"You were born for this, Dec. Your charisma is undeniable. You established rapport with the other on-screen talent, making them comfortable and open. You're athletic enough for the strenuous activities. And wait until the cooking part. The recipes you've already supplied are mind-blowing, and that's before you got here and were actually sampling the food firsthand. I have every confidence in you."

He scrubs his hands across his face, and stands, then paces the room. It's difficult because it's not a large room, at least not by standards at home, and aside from where we were sitting, there's a sofa with a coffee table in front of it, a desk pushed into the corner, but still taking up quite a bit of room, and two wingback armchairs. He gives up on navigating the obstacle course, and stands at the huge picture window instead, pushing aside the heavy drapes.

I walk up behind him and wrap my arms around his waist. This isn't flirting, it's offering comfort.

He puts one hand over my hands crossed over his stomach, and then places the other against the window, leaning forward, taking me with him. "I'm a chef."

"You'd still be a chef."

"I won't leave Dad. He's already losing Knox and doesn't even realize it."

"And you can't do both." I don't phrase it as a question because we both know he can't. As it is, Declan's spread thin and even when the competition is over next month—if they make it past the next round which they will—it would be impossible to film full-time all around the world, and work at Everheart Bar and Fine Dining too. We've worked on the schedule together, and as it is, he'd only committed to being on set the entire time in a little over half of the shoots. If he's our above-the-line talent, missing a location wouldn't be an option.

"No, I can't." His breathing is deep, as though he's trying to calm himself.

I lay my head on his back and squeeze my arms tighter around his torso. "Will you at least think about it? Or can we talk about it some more? Maybe figure something out."

He shrugs and takes in an even deeper breath.

"I'm not trying to stress you out, but you must see that you're made to be in front of the camera."

"I always thought of that as Knox's calling. He got us on that show."

"Yeah, but that's a means to an end. Do you think he really wanted to be on television?"

His shoulders bounce, and a low rumble rolls through his throat before releasing in a sharp bark of laughter. "He did it for a woman. Rowan Townsend. Everything else is icing."

"You're kidding."

"Not even a little bit."

"And you went along with it?"

He shrugs and lifts off the window, turning in my arms. When I try to let go, he reaches behind his back and grasps my hands. "I told you I'd do anything for my brothers. Besides, he wants to leave."

"But you don't?"

Uncertainty colors his eyes. He may not admit it to me, but he's not sure.

"Weston's an excellent pastry chef, but it's not his passion. I can see him going the way of Knox eventually."

"But the restaurant is your passion?"

"Dad needs me."

It's not my place to tell him about selfish fathers. Maybe Flynn isn't like Dad, but I'd bet my trust fund Declan's father is more like Reggie Blythewood than not. "Okay."

There's always tomorrow. He'll be cooking with a local family, and if that doesn't latch him, I won't push the issue anymore. Meanwhile, I keep my fingers crossed that Declan grows a backbone.

WE'VE ONLY SPOKEN about logistics this morning. Even though the car ride was nearly two hours, what felt like straight up, nothing personal exchanged between us. I finish unloading the equipment from the truck that followed us up here then glance around.

Declan's wearing his Peru uniform as I call it. A long-sleeved T-shirt made of breathable material that hangs on him like a long-time lover. His pants aren't his usual designer label trousers although I wouldn't be surprised if they carried a hefty price tag. To me, I'd say serviceable gray Dockers, but I'd more than likely be wrong. His sturdy leather hiking boots are probably waterproof.

I pull on my backpack and look down at my own clothes. I don't need waterproof hiking boots, and mine look more like a cross between boots and tennies. The only difference in my usual athleisure is that my tights have pockets to slide stuff in like my phone.

Fine-ass Renzo is back with us today, wielding a steadicam and a heavy pack of equipment. We have no need for the climbers, but we did hire a translator. A woman treks across the grassy front area and judging from our video chat, this must be Luna. She's striking, with long black hair and luminescent brown skin. I rotate to Declan who looks back at me, eyes wide. He lifts both brows and tilts his head, then shrugs, a hint of a small smile curving his lips.

Yeah, Dec, I know. She's gorgeous.

Something inside me rakes a raggedy fingernail across my gut, releasing a bile I have trouble controlling. I have no claims on Declan, but all of a sudden, I'm jealous as fuck.

"Hello, I'm Luna. You must be Declan and, uh, Kasi." She says this while gaping at Declan, then reaches for his hand.

Yeah, Luna, I know. He's gorgeous.

As soon as she says her name, my ears hurt, the sound of her voice scraping across my eardrum. I release a nervous laugh and cover my mouth. "Sorry, the altitude is messing with me." I offer my hand. "It's nice to meet you in person."

She turns to me, belatedly, and barely grasps my hand.

Declan watches me closely, the smirk firmly in place.

After all the introductions are made, and I've settled into Luna's beauty, accepting I can do nothing if Declan develops a thing for her, we meet the family we came here to cook with. I hang back a bit, allowing Declan to get comfortable with his surroundings including the people. I can't lose sight of what I really want out of this. If I can't convince him to be the talent today, it'll be a lost cause. I'll need to stomp down any misguided jealousy before I allow it to affect my movie.

The husband of the family, Juan, says something to Luna in Spanish, then she translates. "We will need to gather an herb from beside the creek." She gestures toward the flowering meadow leading away from the house on the left. "This way."

Declan, Luna, and Juan walk ahead while both Renzo and I capture the hike on film. After about thirty minutes, I'm feeling the trudge in my chest, and fall behind no matter how hard I try to keep up. The others, this being where they live, aren't winded in the least. Only Declan is breathing hard, although his stride hasn't broken. Even though he and Luna are chatting nearly nonstop.

A few minutes later, and my trailing is noticeable. Declan glances back ever so slightly, then holds his side and stops. "I think I need to take a break. This air is so thin up here and I'm still not used to it."

Juan says something in Spanish, then laughs, pointing at Declan.

Declan only chuckles, good-naturedly, not offended in the least by Juan's teasing.

Luna studies Declan, lips pursed. She knows he's not

tired enough to need to stop.

After a few minutes, Declan casually turns my way. "Sorry for the delay. I'm ready."

I only stretch my eyes, and nod. We're still filming after all.

When we reach the waterfall, my mouth falls open. We've seen so many breathtaking views, but this one is on a whole different level.

Declan puts his hands on his trim hips and shakes his head. "This is incredible."

Juan says something else and points to the river. I know they said creek earlier, and the space is probably creek-sized in width, but the water flows over the rocks in a fast clip.

Luna translates. "Juan says the herbs are right there where he's pointing, but he wants you to get them." Then she displays her dazzlingly bright teeth.

Declan looks from Juan to the creek, then back to Juan.

Juan only smiles and gestures to the creek.

When Declan steps on the first rock, he holds his arms out to balance himself. He moves to the second and wobbles. "Shit, these rocks are slippery." He bends over after stepping to the next rock, barely keeping himself from falling into the flowing water. "Fuck."

It takes everything I have to not giggle loud enough to be caught on camera. I'm the background, the crew. I have no business being seen or heard, but damn, watching Declan struggle through the water-logged path leading to the herbs is almost too much. Especially when he bends over, and the top of his ass crack peeks out from underneath his T-shirt which keeps riding up. This is visual gold. I hope we'll be able to include it in the movie instead of just outtakes when all's said and done.

"Fuck." Declan nearly slides into the water but catches a leafy branch at the last minute and swings, Tarzan-style, to the bank next to the herbs.

My core tightens. If it wouldn't be indecent in front of all these people, not to mention highly unprofessional, I'd reach into my tights right now and rub one out. Damn, what is this man doing to me?

When he picks a small bunch of herbs, he holds them to his nose and sniffs. "Oh, these are wonderful. Very bold." He pinches a bit off and places it on his tongue, then chews.

My nipples harden.

"Also, a sweetness. And floral. My goodness, this is spectacular. Totally worth me almost breaking my neck."

Juan and Luna laugh.

I put my camera down and wipe the sweat from my forehead. We don't need to film him making his way to us, nor the trek back to the cottage. As hot and bothered as I am, the thought is a great relief. *Get it together, Kasi.*

When we make it back to the remaining family, they've set up a pounding station with dried potatoes nearby. All peel potatoes, including Luna, while Renzo and I film. Declan is charming, and initiates conversation with the family through Luna. The mood is generally upbeat and cheerful, with plenty of laughter at Declan's jokes.

He's in his element. Probably like never before. When I visited the restaurant, he was stern and serious in the kitchen, directing the staff with a tense voice, his originality stifled by his father's power. Even when he came over to visit me and

Joy, he was cordial, but there was an edge. Here, with the backdrop of this beautiful landscape, surrounded by ancient Inca ingredients and cooking methods, Declan is relaxed and comfortable, his ingenuity shining through, even while directing the action around him. This will translate beautifully to film and I am so here for it.

Getting Declan on board is a must. Not just for my film, but for him too.

CHAPTER TEN

When she can't help herself.

WE SLOG DOWN the narrow walkway toward the building where our suite is housed. The sun has set but the space is lit with fairy lights strung down its length. It's still darker than the rest of the property, and eerily quiet.

"You know Luna doesn't hold a candle to you?"

I shrug and keep walking. "I hadn't noticed."

"You noticed."

I don't turn, even though he's so close behind me, the breath of his words caresses the back of my neck. "You certainly stared at her hard enough to make that comparison."

An exhale of a laugh puffs my hair held in a high ponytail. "You're jealous."

"Am not." I switch the camera bag I'm holding to my other arm, but don't lose my step. "I could have you if I wanted you."

"Oh, you want me." He takes the burden of the bag from me, and I stop and turn to him.

"I had it."

He steps closer to me. "I know you had it. Now I have it." His eyes are fully charged, his breathing slow and deep.

I take a couple steps back until my butt rubs up against the wall and cross my arms over my hardening nipples. The air is cool tonight, but not enough to account for the pebbles poking through my crop top and underlying sports bra. "Dec, we agreed."

He licks his lips and takes another step closer. "Is that what you still want?"

I study him, my gaze sweeping from head to toe as he's done me many so many times before. I don't linger like him but take him in with one quick pass. His hair is groomed to perfection still, even after he nearly fell into a river and cooked in a small, steamy hut kitchen over a fire. Maybe it's lost a bit of its curl, but probably only noticeable to me because I pay such careful attention. His close beard has grown out ever so slightly over the course of the day, giving him a more rugged than pretty-boy look. His eyes are bright with electricity even under the low lights of the pathway we're on.

My breathing becomes shallow, and the flesh under my skin rises, clawing toward Declan. I raise a hand and curve it around his neck, pulling him down ever so slowly. "That's not what I want anymore."

He doesn't gloat, or smirk, but allows me to pull him closer, his lips slightly parted, his breath ghosting my lips. "Tell me what you want."

"Right now I want you to kiss me."

He meets my lips with a slight brush of his own, not what I was expecting given the passion in his eyes. The kiss is tender with gentle pressure, conveying a certain reverence. My heart picks up the pace with its beats, and my face flushes with want so I drop my hand down his side and pull his body closer.

He groans and dips his tongue into my mouth when I open it for him. Suddenly the kiss is as intense as my desire, and our tongues swirl together, our lips and teeth biting and nipping, our hands roaming and clutching. His ass is as tight as I imagined, and suddenly all I want is to pull his dick out and fuck him against this wall, out here in the open.

"Okay, that's enough." I pull back, trying to catch my breath and clear my thoughts.

"No such thing where you're concerned." He hovers over me but makes no move to kiss me again.

"Dec, what are we doing?"

He barks a small laugh. "I thought that was obvious." After one last squeeze of my waist, he pulls back and lifts the camera bag from the ground. "Let's get to the room so we can unwind and talk."

I follow him down the remainder of the walkway, into our wing of the hotel, and up the stairs. We walk in silence, but it's so loud, I can barely think. I'm not sure I want to think, but I also need to access what I truly want. Besides the obvious. It's not just about the sex anymore and although I still don't think it's a good idea for us to get involved until the film's in the can, I also want him, plain and simple.

"Fuckity fuck."

It's barely a whisper from my lips, but Declan rotates my way when we reach the door to our suite. "What was that?"

"Just a little frustration leaking out."

He searches my eyes, then thins his lips. "Kas—"

"Let's go in, Dec. You're right about unwinding first.

You look fresh as always, but I could really use a shower."

He nods and unlocks the door.

The living room is bathed in the soft light coming through the sheer curtain covering the picture window. I flip the light switch on next to the door and walk over to the window and close the heavy drapes for privacy.

Declan sets down all the bags of equipment, then runs his hand through his hair.

We stare at each other for a moment, then we each turn and walk to our respective rooms.

I close the door behind me and lean against it, taking deep breaths. Relationship decisions aren't something I put a lot of thought into. Normally, I just bypass them. At least that's how it's gone the past couple years since the only boyfriend I've been close to, Gregory, helped Dad screw me over. I've been too busy fighting my way out of forced nepotism to have more than a friends-with-benefits situation. And I'm so close to getting what I want. Now is not the time to muck it up with a guy.

After one last deep breath, I push off the door and stride across the room, past the canopied queen-size bed, kicking off shoes and discarding clothes as I wend my way. When I arrive in the bathroom, I turn the shower on as hot as it'll go, then vanish into the stream, blanking my thoughts, only feeling.

The water cools, waking me from my daze. My thoughts bum rush me all at once, and my gut clenches. Declan was forced on me by his father. Not that I'm ungrateful, but I didn't want a producing partner. Someone watching my every decision and move. But that's the deal I made with the devil, and here we are. Speaking of the devil, in my opinion, he has total control over his son. And Declan doesn't even realize how far up his father's ass he really is. That's not something I can work with, given my own parental pain in the ass. I see the writing on the wall for Dec, but I can't tell him. He has to realize it for himself. Running his father's restaurant is not what he really wants. Until he figures that out, I can't give him even a piece of my heart. The only path with Declan right now is a physical one.

The mirrors are completely fogged up, so I swipe my towel over one just to get a look at myself. My eyes are red from too little sleep, and droopy from the day's excessive activities. I didn't bother to take my hair out of the ponytail, and the ends are drenched, drawing up in tight curls. I don't need the mirror to show me how sore my muscles are, but thankfully the image reflecting my body is no worse for wear. If anything, all the hiking and carting heavy equipment around has tightened my flesh.

I run the towel over my skin, and exhale, rubbing slow circles over my breasts, heat building in my belly. I'll share my body with Declan, but that's all he can have. At least for now.

When I return to the living room, the man himself is spread across the sofa, wearing drawstring pajama pants. The expanse of his chest is smooth, the definition of his firm muscles on full display.

I lick my lips and stare.

He glances up from the screen he's watching. "You're amazing."

I blink. "Huh?"

He swings his legs off the couch and pats the cushion next to him. "Come see."

He's more than halfway through the footage I shot today. "How long was I in the shower?"

"A long time. I was beginning to think you shimmied out the window and scaled the wall."

My face heats with embarrassment, replacing the lust that was just there. He thinks I was scared to come back out. "The water just felt so good."

"Hmmm." He clicks play and the scene of him with the family peeling the dried potatoes flashes on the screen.

Declan is even more spectacular on video than in real life. His movements are easy and his intellect sharp. He picks up on the ancient techniques quickly and incorporates his own training to raise the preparation level. The people around him respond untroubled, secure in his direction, even with the language barrier.

I'm glued to the screen, leaning over Declan to get as close as I can without distorting my vision. The way he takes charge has my heat turning back into lust. "Gosh, you're perfect."

He sets the display on the coffee table, then cups my cheek. "You're perfect."

I close the short distance, and sink my teeth into his bottom lip, then straddle him, pushing him back against the sofa. His growing erection pushes against the seam running the length of my pajama shorts. He clutches the softness of my hips, pulling me closer against his hardness, and runs his tongue over my lips. "I thought maybe you changed your mind."

His voice travels through my lust-fueled fog but it's so distant and distorted. I pull back, concentrating on his mouth. "Sorry, what?"

He kisses down the length of my neck, and I throw my head back for better access. "I said I'm glad you didn't change your mind about us."

I reach between our bodies and rub my hand against his crotch, then grasp his dick through the covering of his pajamas. I give him a wicked grin. "No, I definitely want this. It's the perfect way to unwind, like you said."

He clasps his hand around mine and pulls it away from his erection. "Only unwind?"

The move sobers me, pulling my brain back into my head. "We were supposed to talk, weren't we?" I slide off his lap, ever so reluctantly, somehow knowing this won't go how I want.

He grabs my hand, and holds it, then leans his head back against the sofa, staring at the ceiling. "You know I want more than sex from you, right?"

"Yes, but right now, we're making this movie, and..." I'm not sure how to phrase it. Anyway, if I fix my mouth to say sex is okay, but feelings aren't, that makes me sound like an asshole. "And we can enjoy each other, but let's think about the other stuff after we finish the film."

He squeezes my hand and brings it to his lips, laying a soft kiss on my palm. "No."

"No?"

"I don't want to be your fuckboy."

I snatch my hand back, and sit up, indignant. "That's not what I meant."

"You want to have sex with me, but nothing else. That's what you're saying, right?"

"For now, Dec. That doesn't make you a fuckboy though. I do care about you."

"So what's the problem? I don't see how fucking doesn't get in the way, but a relationship does." He releases a mirthless laugh.

"People always say sex complicates things. That's not it though. It's the emotions behind the sex, usually unsaid. Then feelings get hurt, and issues surface. We can't afford that right now."

"You can't afford that right now."

"Correct. I'm too close to getting what I want. To producing a great series and making your father even more wealthy."

"You don't care about my father."

"You're right. Not even a little bit. But I do care about Tariq. And it's more than that. I want to prove what I can accomplish outside Townsend Productions even with Dad undermining me every step of the way."

He nods and stands. "Right. I get it. It's admirable, what you're doing. But Tariq says he doesn't need the money."

I shrug and stand too, flipping off the switch on the video display. It'll wait until tomorrow to finish watching because there's no way I can have the conversation I want tonight. Not anymore. Whatever this is between us is already messing shit up. "I owe it to him to make good on his investment. It doesn't matter if he needs it or not."

"Alright, Kasi." He walks to the door leading to his bedroom. "I'll see you in the morning. The market tomorrow, right?"

"Right."

He goes through the door and closes it with a soft click.

I just stand there and stare. Then move to the sofa, and sit, and rub my hands over my face.

I have no idea how to make this right, but I can't let him slip through my fingers. Neither professionally nor personally. I look over at the door again, willing him to walk back through.

He doesn't, so I go to my own room and crawl under the covers. I'll sleep on it and come up with a plan tomorrow.

CHAPTER ELEVEN

When they throw caution to the wind.

THE TOWN OF Pisac is only about forty minutes away, but I dread the trip. After last night, Declan won't be happy this morning. And sitting next to a sulking Declan Everheart is not my idea of a good time.

When he opens the door to our hired car and slides into the seat next to me, he turns to me and smiles. "Why didn't you wait for me?"

I blink.

"Did you eat?"

I shake my head, ever so slowly, trying to dislodge the shock built up inside.

"I figured." He reaches into his pack and pulls out a baggie with two croissants filled with mangoes, and hands them to me.

"Thanks." It comes out as a croak, and I clear my throat. "Thank you, Dec."

"You're welcome." He flashes me a quick smile, then looks out the window as we pull away from the hotel. "I'm really looking forward to the market."

I nod, even though he isn't looking my way.

"I've heard there's such a variety of fruit and vegetables."

He chuckles. "Probably more dried alpaca. You really should try just a little. It's unimaginably delicious."

I tighten my lips and cross my arms. I'm unsure how I feel about chatty Declan. I want my serious, arrogant man back. Only, he isn't my man, is he? "What's going on, Dec?"

He swivels his head my way, one eyebrow quirked. He really looks at me now, studying my stiff posture, the way I hold the croissants like they'll bite me, my downturned mouth. "Are you upset about something?"

"Okay, so that's how we're playing it. Fine." I tear open the bag, and bite into one of the pastries.

He watches me while I chew, then slowly slides the smirk into place. "You're having second thoughts."

I swallow and move to take another bite, but realize I'm being immature. "I'm not happy how we left everything last night. You seem unaffected."

He lowers his voice, back to the normal tone I've become accustomed to. "I don't dwell."

"So this…" I wave a hand between us. "This wasn't that important."

"Kas, I don't play games. You seemed to want me to shoot my shot. I did. It didn't work out. I'm not going to beg you."

"Do you want me or not, Dec?" *Shit, what am I saying?* I snort and shove the rest of the bread in my mouth.

He watches me but doesn't answer the question. How can I blame him when I've been running so hot and cold? I hardly recognize myself.

When I swallow this time, I set the baggie with the remaining croissant on top of my backpack resting on the floor. Then I rotate to Declan, and scoot in as close as the seat belt will allow. "I'm not sure what to say. I still don't think it's a good idea, but I want to try if you still do."

"Thank you for forcing yourself into a relationship with me." He snorts and turns away.

"That didn't come out right. I like you. A lot." I rub his arm seductively and bite my lip. "Let's make it work and get this film made without incident."

He looks down at my hand on his bicep. "You're not getting any until you prove yourself." I know I said I missed that smirk, but he's taking it overboard now.

I pull my hand back. "You don't think I mean it?"

"Let's just say your track record hasn't been the best since we met two months ago."

Opening my mouth to protest seems like a good idea until I remember he's completely right. "Fine."

"Fine."

Somehow, I was thinking getting together with Declan would make both of us at least smile. His perpetual smirk matches my scowl, and I can't help myself. I bust out laughing, practically wheezing.

Declan turns back to the window, but his shoulders shake, which is the only clue I have that he's laughing too. After a moment, he circles back to me, his smooth face perfectly composed. Then he dips his head, and I meet him halfway, our lips crashing together. He sweeps his tongue inside my mouth, tasting of mango and sweet butter, and I melt completely into the kiss. The car stops abruptly, shuffling us across the seat, and we both peer through the front window from our position in the back seat.

An older woman, dressed in traditional clothing for the area, crosses the road with an alpaca following close behind.

Declan and I look at each other, and fall back in our seats, giggling. Well, I giggle while Declan shakes his head, the sexy moment lost but not forgotten, judging by the look in his eyes. I'm sure a mirror of my own. We'll see how long he can hold out. I give him until we get back to our suite.

Walking the market is easy and breezy, a weight lifted from my chest. Yes, working everything out with Declan is great although I'm not totally convinced we aren't making a huge mistake. But we've descended about two thousand feet, and I can finally breathe again without gasping.

We're early, but tourists are already filing into the rows of vendors selling their wares. I look up to the mountain nearest us, and a caravan of white buses wend their way down the hill, heading our way. Pretty soon, this place will be overrun with people, perfect for my B-roll shots.

A beautifully carved chess set catches Declan's eye, and he saunters over, picking up one of the pieces.

"You play?"

"Not really. I can play, but Weston's a champ. He would love this."

I pick up one of the intricate pieces, the weight heavy in my hand. The chess set is different than any traditional one I've ever seen. It doesn't contain black on one side and white on the other, but instead is made of both wood and ceramic, and hand-painted in vivacious colors. One side appears to be Inca warriors pitted again Spanish conquistadors on the other. "Wow."

He purchases it for Weston, and my heart swells. It's one

thing for him to say how much he loves his brothers, but quite another to witness his fondness in action. Sure, he's doing the whole competition for Knox, but this just hits different.

I select an alpaca sweater for myself because I don't have any siblings to get mushy over. Then I spot another pullover in vibrant purple and blue, and buy it because those are a couple of Joy's favorite colors.

We stop in a market restaurant and order coffee. I drink it now and again, but don't make a habit of it. We sit on the second floor of the building, on a small terrace, and play footsie under the table. I smile, and Declan actually grins.

After I get some shots of the market and the throng milling about, we head over to one of the huge ovens. A couple hundred years ago, they built a few of these and they're still serviceable today. I marvel at the sheer size of the oven as one of the workers slides a tray of empanadas inside.

My Spanish is super rusty, but I think Declan just ordered a tomato and cheese pastel. "They make just tomato and cheese?"

He nods. "The filling is only limited by your imagination." The wheels are obviously turning inside that fertile mind of his, as he gazes at the oven. He reaches for my hand, and twines his fingers with mine, still watching the entire process of the food being made.

Declan feeds me an empanada when it cools, and I close my eyes in bliss. He wraps me in his arms, resting his chin on top of my head, the camera between us keeping us apart. But I still feel the beat of his heart through my instrument, and I smile to myself. No matter what happens between us, I know that he'll never be the expressive one. Or expend a lot of meaningless words, but somehow I know, I'll always know, how he feels about me.

My chest expands, making room for my growing heart. Maybe making this documentary plus balancing a relationship can work after all.

WE ARRIVE BACK at the hotel in the light of day this time, full on local customs and cuisine. I'm anxious to get inside and review the footage from the day before and today. What I saw of yesterday's was really quite good, and I only wish we hadn't disagreed so much that we couldn't finish it.

This time when we reach the door to our suite, I'm bouncing with excitement. "Let's hurry and change. I can't wait to see what we captured."

He shrugs before walking through the door. "What you captured. I'm just the eye-candy standing in."

I smile, but reserve comment. I can only hope there's some way to convince him to quit his whole life and headline this show. If he does, it won't be the last time his talent will be sought after. He's a star and doesn't even know it.

With the camera equipment set up and ready, I check the time on my phone. "I'm going to grab a quick shower and meet you back here. Okay?"

"Sounds good."

I half hoped he wanted to follow me, and maybe ask to share a shower, but somehow believed he wouldn't. Declan made a stand earlier, and no matter how many touches and kisses we shared today, he'll more than likely stick to it. At least for a minute or two. There's no way I'm sending him back to San Francisco tomorrow without at least a little taste.

The shower feels good, washing away the grime of the day. We didn't have to hike or climb today, but still covered quite a bit of ground, even at a leisurely pace. Seems like whenever we ascend back to the hotel, and the air thins so much, the feel of my skin roughens too. I can't seem to get clean enough.

I pull out the dresser drawer and look between two different night clothes. One set is a mostly sheer white cami with frills and lace covering the matching short bottoms. The other set is similar to the ones I wore last night, red plaid-patterned boxers with a sleeved top similar to a T-shirt. On the one hand, if I wear the first outfit, Declan doesn't stand a chance. I have a feeling that'll make him upset later though. On the other hand, if I wear the unsexy clothes, we'll at least get through the footage without incident.

I choose the boring sleepwear because I don't need to put stumbling blocks in my own way. I want him to concentrate on his performance and really see himself so I can convince him to star in my series. No way that's happening with the lacy pjs.

The living room is empty when I come out of my room. Declan's normally so much quicker than me so I'm a bit surprised. I plop on the couch and wait.

Fifteen minutes later when he finally comes out of his room in a cloud of heated mist, his expression is relaxed. Too relaxed.

"Declan?"

He slides onto the couch next to me and throws an arm around my shoulder, then kisses my temple. "Hmmm?"

I huff. "I can't believe you."

He only shrugs. "I'm strong, but you can't expect me to hold up my end of our bargain fully loaded, can you?"

"So, you made me wait out here while you rubbed one out?"

He doesn't even look ashamed. "No one stopped you from doing the same."

I roll my eyes and release a heavy sigh. "Are you sure you don't play chess regularly?"

He laughs, genuine mirth-filled laughter and pulls me against his chest, kissing my hair. "Let's watch me dazzle some folks."

"You're the worst." He's right though, and I forgot just that quickly. This is why I didn't want to get involved. I already can't hold a train of thought around him. I click play and view without comment, mentally taking notes.

While we watch, sometimes there'll be a small intake of breath from Declan that I barely hear. Sometimes, he'll squeeze my stomach where he's resting his hand. He sees what I see.

When we reach the end of yesterday's footage, I set the device on the coffee table. I don't play what we shot today, or even footage from Renzo's camera, because he's seen enough. He must have. We sit in the quiet room, only our breathing keeping us company. I take in the spicy scent of his understated cologne. Or maybe it's his body wash. My thoughts get sidetracked a moment thinking about all the things I'll get to learn about this amazing man I still don't know yet.

He finally squeezes my shoulders and turns me to face him. "Dad will be livid."

"It's not your father's life though."

"I want to. So badly."

"Then do it, Dec. You deserve this and you're amazing at it. I'm not talking about this one series. This could be your career."

"I like cooking. Creating."

I nod, and smile. "Yes, I can see that. You are absolutely a creative soul. And maybe it would be different if your father allowed you to truly create, but he doesn't. And we both know he never will."

"Never is a long time, Kas."

"Yeah."

"It's too big of a decision for me to make right now. Especially with you warming my chest. I'm not thinking straight."

I snuggle into him closer, climbing into his lap. "I get that, but we need to make a decision soon. We'll need to tell Josh."

"I understand. I'll talk to my brothers."

"What about your dad? This will be good for his investment too. Extra publicity for the restaurant, right?"

He shrugs. "Sure, but he won't see it that way. He'll only see it as losing a chef who happens to be his son. Better to run it by Knox and Weston first."

I smile into his neck, then kiss his pulse point, working my way up to nibble his earlobe.

He turns his head, and captures my lips with his own,

then smiles against my mouth. "That's not going to work."

"What? We can kiss, right? That's not against our contract. Plus, you already took care of your needs."

"That was so I wouldn't be thinking about it. With you draped all over me, I'm definitely thinking it." To put a fine point on it, he nudges my thigh with his erection.

"Then we're on the same page." I move to kiss him again, but he pulls back.

He scoots out from underneath me, and stands, stretching his long body. "How about some dessert?" Then he picks up the phone and fires off an order in rapid Spanish.

I imagine him rolling those r's all over my clit, and my stomach clenches.

Declan has a strong resolve though, so I tamp down my rising libido, and relax against the couch. It's fine. He won't be able to resist me forever.

CHAPTER TWELVE

When it's in service of a friend.

MY VIDEO CHAT lights up and I dive for my phone because although I'm super busy right now, if it's Dec, I don't want to miss him. He has very limited time the next couple days between strategizing with his brothers and actually competing.

I answer and smile when his face lights up my screen. "Hi."

His answering smile crinkles the corners of his eyes. "Hey you. What're you up to?"

"Doing a little storyboarding. How'd today go?"

"It was good. I'm waiting for Weston now so we can get some dinner, then plan for tomorrow. Knox is moping so not much help right now."

"Knox mopes?" I think back to the only time I've met him, and his attitude about having to work while Dec was basically partying with his dad. "Scratch that. I forgot. What's the problem?"

"Something with Rowan as usual. That's the only thing on his mind."

I purse my lips but can't hold back the smile. "What's on your mind?"

His shoulders jump with the release of a blast of air. "Point taken."

"Were the competitions fun at least?"

"The first one was off the charts. Out of the blue, we had to exchange one team member with the other team. The judges picked and Knox had to work on Rowan's team."

"Wow, how did that go?"

"Oh, it was hilarious. She was clearly flustered with Knox on her team. You could see the wheels turning in her head if she'd use him or not. In the end, she only had him pick and wash collard greens. Like five times." Dec wheezes laughing, and I'm momentarily stunned.

Who is this laughing man, and what did he do with my man? Not just laughing, but truly tickled. I shake my head and clear my throat.

"Oh sorry. I wasn't able to laugh earlier because someone's always watching."

"No, don't be sorry. I've just..." I scratch my cheek, thinking how I want to phrase this. "I guess it's just, I don't know, you're more quiet usually. I'm surprised at this side of you."

"You're about to learn I have a few sides, Kas. Hopefully you'll still like them all."

"I know I will." I smile because that's what most people would do in this situation. Not someone emotionally stunted with trust issues like me. Then I huff a small laugh. "I remember thinking when I first met you that you have layers, and that I wouldn't be around to peel those back. Yet, here we are."

"Here we are." His eyes sparkle through our electronic

connection.

I want to kick myself for even thinking I might not like a laughing Dec. What am I, a monster? "I'm happy to peel all the layers, Dec." I offer him a genuine smile because this time I mean what I say. "I miss you."

"I miss you too."

I crack my neck, ridding myself of my discomfort. "So, did you guys win already?"

"We will, but no. There's still tomorrow. Our competition's good, but not nearly as great as us."

There he is. "So, collard greens, huh? How'd she make them?" I'm curious about who grabbed his brother's heart so completely, but he can't even tell her. The brothers may look alike, but Knox is definitely different than Dec in that department.

"I wasn't really paying attention much. It's better to concentrate on your own work with this competition. They've made lots of Creole food so far—gumbo, jambalaya, meat pies."

I wasn't expecting that. Creole, not Cajun. How interesting. "Do you think they'll advance?"

"Who knows. Her family's second competition didn't work out so well. I hope so, otherwise, Knox will be a mess." He shakes his head, but smiles. Talking about his brothers changes his whole disposition. "Let's talk about you. How's everything there?"

I look down at my laptop, then back at the screen. "Not a whole lot of movement since I saw you yesterday." I don't mean to scoff, but anything I'm doing hinges on who will be in front of the camera. Planning for Dec will be a completely different ballgame than planning for Josh. Dec will do all the cooking on-screen along with the people we showcase. Josh will help with cooking. There's a huge distinction.

"Sarcasm can't be your go-to with me, Kas. You're upset because I haven't given you an answer. I get that. But hopefully you understand I need a little time. It's a huge decision."

I shrug. I get his point, but I don't understand why it's such a huge deal. He's a grown man. "People change jobs all the time. I guess I don't get it."

He runs a hand through his hair, and sighs. "It's not just a job. My whole life, all I've ever wanted was to be a chef and run Dad's restaurant someday. These last few weeks have really spun my head around and opened my eyes." He looks up at the ceiling like he's reaching for words.

"I get that. But you don't really enjoy the work, right?"

"It's not what I thought it would be."

"And neither is being in front of the camera. In a good way though."

He nods but doesn't say anything.

"You want me to use my words, so I'll just say that obviously this is something I really want. I know it's selfish, but I also care about you. And you're in your element out there. You can deny it all you want, but this is what you were born to do."

"Hold on."

He sets the tablet down and the ceiling appears for about a minute. There's talking in the background, then he picks the screen up again. "Sorry, that's Weston. He's ready."

Weston's kind face appears behind Dec and he waves, a

huge smile splitting his face. "Hi, Kasi. It's good to see you."

"Hi, Weston. Are you having fun?"

"It's been a blast." He smiles, and his blue eyes light up.

I compare the brothers. Although they have nearly the same features, they're so different in appearance. Weston's eyes are more blue to Dec's deeper blue with a hint of gray, but it's more than that. Weston is perpetually sunny and open. Dec is...well, Dec isn't sunny and open.

"I won't hold you. I know you're heading to dinner."

Dec leans forward, taking up the entire screen. "We'll talk later, okay?"

I nod.

He reaches to click the tablet off, but I hold up a hand. "Wait, Dec."

One of his recently trimmed eyebrows raises.

"I just want you to know that I'll support whatever decision you make."

"Good night, Kas."

"Good night."

When the screen goes back to my original background— a picture of me, Joy, and Tariq—I just stare. I meant what I said, and if he chooses to stay with Everheart, I will support him. I'm just not sure how long we'll be able to make it work because that decision means he's stuck to his dad even though it isn't what he wants. There will never be anything I can do to compete with that.

MY DREAM IS so good, but my consciousness is swimming to

the surface, and I can't capture the threads. Damn. I look up at the ceiling in my room and think about the day ahead. My mouth is full of cotton, but when I look over to my nightstand, there's no water. Maybe I should just turn over and get an hour or two more sleep.

My hand hits flesh, and I yelp, then sit straight up.

"What the hell, Kasi? I'm sleeping here. Damn."

"I am so sorry, girl. I completely forgot you spent the night."

Joy flips over, putting her backside to me, and settles back into the mattress.

No wonder the inside of my mouth is ashy. We went through a whole bottle of whisky last night. And that was after a couple bottles of red. We had Tariq's help though.

I roll out of bed and head to the bathroom to brush my teeth and hydrate. At least my head isn't hurting. When I'm done, I eye the shower, contemplating. There's no way I'll be able to go back to sleep now anyway. Too much work waits for me. I turn the knob, and take off my pajamas, then put a shower cap over my hair. I need to get my locks braided bad, but things just keep getting in the way. I could go to my cousin's later today, but she lives in Compton, and that's too far to drive in my current state. Plus, sitting for multiple hours will put an unnecessary crook in my neck.

When I return to the bedroom, wrapped in a towel, Joy swings her legs out of the bed. "Morning."

"Girl. Why did you let me drink so much?"

She laughs, but then holds her stomach. "I'm the one. You know my gut is delicate."

I won't forget Austin and her food poisoning any time

soon. "It was all in the service of a friend."

She frowns, then stands and rotates my way. "I still can't believe Ashley."

I snort, then cover my mouth, hoping I'm not loud enough to wake Tariq sleeping in the spare bedroom. "I always knew what was up. She had gold-digger vibes from jump."

"You always did say that."

"Some people have to touch the stove though."

"You're so right. It's a shame though. And how do you bring kids into the world knowing you really don't want their daddy? You have a five-year plan then you jet?" Joy puts her head in her hands. "Oh, and that mess of a prenup. I begged him to let me tighten it."

I smirk at the thought of how dumb Tariq was. Or maybe just in love, but we all almost fell out about the whole thing. "He made his decision, now he's living with it, but I sure hate it."

"You know I can hear you, right?" Tariq calls from the other room.

I don't bother to dress but just head into his room. "Sorry, bud. But you were stupid. And we love you."

He's still in bed, the covers pulled all the way up around his neck. "I know. To all of the above. Lesson learned."

"Yeah." That's a tough way to learn a lesson, but I don't voice it. What's done is done. "I'll make us some breakfast."

He groans and pulls the covers over his head.

I walk back into my bedroom to dress. The water is running in the shower and Joy has disappeared, so I'll have to decide what to make for breakfast on my own. I wish Declan were here. Not just because he makes amazing pancakes, but just because.

After throwing on tights and a tank top, I stroll to the kitchen and open cabinets. Even though I've been home for two days, I never have made it to the grocery store. Not satisfied with anything in the cabinets or in the fridge, I pick up my phone and order veggie omelets for all three of us with plenty of spinach. In my vast experience, eggs and spinach help with a hangover. I'm tempted to add orange juice, but knowing us, we'll turn it into mimosas. Hair of the dog, and all that.

Joy drags herself into the kitchen and plops down on the breakfast nook bench. "Coffee?"

Ugh, coffee. I open the app again, and order something from the coffee shop a block over, situated in the strip of shops and restaurants bordering the beach. "Okay, it's on its way."

"You know we could have just walked next door, right?"

I grumble and sit on the bench next to her, taking in her smell of my lemongrass body wash. "I know, but I still have whisky-brain."

She leans her head on my shoulder. "Poor Tariq."

"Yeah."

"All we can do is be here for him."

"Yeah."

There's a knock on the front door, and I shake my head. We really could have just walked next door.

When I return with the lattes, Tariq has joined out little pity-party. It's only right since he's the guest of honor. "Oh good, coffee."

"Here, buddy. I got you an extra-large."

He gives me a good long stare, then grabs the coffee cup. "I swear, if you call me that one more time…"

I twist my mouth to the side, thinking of my smart-ass reply, then I remember why he's here. "I'll try to remember. But you're like my five-year-old brother who fell off his bike and scraped his knee."

"Says the only child."

"Fine, whatever. Sorry." I take my cardboard cup out of the drink carrier and pour the coffee into a ceramic mug that reads *Don't trust a filmmaker that doesn't say fuck a lot.* I laugh thinking about Peru.

Tariq looks over my shoulder, then shakes his head. "It's not that funny."

"I was just thinking about Declan cussing up a storm whenever he got in a tight spot. Like getting ready to fall off a cliff, or his inability to breathe because of the thin air, then almost falling off a cliff." I take a tentative sip of my coffee, then set the cup of hot liquid on the table. "He always managed to collect enough air to say 'fuck' though."

Joy and Tariq share a look.

I cut daggers between the both of them. "I saw that."

"We weren't hiding." Tariq sits his big self down on the bench next to Joy and slides her over with his hip.

Joy shoves his shoulder and laughs, then grabs her stomach. "Dang, big ass." She looks up at me where I'm hovering over the table. "You really like this dude, huh?"

I snicker. "Nah."

Two pair of eyes roll in unison.

After I plop on the bench opposite them, I take another

small sip of my coffee. "He's a'right."

Two pairs of arms cross over chests.

"You spend way too much time together. You're like the Bobbsey Twins." I tear up the napkin sitting under my coffee cup and wait for someone to change the subject. When I look up, they're only staring at me. "Fine, I like him. Happy?"

Joy's lips turn up in the corner very slightly. Almost like she wants to smile, but isn't sure my revelation is a good thing. "Are you?"

I let out a sigh because in truth, this is a complicated question. "I'm happy when we're together, just being around each other without thinking. We're compatible, I think. But then I get in my head, and I'm worried he'll disappoint me."

Joy looks at Tariq out of the side of her eye, then grimaces.

Tariq pats her on the shoulder. "Talking about Kasi's love life doesn't bother me. If I'd listened to you in the first place, I wouldn't be where I am now. Maybe you can give her some good advice that she'll listen to."

I reach across the table and squeeze Tariq's hand. "Thanks, budd...uh, bruh." I take a good deep drink of my cooled coffee to hide my smirk.

Joy does giggle. "You two are a mess. Anyway, what I was going to ask is why do you think he'll disappoint you?"

I say, "Daddy issues."

Joy quirks an eyebrow. "What do your daddy issues have to do with Declan disappointing you?"

No, this heffa didn't. I cock my head to the side. "Excuse you?"

"What I say?"

"*I* do not have daddy issues. My daddy just happens to be an ass. That's not my issue."

Tariq and Joy both put their coffee cups up to their lips and hold them there in the longest drink of coffee ever recorded.

"Think whatever you want. Declan is the one with daddy issues. His father's an ass, and he doesn't even know it."

Tariq says, "Maybe you two should go to counseling."

I stretch my eyes at him. "That's your advice?" I slide my gaze over to Joy. "I hope you have something better."

"Listen, I think Declan's a good guy. Obviously I'm only going by my outside impression of him, but it's not like you're going to marry him tomorrow." She gives Tariq a quick glance with a grimace, then looks back at me. "Just take it slow and see what's what. The main thing is to keep the lines of communication all the way open and remember you're both grown."

I nod. "Solid."

In my opinion, Dec and I have both been open about what we want and don't want. I'm not trying to come between father and son, but it's time to see what's what, just like Joy said.

CHAPTER THIRTEEN

When maybe things come together.

I SWEEP MY front porch, expending nervous energy. It's been so breezy the past couple days that leaves have flown into my yard from some unknown place. There's only a few but sweeping gives me something to do while I wait for Dec to get here. I should have insisted on picking him up from the airport. His way is causing me more anticipation than I bargained for. It's only been four days since I've seen him, and he can only stay overnight, but I'm buzzing with excitement. Not to mention being horny as fuck. Please, Lord Jesus above, let this be the night we finally do it.

When there's not even a speck of sand left to sweep, I set the broom back in the entryway closet and throw myself in one of the high-back chairs next to the front window, giving myself a good view of the gate. Hours pass. I check the time on my phone. Okay, minutes, but it seems like hours. He should have been here by now.

I can't wait any longer, so I type out a text. *How far are you?*

No immediate response. Ugh.

A hand reaches across the top of the gate and springs the latch.

I shoot out of the house and make it to Dec just as he's closing the gate behind him and jump him right there in the yard.

He catches me easily, grabbing two big handfuls of booty to keep me lifted off the ground, my legs wrapped around his waist.

Once I release the grip I have around his neck, I lean back and get a good look at him. He's a little tired around the eyes that aren't quite red, but on the verge. His hair is neat in its usual style, but his beard has the all-day growth look I've come to know. I lean in and place an easy kiss on his lips.

Dec smiles against my mouth. "Looks like you missed me almost as much as I missed you."

I rest my forehead against his. "I guess so." I slide down his body until my feet hit the ground before I break his back.

"I got your text, but I was getting out of the rideshare."

"Dang, if I'd waited one more minute, you wouldn't know I was parked in the window with my eyes glued on the gate."

He takes hold of the handle of his roller, then grabs my hand with his free hand, and we stroll up the walkway. "I think I would have known when you tackled me before I could get in the gate." Oh, how I've missed that smirk.

"Whatever. Don't forget you altered your whole flight plan to spend one night with me, so I wouldn't be getting too far up my own ass if I were you."

He chuckles and follows me through the front door. "Guilty. But I wouldn't have been able to swing it if the restaurant hadn't flooded."

"I'm glad it's not too serious. Are you hungry?"

"Definitely. We left the studio and went straight to the airport. I had a stroopwafel on the airplane, and that's it."

"A who what now?"

"Kas. They're a Dutch cookie. We're really going to have to brush up your culinary knowledge before we venture out again."

"I have no intention of going to the Netherlands to shoot. They're not really known for anything other than windmills and tulips. Definitely not food. Besides, Scotland is basically covering that region and we'll be there next week."

Dec falls onto the sofa and closes his eyes. "I'm looking forward to it."

He's carrying a heavy workload right now, and I hate it for him. If he would just grow a pair and tell his father the deal, his life would be so much easier. "Don't go to sleep. Let's get you some sustenance first. We won't go far. Seafood okay?"

He takes a deep breath, then hauls himself into a sitting position. "Seafood sounds perfect."

I've dressed up today, at least my version of dressing up, in a blue sundress and sandals. They're flats but show off the toenails I painted bright orange last night.

Dec takes a quick shower in the hall bathroom to wash off the unscented plane odor he swears he smells, and changes into a different pair of expensive slacks, but with a T-shirt. No screen T with a snappy saying or superhero on the front for our stylish Dec though. It's plain pale blue but hugs his muscles in all the right places.

"Blue is my favorite color, you know."

"I did know." His eyes crinkle as he gives me a warm smile. "How was your day?"

We make it to the host stand of the restaurant, and they seat us right away since we're a little past the height of the touristy dinner crowd. We occupy a table next to the front window where we can watch the sun sink into the ocean. "I never get tired of this view."

"It's gorgeous."

"It really is." I turn back to him. "So, what were you asking me when we got here?"

"I was wondering how your day went."

"Oh, that's right. I got everything booked for our trip to the Highlands next week. We'll fly into Edinburgh and drive over with someone from the local studio there. They've really built up their film presence so making the arrangements was so much easier than Peru."

"And no need for a translator this time." He raises his eyebrows, then shoots me a wicked grin.

"Too bad. I'd loved to get one of those Jamie Fraser types in a kilt."

His grin falters. "Jamie who?"

"You know. *Outlander?*" He shrugs, and I shake my head with as much disapproval as I can manage. "Never mind."

"Luckily you won't be needing this Jamie or anyone else in a kilt. I hear they speak a lot of English there."

"Maybe we can dress you up in a kilt." I wag my eyebrows and laugh at his answering expression. "We'll see. I don't think we should take it off the table just yet."

He snorts and looks at the menu.

I already know what I want so I just look at him instead. "How was your day?"

"It was fine. Other than finding out about the flood, I already told you we go on to the next round, so there's that."

"You don't sound happy."

"There's so much going on in the background. It's difficult to be excited for Knox right now."

"Is he not being appreciative?"

He shakes his head. "Nothing to do with us. Rowan didn't make it through. My baby brother is extremely unhappy."

"But if he was trying to win the prize, and have his own restaurant, why would it matter if she didn't make it?"

"It's so complicated. He may not even want the restaurant now, not that Dad would let him have it." He shrugs and puts down the menu. "I'm just going with the flow. One more round and we're done. However it works out."

I study him for a moment. Normally, Dec doesn't get too bothered about anything, and his expression reflects that. But his face is stiff which tells me he isn't being completely truthful. It's not that he's lying, but he's not telling me everything either. And what's that crack about his dad *letting* Knox have it? What's Flynn got to do with it?

THE SUN HAS good and set by the time we make it back to my place. I go around opening windows and letting the breeze flow through. When I'm here alone, I don't sleep with the windows open—the bat will only help me so much—but this is an added treat with Dec's visit.

"Do you want something to drink?" We both had Pinot Gris with our fish, and it seems to have perked him up a little. More may put him on his behind though.

"I'm good." He sits on the sofa and pats the cushion next to him. "Unless you want something."

"Nah, I'm good too." I curl up next to him and lay my head on his shoulder.

He kisses my temple, then rests his arm over my shoulder, rubbing his hand up and down my back. "This is nice."

"Hmmmm." It is nice, but temporary. Tomorrow morning, he'll fly back to Austin, and we'll be back to video chatting. It's not that I'd mind the distance if there was an end in sight. Dec hasn't even mentioned if he talked with his brothers or not.

He leans away and catches my gaze. "Why are you getting all stiff?"

I frown because I hadn't realized. "I'm not sure."

"What's on your mind, Kas?"

I think back to a couple days ago when Joy gave me that excellent advice about communication. I obviously need to release my thoughts into the universe and see what it spits back. "You haven't mentioned if you talked with Weston and Knox about my proposal."

"Proposal? That's a pretty innocuous word for you wanting me to upend my entire life and abandon my family."

Somehow I must have missed the swing of his arm because the punch he just landed to my gut was a doozy. I clench my stomach to guard against the pain threatening to settle there. "No, Dec. This is just a business proposal. That's it."

"That's not it, Kas, and you know it."

"Even if I didn't care about you and want to see you living your best life, as a director and producer, I would still ask you to be in the movie. Why can you not see this is what you're meant to do?"

"I was born into a family of chefs. Did you know even my mother was a chef?"

I shake my head because he doesn't talk a whole lot about his mother.

"She was a pastry chef."

"Like Weston."

"Exactly. My parents met in culinary school. Then had three sons, all chefs, even though Mom died well before we were old enough to decide." He leans forward and rubs his hands across his face.

"Are your grandparents chefs too?"

He snorts. "Not at all. My maternal grandparents are retired now, but they both worked for the city. My aunt can't cook a lick." He frowns and sinks back into the couch. "My father's family are all in health care. My grandmother is a surgeon, my grandfather an anesthesiologist. Both uncles are also doctors."

I sit cross-legged on the couch and study him. His posture is stiff, and his eyes closed. "Wow. What do they think of your dad?"

"He's the black sheep of the family. Obviously."

"Obviously? He's a Michelin-starred chef. Do they not understand what a big deal that is?"

"They know. And think it's frivolous and throwing away

his inherited talent."

I try to read between the lines of this story. "So you're afraid to use your talent because you'll be labeled the black sheep? That doesn't make sense though because if anyone should understand forging your own path, it would be your father."

He opens his eyes and stands, swiftly raising himself off the sofa as if puppet strings pulled him up. "You obviously don't know my father very well."

He's right. I don't know him. Dec is getting more agitated by the moment, pacing from one end of the living room to the other. "I don't, but if he made his decisions, even though they were against his family, what does it matter if you make yours? He can think whatever he wants."

"I don't want to go a year without speaking to my father, Kasi."

I move my lips, but nothing comes out. My throat has tightened, and I can't gather enough air to speak. I race to the kitchen and pour myself a glass of water and gulp it down. When I return, Dec is standing by the television, with his hands on his hips. "Just like I don't really know your father, you don't really know mine either."

"It's the truth though. You've fallen out with your own father and won't speak to him. My family isn't like that and I don't want to start now."

"Wow, I'm only trying to help you out. You're the one floundering around without a purpose in life because you can't get out from under your daddy's thumb. You could be doing what you really want to do if you'd grow up."

He releases a huge puff of air. "You're just as bad as Dad,

you know that right?"

"What's that supposed to mean?"

"For some reason, in the couple months you've known me, you think you know better than I do what I should do with my life. At least Dad's had thirty-two years to come to his conclusions."

I throw my hands in the air, expending all this energy I've built up. "You know what, Dec. It's fine. You're right, I don't know what you really want. I only know what I see. But hey, you do you, babe."

He walks across the room in the direction of the hallway.

"You're leaving?"

"I'm going to bed."

And just like that, poof, he's gone.

I WAKE EARLY and dress like it's a normal morning. Like I didn't get but an hour or two of sleep last night, if that. I started the night so angry, mostly because Dec gave up so easily. Then I ran everything over and over in my mind, and finally realized he may be right. In a way. I'm projecting my family situation on him, no doubt. But only because our fathers are so alike. But more than anything, he's right that he needs to make his own decisions for his life. That's really all I was trying to tell him because right now, his dad is pulling all his strings. But hey, if he likes it, I love it.

The house is still quiet when I go into the kitchen and pull out the French press and the mortar and pestle to grind some beans. Dec's plane leaves in a few hours so we don't have much time to talk this morning. Hopefully he got more sleep than I did last night.

Once I press the coffee, I pour it into a mug with the slogan *Producing doesn't build character, it reveals it.* I pick up my own mug of English breakfast tea and travel the length of the hall until I get to the guest bedroom, and use my foot to bang on the door as lightly as I can without accidentally kicking it in.

"Come in."

"I can't. Can you open the door?"

Light footsteps slap against the wooden floor. His steps are heavier than I've ever heard even though they're barely audible. He normally moves like a cat which makes me wonder if he didn't sleep all that well either. When Dec opens the door, wariness colors his eyes until he sees my peace offering. "Thanks, Kas." He takes the cup from me and moves across the room to sit on the bed. He's still wearing his pajama bottoms but has an undershirt on instead of his usual bare chest.

I sit next to him on the bed, and the scent of his strong coffee overpowers my tea easily.

Dec squeezes my knee. "I'm sorry."

"Me too." I look down into my mug and form my next words. "I am sorry about the way I approached it. And if I'm pressuring you. I'm not sorry about talking about it though. You walking away was ..."

"I know. I don't like to argue."

"Me eith—"

He snorts.

"Look, obviously I don't shy away from an argument,

but I don't enjoy it. Sometimes I can have a bit of a temper though."

"You don't say."

"Dec."

He smiles, then takes a tentative sip of his coffee. "Knox is already having arguments with Dad. I'm not sure how, but Knox leaving didn't occur to Dad before. He assumed we were in the competition for a second location for Everheart Bar and Fine Dining."

"You're kidding."

"Afraid not. Dad was apoplectic when he found out that's not what my brother had in mind. Knox is playing the long game. He knows exactly how Dad is, so he's setting his plans in stone before springing them on him. There's already so much family drama right now."

"I'm impressed with Knox's skills."

"Knox is impressive." He takes another sip of his coffee, avoiding my gaze.

Another conclusion I came to last night: Dec may exude confidence, but deep down, he's unsure of himself. He questions his own talent. As well he should because being a chef is not his talent. He may be good at it, but that's just competence from training. His talent lies elsewhere and there's the crux of the problem. Knox is an exceptional chef and Dec isn't. And he may not resent his brother for it, but it causes a weird dynamic because he's constantly trying to prove himself to his father. But he's a natural in front of the camera. His charisma pops off the screen. And he's so original in his thinking that even though he may not be an exceptional chef, he creates exceptional food. "Maybe talking it out with at least your brothers will help. You were all in for Knox and this competition. Surely he won't mind hearing you out."

He nods. "Yeah, I'll speak to them when I get back this afternoon."

"Is that a promise?" I slide a bare leg over his, and scoot closer to him.

"What am I going to do with you?" He sets his coffee mug on the floor, then reaches for mine, placing my cup next to his. Then he pulls me all the way into his lap and hugs me close.

"I only want to help, Dec, but I'll stay out of it. We'll go to Scotland next week and continue with our plan. You'll have to give me an answer after though. It'll be totally up to you, and I won't have anything to say about it."

"Okay." He sighs and places his chin on top of my head. "I appreciate you, Kas. Even if it doesn't seem like it."

I squeeze my arms around him. There's really nothing for me to say to that because even though he may believe that, I'm not sure it's true.

"You're really beautiful, Kas." He cups my cheek and strokes a thumb across my lips.

I smile and sink into his touch. "Thanks. So are you."

He grins and leans in.

I meet him halfway and graze his lips with my own, then lick the seam of his mouth, tasting the hazelnut coffee he's been sipping on.

He slips his hand around my neck, pulling me even closer, and nestles the other on my lower back.

I glide my fingers through his already messy hair, the

silken strands are so soft against my hands. "Hmmm, you feel good."

His lips meet mine again and I open for the tongue he dips in my mouth, and I suck on it, drawing it into my depths. My stomach clenches, and my skin flames. Somehow he pulls me even closer, and slips his hands under the band of my sleep shorts, rubbing the top of my ass. Desire burns through me and I slide my hands from his head down to his back and pull him with me as I lie back on the bed.

Dec groans in my mouth and settles his hardness between my legs, moving ever so slowly against my covered slit. I lose myself in his movements, grinding myself against his erection, the fabric of our clothes creating a delicious friction. I grab his butt and pull him harder and faster against me until my swollen clit finds some relief. "Yes, right there." My stomach clenches as the pull between my legs tugs against it, and my orgasm spasms through.

A loud noise breaks the silence in the room before I can come all the way down. "What the hell is that?"

Dec groans again and rolls off me, grabbing his phone from the dresser. "My alarm. I have to get dressed and get to the airport."

"No. You can't be serious." I don't recognize my own whiny voice.

He lies next to me and pulls me in his arms. "I wish I wasn't." He snorts. "You have no idea."

I kiss him and run my hand down his stomach, heading decidedly south.

He catches my hand before I hit gold. "If you need me, I'll be in the cold shower." He rolls off the bed and out of the room, presumably to the bathroom to get that shower. If he'd given me five more minutes, he could have at least had a little relief. As it is, I suppose he'll have to blue balls it back to Texas.

That's not really how I want to send my man back home, but there's no help for it I suppose.

Hopefully he'll let me make it up to him when we go to the Highlands next week. I flop back on the bed and listen to the water flow through the pipes, and think about all the nasty things I'm going to do to one Declan Everheart the next time we're together.

CHAPTER FOURTEEN

When everything seems good, but it really isn't.

I STARE AT my phone with tears pricking the back of my eyes. *Hold it together, Kasi.* "Hold on."

After running to the bathroom to take a couple deep breaths, then washing my face with cold water, I blow my nose and walk back to the living room, and pick up the phone, Declan's smirking face transmitting through. "You're not messing with me, right?"

He shakes his head and almost smiles. "I wouldn't mess with you about something this important, Kas."

"Wow, I'm just…shocked."

"Ouch. It's almost as though you didn't believe in me."

I frown because although I'm deliriously happy, he's right. I didn't a hundred percent believe he'd follow through. "Sorry, my bad."

"It's okay. I don't blame you."

"But, on another note, oh my gosh, I'm so damn excited, Dec. For me and the film, but most of all for you."

"I'm pretty excited myself."

"Tell me everything."

He actually smiles, the corners of his eyes crinkling, and his eyes sparkling with excitement. "We've been prepping for the show's visit this weekend. It'll mostly be business as usual, but also figuring out how to keep Dad out of the way while they shoot B-roll footage."

"Right, you mentioned."

"Yeah. Thankfully we have Ryan because she's been running interference and has figured out how to keep Dad out of the restaurant Saturday. By the way, Weston definitely has a crush."

"Whoa, really? I thought no fraternization."

"Definitely not. I don't think she even realizes."

"Oh, interesting. Okay, enough of that. Get to the good stuff."

Declan leans over out of view, but when he comes back, his face is alight with delight. "You are the worst."

"I know. But still, get on with what I'm interested in."

"So the three of us were in one of our back rooms early this morning, basically choreographing how everything would go, when Knox told us he got a new job."

Wait, what? I blink my way into understanding. Or at least try to because I don't quite grasp what he means.

"I can see by the expression on your face that I've thrown you off your game."

"What the actual fuck, Dec? You could have led with that."

"I have to keep you on your toes, Kas."

"Knox quit?"

"Not officially yet, but Ryan knows so she's preparing to lose him. That's a huge loss and you could tell by her demeanor that she wasn't happy about it, but she's the utmost professional so she didn't say anything other than she'd start looking for a replacement who would satisfy Dad."

"I can't imagine that's an easy task."

Declan snorts, then widens his eyes. "No, not at all, but if anyone can do it, Ryan can." He's somber for a moment, then shakes himself, and rolls his shoulders. "I told her while she was looking, maybe find two. You should have seen the surprised eyes swinging my way. Weston nearly fell out of his chair."

"I can only imagine. Then what happened?" I'm anxious to hear how Knox handled this revelation.

"Then I said I think I've found a different calling. Something that I enjoy much more, and maybe have a more natural talent for. Plus, replacing me won't be as big a task for Ryan."

I shake my head because he still doesn't believe it with all his heart. Or maybe he does but hasn't embraced it yet. I can't tell because I'm used to confident, arrogant Declan. I'm not sure how to navigate this guy's emotions. "You have a tremendous talent for it."

He smiles, and nods. The barest spark of conviction lights his eyes. "Yeah. Knox only said that he was happy for me and that I should follow my dreams. He was surprised that I'd leave Dad, but he was also proud of me."

"Wow."

"I told him how proud I am of him too since he's going to be doing something he really wants to do. Even though his talent is off-the-charts as a chef, he'll do well advising the process. Remember that hearth was his idea and he's had a thousand more like it, but Dad hasn't taken any of them into consideration."

"Good for him. What about Weston?"

"He didn't have much to say other than I should go for it. He's usually so expressive so it was weird seeing him clam up so much. I'm not sure if he's thinking about being there alone with Dad, or maybe thinking about leaving too. Did I ever tell you he writes fanfiction as a hobby?"

I twist my lips to the side, and glance at the ceiling. "It maybe sounds familiar."

"Yeah, I don't know a whole lot about it, but every spare second he gets, he's tapping out on his computer. Or writing longhand on napkins. That's his true passion so I hope he'll figure out a way to do it full time someday."

"Do you think you should talk to him about it?"

"Maybe. First I have to get my own stuff figured out."

My skin prickles, and I hold my breath. "I thought it was figured out."

He looks at me a good long time, then shakes his head. "I still have logistics, Kas. I haven't told Dad yet. I'll follow Knox's lead and wait until Ryan has someone lined up. Then there's the matter of living arrangements. Do I keep my house and get something out there too? Do I keep my house, and lease it out? Do I sell my house and cut ties with Austin?" He frowns, the lines around his mouth deeper than I've ever seen. "I don't want to do that, Kas. I can't imagine living full time without my brothers."

"You'll be traveling a lot, but these are things you can figure out. You have time."

"Knox's new job will have him traveling all over the world too." He scrubs his hand across his face slowly, stretching the skin under his eyes like a melting mask. "Everything's changing."

Even though it's not my strong suit, I want to reach through the phone to comfort him. I know in my soul this will be best for Declan in the long run, but I didn't think how much he'll miss his brothers. "You'll still see them. And hopefully it'll be in a more relaxed atmosphere than now."

He doesn't say anything and looks off to the side.

"Listen, I don't have any siblings so I shouldn't have even said that. I only hope that pursing what you love will make up for the loss of seeing your brothers every day. Sounds like Knox won't be around anyway, so hopefully you and Weston can still spend time together. Also, as a plus, you'll be nearer your mom's family. Hopefully that'll be a comfort."

He nods his head but continues to look off in the distance. After a few moments of silence, he rotates his gaze back to the screen. "I notice you haven't mentioned Dad."

I take a deep cleansing breath because although I think his father is controlling and unreasonable, Declan hasn't come to that conclusion. "I'm not sure what to say. I know you're close with your dad. I'm sure he'll miss you." My gut clenches and suddenly I have to examine why. *Do I miss my own father?* I mentally shake myself. That can't be right. My father is basically trying to destroy any career I have outside his reach. No way I miss that.

"Yeah. Hey, I have to go. Dinner starts soon, but just wanted to let you know the news." He smiles, but it's tinged with sadness. "I miss you."

"I miss you too. I can't wait to see you Monday."

"Me too. I'll call you later tonight if we close on time. Or tomorrow when I think you're up."

"Okay, sounds good." I raise my hand in goodbye and watch as the screen transforms back to my screensaver. An ache settling in my heart.

I should be elated that Dec's agreed to be the talent, but there was a deep sadness in his eyes I hadn't anticipated. Maybe I just didn't get that family gene. Or maybe it's because I don't have siblings. It's hard for me to imagine something like that holding me back. I think about my relationships with Joy and Tariq, friends I've known and loved most of my life. They're as close as I come to people I wouldn't want to live without. My eyes mist again with the thought of not seeing them at least every week or so.

I take a deep breath and send a text to Joy. *Please get the deal memo over to Declan.*

She responds with a thumbs-up emoji.

THE HOSPITAL DOORS swish open on my approach, and I enter, looking around wildly, until I spot the bank of elevators. I press the button three times, one after the other, willing one of the doors to open. When an elevator does open, Joy is there on the other side of the doors and pulls me into a tight embrace as the elevator closes behind us.

I wipe my eyes and look at her. "How bad is it?"

"Bad enough. He doesn't have any life-threatening injuries but does have a concussion. His left leg was completely crushed, and he tore the ACL in his right knee. It's too soon to tell, but unlikely he'll play again." She sags against the wall of the elevator.

I straighten my spine, preparing for the doors to open, but can't help feel some relief that he'll eventually be okay. Losing Tariq isn't an option. "What an asshole."

The doors swish open and Joy pinches me as she passes. "You're the asshole. Come on."

Thankfully I haven't spent much time in hospitals because the strong smell of antiseptic masking blood is enough to make me gag.

"Get it together, Kas."

We trudge down a long corridor of rooms. I'm anxious to see Tariq, but I'm also filled with dread. Some doors are open all the way revealing all manner of injured people alone, just lying there, watching the hallway for passersby. Other doors are cracked open enough to display patients with visiting families. Still others are closed completely. When we stop in front of a closed door, my heart drops. "I don't think I can."

Joy looks at me and frowns. "Oh, you will. He's sedated, but you better get yourself together right now. Now that Ashley left him, he doesn't have a whole lot of close family. Only his dad, and you know about how that'll go. He needs us, Kas."

I suck in a deep breath, then immediately regret it, sputtering as I exhale the septic smell. "Just give me a second." I try closing my eyes and finding my happy place. In all these years, I haven't been able to figure out where that is, but suddenly an Andes Mountain comes into view, and Dec dangling off it. He's cussing up a storm and struggling to catch his breath, but his bright smile lightens me.

When I open my eyes, Joy nods. "Okay then." She pushes the door open, and I nearly lose it again, but blink back my doubt. I can do this.

Tariq is lying in the bed, eyes swollen closed although Joy said he's sedated so his eyes wouldn't be open anyway. I spare a moment to be thankful he's not awake. One leg is bandaged and suspended in the air. The other is hidden under a sheet. I whimper and slap a hand over my mouth. How could a Jet Ski accident cause this much damage?

Joy pins me with a stern glance.

We're quiet as we both stand over him, on opposite sides of the bed. The more I stare, the angrier I get. When I've had more than I can bear, I walk out of the room and down the hall until I get to a waiting room, thankfully empty. There's an old-fashioned landline set on an end table bordered by two couches. A television posted on the wall is turned to a kid's cartoon. I shudder with the thought of children having to wait in this room while a loved one is somewhere looking like Tariq.

I fall onto one of the sofas and put my head in my hands. Where are Tariq's children? Not here, thankfully, but do they even know what happened to their dad?

I look up when the door to the room opens and release a relieved sigh when Joy steps into the room. She's probably here to berate me, but even that would be some comfort. "Sorry."

She slides onto the sofa next to me and puts an arm around my back. "Why are you sorry? I understand how hard it is seeing him like that."

"I'm sorry because I *am* an asshole. The first thing I thought of when I saw him was how stupid could he be? Then the guilt set in because I've been so wrapped up in my movie, I didn't pay close enough attention to him after Ashley bounced."

"He's a grown man, Kas. And you're not his mother."

"No, but his mother is nowhere to be found." My lungs seize and my eyes prick. "Oh, God, I should have made him move in with me."

Joy pulls me closer, and we hold on to each other dearly, our tears mingling together in our laps. After we let it all out, sobs breaking that can probably be heard all the way to the nurses' station, Joy grabs some tissues from the dispenser and we both clean up.

She gives her face one more wipe, then applies some lip gloss. "You know that it's probable that if he had told either of us he was going Jet Skiing, we probably wouldn't have batted an eye. It's not usually a dangerous sport."

"Not the way we do it." I shake my head and let out a last shuddering breath, pulling myself together. "You know that if he'd told us, we would have put our foot down. Since he started being recruited in high school, he wouldn't even play touch football with us for fear of injuring himself. He wouldn't take a risk like this if it hadn't been for fucking Ashley."

"You're probably right." She falls backward into the sofa and crosses her arms. "It's over now. We just need to figure out what to do next."

Guilt seizes my gut. I'm supposed to fly halfway around the world in a couple days. If I leave in my best friend's time of need, I'm the world's worst person who ever lived. If I don't go, I let down someone I've just convinced to upend his life and follow me. "I don't know what to do, Joy."

She huffs. "I know what you're thinking, but here's what you're not going to do. Don't even think about missing your trip. I've got this."

"You don't have this by yourself."

"Yeah, well Tariq's sorry daddy will have to help. And you won't be gone that long. He may not even be out of the hospital before you get back."

"Okay sure, but there's a lot that needs to be done before he's released. All that needs to be figured out."

"Yeah, and we have a couple days to get started before you leave. We'll get a plan together and I'll execute it. We already know the first step is to hire a full-time nurse."

I sink back into the couch because the thought of hiring a nurse just sparked another thought. Tariq has violated his contract in the worst way. They won't have to pay him another cent. Plus, now that Ashley is taking at least half plus a hefty child support check, his money is flying out the window at a quick clip.

Now more than ever I need to honor my commitment to him. He would never ask, but he needs his investment back, and I mean to make it happen, no matter what it takes.

CHAPTER FIFTEEN

When they bagged a Munro.

"WE'LL DO WHAT they call the summer scramble."
Dec loads his backpack in the living room of
the lovely cottage we rented in Mallaig, near Fort William.
"Okay, what does that mean?"

"I'll explain on the car ride over." I heft my pack onto
my back and steady my camera in front of me. Like Peru,
we'll have a local with us to provide backup shots. And this
time, a third person to help us transport all the equipment
up the side of a gigantic mountain. "I guess I still don't
understand why we have to climb the absolute highest
fucking mountain in Britain. There's literally like more than
two hundred mountains we could have gone up in Scotland."

Dec smiles, and I'm buoyed that he's back in his element
and happy, and he's made the right decision. The whole
Tariq thing has really thrown me off my game, having me
thinking maybe *I'm* not making the best decisions.

Dec easily lifts his backpack with one hand and takes my
second bag with the other. "Bagging Munros, Kas."

"Bagging Munros, climbing mountains, same difference."

He kicks open the screen door and walks over to the car. "It's a good thing you're not the one in front of the camera I suppose."

I drop my backpack by his feet, and carefully place my camera in the back seat of the rented Land Rover. "You don't know the half of it. Trust me." The memory of the first year of film school slaps me upside my head. We had to rotate positions so everyone could learn and appreciate the other. Not only directing, and producing, but I also had to write, and be the on-camera talent. What a clusterfuck. "Just ask Josh sometime how that went."

"I've been meaning to ask how Josh took the news." Dec says this with a little too much glee.

I've been wondering what his deal was with Josh, but now that he's not our talent anymore, I haven't spared another thought for Dec's hesitation. I have way too many other things to keep track of these days. "Honestly? He sounded relieved. I'm beginning to think he was only doing it as a favor for a classmate. He has a few other projects lined up."

"Good for him."

I smile and slide behind the wheel of the SUV. "Get in, Dec."

He walks around the car and gets in on the passenger side. "Sorry, I can't help with driving."

"I'm almost relieved. It'll be a long time before I forget your reckless-ass driving that time in Austin. You on the wrong side of the car, on the wrong side of the road is a recipe for disaster."

He fastens his seat belt and shrugs. "I just need a little

practice."

"I'm surprised you've never driven like this before."

"I don't know why. I've mostly only traveled with Dad who always hired a car. No opportunity, not that I wouldn't have loved it."

I paste a smile on my face because I have no intention of going there this morning, especially since we're about to shoot. Ticking off another check mark on where Flynn is controlling wouldn't be welcome today. Or probably any other day.

"You're wearing your fake smile."

"You don't know my life."

"I know you enough to recognize when you're placating me."

I concentrate on the road "You know where I stand on your relationship with your father. You also know I've washed my hands of it and am leaving you to it."

"Which is where?"

"The same place I am with my father. Only I'm doing something about it. But hey, let's not argue, okay?"

"It's fine, Kas. So tell me about this summer scramble."

Because he couldn't get away earlier, Declan just arrived from Austin before it was time to leave again so I explain the day to him on the thirty-minute drive where we'll meet the rest of the crew. When we park and get out of the car, I marvel at the mountain we're expected to hike. The sky stretches above it, blue as can be in all directions. Even though it's May, there are white caps at the very top, and I shiver at the thought of ending the trail in snow considering the current mild temps.

"Don't worry, by the time we get to the snow, you'll be good and warmed up."

I spin to meet the man whose voice just spoke.

He reaches a large hand out to me. "It's nice to meet you in person, Kasi." I shake his hand with the firmest grip I can muster. When Ian and I tried video chatting, he could see me, but on his end, there were technical difficulties. It made for an awkward conversation to say the least.

"It's nice to meet you too, Ian. And great to get to see your face."

We laugh, and he taps my shoulder good-naturedly.

Dec reaches his hand out as well.

"Oh, and this is Declan Everheart. He's a producer and the talent. Dec, this is Ian Balfour, our second camera operator, and contact while we're here."

"Very nice to meet you, Declan. You've picked a fine time to bag your first Munro."

Dec nods and withdraws his hand after the shake. "Nice to meet you as well." He cuts his gaze my way very briefly, then looks away.

I'm not exactly sure what was in his eyes, but I'm guessing something similar to what was in mine when we saw Luna in the flesh for the first time. Ian is every bit as beautiful as Luna, but in his own unique way. Luna was petite and brown-skinned with dark eyes and hair. Ian is extremely tall—like Tariq-tall—and ivory-skinned with green eyes and blond close-cropped hair. He's built with muscles on top of muscles which makes sense considering his profession.

I'm here to shoot a film, not placate Dec's insecurities, but then I think back to how I felt with Luna. They were so friendly and chatted the entire time. And that was before Dec and I got together. I turn to him and give his hand a squeeze, and a sexy smile only he can see. "You ready to bag this Munro, babe?"

He quirks a freshly trimmed eyebrow. "Uh, yes?"

Okay, maybe the babe part was taking it a little too far. I may as well have stamped boyfriend on his forehead.

Ian slaps his hands together rather loudly. "Excellent. Very good."

Two other men walk up and greet Ian. One is dressed like Dec in waterproof hiking boots, sturdy trousers, and layered shirts. The other is dressed a bit more rugged like me and Ian since the three of us will be behind the camera and carrying most of the equipment. Dec has a few survivalist items in his backpack like extra socks and a flashlight, but I didn't want him too weighted down.

Ian slaps the well-dressed man on the back. "You made it."

"Aye, we ran into a little trouble, but here we are." He speaks with the perfect amount of Scottish brogue, and will work so well along with Dec in front of the camera as Dec's guide.

Ian says, "Declan, this will be your partner up the Munro. Drummond, this is Declan, the star of the series."

I swear Dec's chest puffs just the slightest. It's probably not noticeable, but I was looking for it.

Ian continues, "And this is Crom. He'll be in the background with me and Kasi."

Everyone shakes hands again, and we finally get set up and settled, then head up the trail. The air is different here than in Peru, but thinner than home. And so dry which I'm happy about because I'd hate to have to try and balance all this equipment in the wet. It's bad enough that we'll be in the snow briefly. However from my research, there shouldn't be any ice. We shouldn't have any rain today either.

As usual, Dec is being his athletic self, walking and talking with Drummond. They highlight different spots on the path that are of interest, then converse about Munro bagging in general, and Ben Nevis specifically. It's Drummond's forty-seventh time but he still has a great affection for it. Dec absorbs every word and asks compelling questions. The trip up is uneventful, but still makes for captivating footage.

After about four hours of walking and taking breaks here and there, we make it to the summit, and I take it in through my lens. The valley below has a wide ice-blue river running through it. It's crisp up here, but as Ian said, I don't mind the cold.

The snow is shallow, but Dec digs his waterproof jacket out of his backpack, then stands on top of the world as he shrugs it on, spinning in all directions to take the vistas in. Dec smiles wide. "Incredible."

I want to stand near him and hold his gloved hand, or circle our arms around each other, but we're filming and that's not why we're up here. Maybe one day we'll come back and bag a few Munros together on our own time.

Instead Dec and Drummond clap each other on the back, all smiles. Then Dec fist-bumps Drummond. It's a glorious shot, and for the first time (and probably the last), I'm envious I'm unable to be in front of the camera.

When we've wrapped, we pack up all the equipment and

hike back down. It takes considerably less time downhill, mostly because of gravity, but also because we're not filming anymore. We agree what time to meet tomorrow and say our goodbyes to the other men.

Dec is quiet on the return trip to our cottage.

I stare at the road ahead of me, running shots through my mind. When I kill the engine, I turn to him. "Everything okay?"

He shakes his head, then shrugs. "It's awe-inspiring. And I guess I'm wallowing a little too. I can't believe I've been wasting my life in a restaurant when I could have been out here doing this instead. I'm thirty-two, and before today, I'd never heard of bagging a Munro even though hiking is the number one thing I love to do. And it's because I was satisfied with following Dad's lead. When we did vacation, which was not often, we traveled in luxury, staying at the best hotels, and dining in the finest restaurants. Back home, I thought I was really doing something by hiking the hills around Austin." He shakes his head again, then opens the door.

I'm left staring at the door he just closed, wondering if he's happy or sad. It was difficult to tell.

My door opens, and I'm jolted from my thoughts. Dec reaches over me and unlatches my seat belt, then offers his hand. He pulls me from the Range Rover and wraps me in his arms. "Thank you, Kas."

My heart squeezes and tears prick the back of my eyes. This has been an emotional few days, and Dec's simple gratitude is almost enough to undo me completely. I don't speak because I don't think I can, so I hold him tight, and we rock together on the walkway.

BEFORE WE OPEN the front door, we walk on the path leading around the house, and take in the view. It can't compare to being atop Ben Nevis, but it's lovely just the same. Because Dec didn't get here until early this morning, he was rushed and barely had time to set his luggage down, less known take precious minutes to look outside, or even too much inside.

He wraps his arm around my shoulders and pulls me into his side. "We should move here."

I snicker.

"I'm serious."

I turn into him and secure my arms around his back, while looking up into his eyes. I want him to know that I really care about him, but also am not going to be bothered with his bullshit. "We just argued about you moving a thousand miles from your family and now you want to move nearly five thousand miles away to a whole other country. To a small fishing village." I lay my head on his firm chest. "Help me make it make sense."

He sighs and returns my hug. "It doesn't, but suddenly I feel free and I want to do everything."

"Let's finish this show first, then we can discuss whatever you want." I rub his back, clearly placating him, but I'm not sure what else to say. I love that he's got a new outlook on life, but we only met a couple months ago, and although I like him more than anyone I've ever been with, I still don't trust him a hundred percent. There's a niggling at the back of my neck, right where it meets my scalp, and I can't make it go away no matter what pretty words Dec says. Maybe once he's told his father, that worry will magically disappear, but until then... If I cut my heart into three pieces, he almost has the second one secure. Time will tell if he can have them all.

"You're right."

I turn in his arms and look out at the harbor below. Tomorrow, Dec will don a wet suit along with Ian manning the underwater camera, and dive near Arisaig.

Dec's stomach rumbles, vibrating my back. I angle my head to see his face. "Eat out or order takeaway?"

"Definitely takeaway." He smirks, and I don't miss the heat in his eyes.

That heat travels right through me directly to my clit. "Takeaway it is."

We walk back around to the front of the house, a greater sense of urgency moving our steps. When we tramp inside, Dec's bags are still in the living room where he transferred some items to his backpack. Although it's late afternoon, the room is very bright due to the huge windows, white walls, and colorful yellow-toned accents.

Dec lifts his bag without closing it. "Where to?"

I bite my lip because I'm not certain how to answer. "Well, there's two bedrooms right next to each other. Follow me." I lead him down the hallway that ends with an open door. "Only one bathroom there."

He peers into the large room with a modern shower and large tub that's obviously been upgraded recently. "Okay."

I open the door to my room, and vaguely gesture to what's inside. "I put all my stuff in here."

Dec studies me, then the smirk appears. "Do you want me to stay with you?"

I lean against the doorframe, and shrug. "You can do whatever you want."

He narrows his eyes, and the smirk deepens. "Can I?"

After placing my hand on my generous hip, I point to the dresser. "Just put your junk inside." I slap my hand across my mouth at that double entendre I just launched.

He passes me to get into the room, but lingers as his arm brushes against mine, his eyes hooded. "I'll gladly put my junk inside."

I whisper, "Finally."

Dec's faint laughter follows me down the hallway as I go to find my phone so I can order us some food. I want him to have plenty of sustenance because I plan to wear him the fuck out later.

I search for takeaway restaurants nearby and come up with two that probably won't satisfy Dec's superior palate but are the best candidates to get the job done. "Pizza or fish and chips?"

He comes back into the room, having shed several layers of clothes, and walks up behind me. He looks at the phone over my shoulder, pressing his body against me ever so slightly.

My stomach clenches at his casual touch.

"I'm guessing they know fish better than pizza. Okay with you?"

"Perfectly okay." He doesn't move as I click through the

pages, ordering our food. I throw in some veggies for good measure. "Be here in thirty minutes."

He moves my hair to the side, his breath warm on my neck. "What do you want to do while we wait?"

I rotate to face him and grab the collar of his shirt. "I can think of a couple of things, but I think we both need a shower."

The right side of his mouth quirks up ever so slightly. "Together?"

I walk backward, pulling him along. "Sure, why not?"

"I can't think of a single argument against it."

I turn and race down the hallway, confident Dec is right behind me. The last time we talked about it, he was set on waiting until he was sure of me. I spare a moment to wonder. As much as I want to jump him here and now, a small conversation could go a long way.

Once the water runs out of the taps, warming, Dec and I stare at each other.

I release a small sigh. "I really like you, Dec."

He narrows his eyes and bends his head to the side. "What's wrong?"

"Nothing. Nothing at all. I just want to check in because even though you humped me to oblivion last time we saw each other, we didn't really talk much before."

"I remember a heartfelt apology."

"Right, but the time before that, you said you wanted to wait on anything physical until you were sure about me."

He unzips his pants and pulls the final layer of the combination of merino wool shirts he was wearing over his head.

My mouth goes dry at the sight of the planes and angles

of his muscular tattooed chest. His arms flex as he discards the shirt onto the floor. "Hmmm."

He strides over to me and palms my cheek, his gaze intense. "I'm sure about you, Kas. Try not to break my heart, okay?"

That brings me up short. I've been so busy protecting my own heart that I haven't spared a thought for his. My skin gets all prickly. I'm not certain I want this responsibility. "I would never intentionally hurt you, Dec."

He nods and caresses a thumb across my lips. "Right. But maybe go out of your way to not unintentionally hurt me either." He smiles, but his eyes are serious.

"Okay."

"Okay." He leans in and I meet him the rest of the way. He runs his soft lips back and forth against mine and closes his eyes.

I absorb the touch of his mouth, his slow breaths, and the spicy smell of his skin so familiar to me now.

The room fills with steam, and Dec leans back. "Let's shower before the doorbell catches us in a bad position."

He's right, but I don't want to move from this spot. The tenderness of his touch isn't the first thing I usually think of when Dec comes to mind. His brashness and arrogance, unbelievable creativity and originality, his air of confidence that hides his inner need to be wanted, that smirk. Those are what he presents to the world, but his gentleness is all mine.

I stare at him for a moment, then reach for his hips, sliding his pants and underwear down his legs, freeing his erection.

He reaches for me, but I step back until my back hits the

wall, and shake my head, then unbutton my shirt painfully slowly with excited hands, finally releasing my breasts from my sports bra.

Dec's skin pales, and he takes a step.

I shake my head and momentarily marvel at his control. And mine because his dick bobs with every deep breath he takes, and I ache to wrap my hands around it. My mouth waters at the thought of tasting him. But I remember myself and slide my cargo pants down until they hit the floor, then step out, followed by my panties. Then I hold out my hand, and when he grabs it with urgency, I lead him into the shower.

I glide my hands over his smooth chest then down his stomach, feeling the dips and crevices of his abs.

He shudders then reaches for my breasts, cupping their heaviness. "So beautiful."

I soap up a washcloth and hand it to him.

"I don't need that."

"You do if you plan on washing my body."

I turn around and he glides the cloth across my back but reaches a soapy hand around me and cups my breasts again. He kisses the back of my neck, then slides his hand down my stomach, all while washing my back. "You're very talented with your hands."

He grins against my neck. "Wait until you see what I can do with my tongue."

I brace my hands against the tiled wall. "I can hardly wait."

He uses the towel to wash my butt, trailing it down the crack of my ass.

I suck in a breath from the rough sensation, then grab another washcloth and soap it up, and rotate in his arms. "My turn."

He watches me from under hooded eyes, his dick at full attention. I move the washcloth across his skin with a greater urgency until I reach his hardness where I take my time. He closes his eyes, and hums, grinding against my touch. I drop the cloth and take him in my bare hand, pumping him from root to tip with steady, pressured strokes.

His eyes pop open, and he opens his mouth to say something, but a groan escapes instead. He slides his fingers through the slick folds between my legs and inserts two fingers. I grasp his erection harder, never slowing the motion even though the delicious way he stretches me makes me want to lean back and enjoy it selfishly. He finds the swollen nub of my clit with his thumb and circles it with exquisite pressure and continues to stroke inside me adding a third finger.

I lick my lips and stare into his eyes while I pump his dick. He returns my gaze with a heated one of his own, never losing eye contact or the rhythm of his hand. I add my other hand to the mix and cup his balls. The move presses our bodies together, and the new angle is my undoing.

I lean my head against his hard chest. "Shit, Dec." My release comes quickly, vibrating through my stomach and shooting out my clit, the walls of my pussy pulsating around Dec's fingers. My knees buckle, but he's there to hold me up, and take over to find his own release.

He pumps into his own hand a couple times before gripping me against him. "Fuck."

I'm working on catching my breath, but I can't speak yet. I can only muster a thought. *Tell me about it.*

We rinse off and exit the shower just as the doorbell rings.

I sit down hard on the towel-covered toilet. "You have to go."

He only smiles and leans down to give me a quick kiss. "My pleasure." He wraps a towel around his waist and leaves the bathroom.

I just sit there and get myself together. I laugh because while I wanted to build up Dec's energy with food, I'm the one who ran out of gas. It's okay though because I'm about to fill the tank all the way up for round two.

CHAPTER SIXTEEN

When they get the deed done.

M Y STOMACH IS tight from eating too much and I realize I've made a tactical error. "Ugh, I'm too full." Even the shorts I changed into after the shower are pressing hard on my belly.

Dec pulls me against him on the living room sofa, and exhales. "Me too. It was surprisingly good."

"Yeah, it was. But now my stomach hurts and I can't fuck your brains out like I planned."

His diaphragm vibrates against my back, and he strokes my wet hair that's slowly turning into a rather large Afro. That's what I get for paying more attention to Dec's dick than covering my hair before we got in the shower.

"It's not funny."

"Don't worry. You have plenty of time to fuck my brains out tonight. It's only seven."

"Really? That can't be right." I strain to sit up and grab my phone from the coffee table covered in empty cartons. "It really is seven."

"Told you."

I lie back and relax into his arms. "This is very good news."

"I agree. Plus, it gives us some time to watch what you shot today."

I chuckle and shake my head. "You really are leaning into this life, aren't you?"

"You'll find I don't do anything in half measures."

"Good to know. Let me contact Joy first, then we can set up the playback." I notice there's a missed call from Mom so I text her to let her know it'll cost me too much to call her back, and see what she wants. Next, I text Joy to find out if there's anything new with Tariq. He's not due to be released until I return, but I don't want to drop the ball if I'm needed for anything before then.

"Okay, I'll get the equipment." He removes the cartons from the table and heads in the direction of the kitchen.

I turn my attention back to my phone. *How's Tariq?*

As well as can be expected. The doctors are hopeful though so that's good.

I bite my lip, deciding how to word my next question. *Has he said anything about anything?* Okay, I prolly should have flushed that out a little more.

He hasn't said a whole lot. He agreed to let us take care of everything though. He doesn't want to see the kids like this. Did that cover what you're asking?

Yes, thank you, Joy. I appreciate you so much.

Dec sets the equipment on the table and sits back on the couch next to me.

It's all going to be okay.

I nod even though she can't see me. *I love you.*

You too, sugar.

I set the phone down next to me on the couch in case Mom texts back and push my fingers into the thickness of my hair, scratching my scalp.

Dec rubs my back. "How is he?"

"Joy says the doctors think he'll be okay."

"I'm glad."

"Me too. I'm just so worried about what's next for him. His kids and football are basically his life. Ashley plans to move to NoCal near her parents, and football is a full-stop no-go."

"The doctors are sure he won't play again?"

"Yeah."

He releases a long sigh. "He seems like a really great guy. I hate to hear it."

My phone lights up with a text and I grab it up. "It's my mother."

"Everything okay?"

"Just asking about Tariq." I tap out a quick response of what I know which isn't much of anything.

"You and your mom are close?"

I mull the question a moment, deciding how to answer. I sit up and turn to him so I can watch his reactions. After today's response to shooting and a reaffirmation of his intentions, I've given Dec closer to two-and-a-half of the three pieces of my heart, but that last half is still reminding me about his relationship with Flynn. "We're as close as two people can be when there's a third person pulling at us in different ways."

He doesn't react, but a slight confusion bends his brow.

"Dad is telling her one thing but doing another. Which means she believes him, and thinks I'm blowing things out of proportion."

Dec opens his mouth to say something, then closes it again.

"I'm not, if that's what you were going to ask. He convinced my mother that he's only making moves against me for my own good. That I need to embrace his legacy and keep it moving. He doesn't care that I want to walk my own path."

He nods, understanding lighting his face. "This is bringing a lot of things you've said into sharper focus."

"Yeah, my daddy issues are different than yours though."

"How so?"

"Because unlike you, I don't want to work for my father. Plus, unlike Flynn, Reggie will sabotage me at every turn."

Dec snorts. "Clearly you don't know my father."

My heart vibrates, threatening to snatch that half piece back. "Are you worried he'll do something when you tell him?"

He smiles, but it's sardonic and sad. "No. I'm more worried about Knox."

I want to ask if he's accepted Flynn will never give him the affirmation he's looking for, but it's not the best time. Plus, that's probably something he should work out with a therapist. Between this documentary, Tariq, and my own asshole father, I don't have the bandwidth right now. "That's too bad. Parents really should be better."

He shifts and stiffens a bit, then clears his throat. "I'm sure you'll take that lesson to your own kids."

"Lord no. I have no intention of ever having children."

"Oh, thank goodness." He releases a harsh but relieved bark of laughter.

"Is there anything about me that screams maternal? I mean, seriously."

"I think you would make a wonderful mother. You'll exceed in anything you put your mind to." He rubs the back of his neck, as if relieving the last bit of pressure. "I'm just happy you don't want that."

"Yeah, I suppose. It's just not my jam. I'm assuming that means you don't want kids either."

"I never have. And my decision is reaffirmed now that I've seen what else is out here. I have a lot of time to make up."

I check in with my stomach to ensure it's no longer full. Satisfied, I turn around and straddle Dec's lap. "You know, just because we don't want to make an actual baby, doesn't mean we can't pretend."

"I'm already ahead of you." To accentuate the point, he makes his erection known by pulling me closer against him.

"Indeed you are." I place the palms of my hands against his cheeks and draw him to me, then press my lips on his, relishing the soft pillow of his lower lip. He tastes of greasy chips as they call them here, and fried fish, but I don't mind. He grinds against me, but this will not be a humping session.

Not this time.

I break the chaste kiss and pull my tank top down to release my breasts, then reach between us, fumbling with the drawstring of Dec's pajama bottoms.

He doesn't waste any time circling my nipples with his fingers and lips, pulling one deep into this mouth. I lose my concentration for the barest of moments then get the dang string untied. Before I can reach inside his pants, he pulls my face down for another kiss, parting my lips with his tongue, then delving inside. He explores my mouth, and our tongues tangle, swirling and sucking. He moves away from my mouth, and trails kisses down my neck, nipping at the sensitive skin behind my ear.

With strong hands, Dec lifts us both from the couch and carries me down the hallway.

I giggle and wrap my arms around his neck, hanging on for dear life. "Don't you drop my ass."

"That would really defeat the purpose." He smiles against my neck, then does drop me on the bed. His pants slide down his legs onto the floor once he releases me, and I make quick work of my shorts which he gleefully takes from me and tosses on the floor.

He looks down at me with unbelievable heat in his eyes. The blue has almost turned completely gray. When I reach for him, he shakes his head, and grabs the backs of my knees, pushing them up, before settling his head between my legs. My whole body tenses, and my skin tightens everywhere he licks. First my inner thighs, then up to my stomach, and back to my nipples where he takes his time. My breathing becomes labored and hard, and all I can do is sink my fingers into his scalp and hold on for the ride. "Fuck, Dec."

He smiles against my breast. "I intend to. Give me a minute."

"Dick."

"That too." He trails his tongue back down my stomach, then slowly licks and kisses until he reaches my drenched pussy, and drags his tongue through my wet folds, ever so slowly, setting my blood on fire. I let go of his hair and clench the sheet for better purchase. He takes that as an invitation to get comfortable and slides his arms under my thighs and grips my hips, securing me in place for the long haul. He works his magic tongue on my clit, circling and tugging, then inserts a finger, curling it inside as he presses my clit with his mouth. I don't have time to brace myself as the orgasm splits me apart, leaving me gasping for oxygen.

Dec squeezes my thighs, then lifts himself off the bed. "Be right back."

I can't do anything but nod which he probably didn't even see because even though the sun hasn't set, the bedroom, with its heavy drapes, is nearly pitch-black. He rustles for something in a bag on the dresser, then comes back and climbs over me, trailing kisses up my stomach.

I wrap my legs over his strong thighs and drop my arms over his back while he gives more attention to my breasts. I'm completely spent from that mega-orgasm but my core tingles again, coming back to life with every suck and lick to my nipples. "Come here, Dec."

He obliges, and I kiss him with everything I have, tasting my salty flavor on his tongue.

I grab his taut ass and squeeze, pulling him closer to my center. "I sure hope that was a condom you were rummaging around for."

He sits back on his haunches and rubs his hand across the blanket until he finds what he's looking for. "A whole row of them." Before I can laugh, he runs a finger across my nub, and I gasp from the sensation. "Not quite ready, I see."

I sit up and ease him down to where I was just lying. It's true that my clit is still sensitive, but I don't want to just sit around waiting. I lie back next to him, but position myself lower, where my head lines up perfectly with his stiff dick. It's practically waving at me, so I scoot a little closer to say hello, licking from the root up the bottom of the shaft until I get to the top. Dec's intake of breath urges me on, not that I needed the encouragement. I swirl my tongue around the head and take him deep into my mouth, swallowing his length down my throat. "Oh my fucking God."

My mouth's too full to smile, but I give his thigh a little squeeze of acknowledgment, then set to work bringing him to the edge, relishing his movements and sounds of pleasure. It doesn't take long so I release him before he goes too far. "Oh no you don't. I want you inside me. Now."

He grunts as he sits up, searching for those condoms again. When he tears one open, I stretch out next to him, and wait for him to roll it on, rubbing my hands over my own body. "Hurry."

"I got you." He settles between my legs and pushes the head of his dick against my opening, stretching to fit him. With a deliciously slow pace, he sinks into me, filling me all the way, and I clench around him from need. He bends down to kiss me, and our tongues grind against each other as he drives into me. I match his movements, pounding against him, relieving the itch I've had deep inside me since I first met him.

"Yes, this is perfect, Dec." He catches my words with another kiss, holding my head in place with his hands while balancing above me on his forearms, pushing deeper and deeper inside. I'm close again so I wrap my legs over his thighs causing him to grind against my clit as he pumps.

That's all it takes, and my stomach clenches, the heat and intensity building there before traveling decidedly downward, filling my core with vibrations, causing my walls to clench around his dick, pulsating out my orgasm.

He buries his head into my neck, grasping my shoulders as he comes, pressing his pelvis into me and holding still before finally relaxing. "Jesus."

"Yeah."

The weight of him presses me into the mattress despite balancing on his elbows. I don't mind it though. The feel of his body engulfing me completely is potent, and there's no place I'd rather be.

"FUN FACT, HARRY Potter was filmed here. Well, the railway station parts." Ian smiles, extremely proud of that tidbit of information.

"Is that right?" Dec smiles back, but I'm certain from the gleam in his eye, this is a detail he already knows.

We pass shops on our way to the train that will take us the short trip to Arisaig for a day of scuba diving. We could have driven, but we both wanted to travel this way to see a bit more of the interior of the surrounding area, instead of riding down the coast.

Ian lifts a burly arm and points at one of the shops. "They still sell genuine oak-smoked kippers from the factory shop there."

Dec nods. "We'll have to get some for sure. I'd love to try them."

I nod too, but I'm not sure about kippers. I'll try them, of course, but I'm not looking forward to it like Dec is. After last night's physical activities, I'm feeling it—from the soreness between my legs to the lack of sleep—but Dec has a bounce in his step despite using three of the condoms on the roll. I smile to myself because although it took a while to get together, I'm not in any way disappointed.

When I look up from my thoughts, Dec is studying me, a smirk shaping his mouth.

I only shrug because I'll let him have this one. He definitely wore me out as promised.

During the train ride, we don't pass anything significant, but the landscape is beautiful and lush. Dec leans close to me and nuzzles his nose in my neck. "You smell like me."

I laugh because despite scrubbing myself in the shower this morning, his smell is all over me. "Maybe it's because you keep licking my dang neck."

He gives me one long lick from my collarbone to my ear, and I squeeze my legs together to tamp down the desire stirring there.

Ian clears his throat, having just come back from the bathroom, and sits across from us. "Fancy a drink? Some tea maybe? Or coffee?"

"I think I've had enough. Thanks."

Dec adjusts himself beside me, then clears his throat. "I could use some more, but I'll wait." His sly grin broadcasts exactly what he's talking about. And it's not coffee.

Ian runs through the events of the day, and I half listen, half watch the passing scenery outside. Only Dec and Ian will be diving, and while I'm interested, my thoughts are leaning in another direction. I'll wait on the boat and take some shots of them going in the water and coming out. Plus, cooking and eating right on the boat whatever they catch down there.

A smiling, excited Dec is actually growing on me. Maybe because I actually care for him now. The moody, stern appearance was edgy and fun for a surface relationship, but taking a deeper look inside has me a little in my feelings. As if sensing my mood, he doesn't break his exchange with Ian, but reaches for my hand under the table and holds it, rubbing circles on my palm.

After loading all the equipment onto our charter, more conversations happen with the guide, Mysie. Dec has experience, but we'll still need to defer to the experts.

Mysie instructs Dec on putting on his wet suit, a tight dark green and gray affair, and although Mysie is attractive, I don't get the jealous pang I did when we met Luna. I recognize Dec and I are in a better place this time.

Laughter draws my gaze from setting up my camera to Dec and group getting all of their apparatuses and spears together. Mysie even has an underwater bow and arrow which I raise my brows at. I realize, too late, I should be capturing this camaraderie before they drop below the surface. I bite the inside of my cheek to focus my thoughts. Daydreaming about Dec is not going to help get this show done. This is why I didn't want to get involved in the first place. Well, one of the reasons.

Ian and Mysie shove off the boat into the water, and Dec hangs back. He watches me from behind white plastic goggles, but between the heavy equipment and tight inflatable jacket, he can't move his arms to give me a clue what he wants. He smiles from around his mouthpiece, then shrugs, and glides into the water with the others.

I finally get myself set up enough to capture them sliding beneath the surface. There's nothing else for me to do but chat with the other crew members and wait to see what they come up with from down below. A pod of dolphins swim by with grace and energy. They're not the kind I'm used to seeing but are smaller and have shorter beaks, and more rounded foreheads. I sidle up to one of the crew members who's pulling at some ropes. "What kind of dolphins are those?"

"Them? They're what's called the common dolphin, lass."

"Common?"

He nods and goes back to his task.

I fish around for my phone in my bag, and search for common dolphins and sure enough, that's what they're called. Even though they are the largest number of all the dolphins, they're not the typical prototype of what we usually think of. "Hmmm, learn something new every day."

"Lass?"

I shake my head because I was really talking more to myself anyway.

While I have my phone out, I notice a message from Mom. *We've all agreed to move Tariq here. More details when you're stateside.*

What the actual fuck? I don't type that out, but I sorely want to.

Instead, I tap out a text to Joy. *What the actual fuck?*

I see you've heard from your mother.

Yeah, sure did. What in the world is going on out there?

We'll talk about it when you return. You know how your mom is and ultimately, it was Tariq's decision.

I grip my phone so hard, I have to drop it in my bag or most likely break it. How dare she put Tariq under the same roof with the man who stole his money? I fume, pacing the boat, and the others aboard seem to find something else to do far away from me.

After a few minutes pass, I finally work the negative energy out, and return to my equipment. Dec and crew should be breaking the surface any time now and I don't want to miss it. I'll have to backburner the Tariq situation until I get home. I sigh and shake my head. Well, at least until we get back to the cottage. Business first.

When the divers do come back up, the crew members help them with their haul while they're still in the water. There are a couple of wicker baskets filled with what looks like crabs and lobsters, and some small shell-encrusted sea fare. Next come bags filled with fish.

Dec comes aboard and pulls his gear off, panting, but smiling. He looks directly at me and opens his mouth, before he realizes I'm pointing the camera his way. Instead, he turns to Mysie and fist-bumps her. "That was incredible. Did you see when the shark came our way?"

Wait. What? I pretend my feet are in concrete so I don't run to him. I patiently wait for an explanation.

Mysie must recognize the look of horror on my face because she turns to Dec, all smiles. "Oh, mate, that was only a baby."

Dec's eyes round to saucers. "A baby? It was almost as

big as me. And that mouth."

"Well, you're lucky that was only a baby because the parents are quite large." She slaps him on the back then bends down to pick up something out of one of the baskets. She slides out a knife from a pocket of her suit and cracks the shell open, producing something white inside with bright orange on the end. She hands it to Dec. "Try that, mate."

"You mean eat it? Right out of the shell?" I expect him to look as repulsed as I feel, but he reaches inside and pops the thing in his mouth, then closes his eyes in bliss. I recognize that look. I saw it last night. "Oh my, that's the sweetest scallop I've ever had."

One of the crew picks up a bag of fish, and Dec smiles so hard, it's a wonder his face doesn't freeze that way. He turns to the camera again, brandishing his spear, but speaks aloud as though addressing the whole boat. "I speared several flounder, and we'll steam those for lunch."

Mysie claps him on the back and walks to the stairs leading down to the bathroom below.

I stop filming and walk over to Ian. "Did it go okay down there?"

"Oh, aye. I got some spectacular shots." He rubs his hands together in anticipation, then picks up the camera, and hands it to me. "You'll really be pleased." Then he goes over to Dec's discarded equipment and pulls off the camera we attached to his helmet. "This should make for some fun footage. Your lad was quite daring."

My face heats because despite trying to maintain a level of professionalism, we're not fooling anyone. I take a breath, and turn to Dec. "Great job."

He walks the few steps and grabs me by the upper arms. "I can't wait for you to see what it was like down there. I've dived many times before, but never for food. This was the best day ever."

"I thought you said yesterday was the best day ever."

He tempers his enthusiasm as best he can, and leans in, and whispers in my ear. "Every day with you keeps getting better."

Those pretty words shouldn't matter, but my insides turn to mush, and the back of my eyes prick. I lean into him, and exhale slowly. "You. Are. Killing. Me."

He gives my temple a quick kiss, then goes over to help the crew members scale and clean the fish.

Ian elbows me out of my trance. "You have yourself a good one."

I'm not sure how to respond. I've never *had* anyone to this extent before. What does that mean, having someone? I just answer, "Thanks."

He nods and sets at his task of cataloging all the equipment.

I squat next to him and help, my mind drifting with the mindless exercise.

Do I want to have someone?

CHAPTER SEVENTEEN

When he still hasn't signed.

M Y CHILDHOOD HOME is mostly invisible from the street. I park in the driveway then look down the hill at the sprawling house below. After taking a deep, cleansing breath to chase away the butterflies in my stomach, I trudge to the door all the while hoping Dad isn't home, but knowing my luck isn't that good. It's never been.

Instead of punching in the code and using my spare key, I buzz the intercom. A few moments later, the gates protecting the front porch click open, and by the time I make it to the front door, Mom is there swinging it open. "Hello, dear."

I step into her waiting arms and give her a brief hug. The soft material of her blouse makes me want to linger, but I step back anyway. I look down at her feet and smile, shaking my head. "You will never change."

"I certainly have no intention to." Her kitten heels slap against the tiled floor as she moves from the vestibule to one of the hallways leading away from the front door. We're headed to the first-floor guest wing which isn't a surprise. Lodging Tariq on any floor except the ground one wouldn't make sense.

"How is he today, Mom?"

She stops in front of a closed door, and knocks. "You can see for yourself."

A muffled voice comes through the thick entrance. "Come in."

Tariq is propped up in his hospital bed, with one leg still hanging in the air.

Mom answers my confused stare. "We had the bed moved out. This is easier for him."

The bed in question isn't your normal hospital bed. It must be the Cadillac of beds because it's plush and comfortable, yet has every gadget known to man hooked to it.

The man on top of it is in better condition than when I left him nearly a week ago. "Hi."

I rush over to him, intending to throw my arms around him, but catch myself at the last minute. Instead, I pat a shoulder that doesn't look to have been damaged. "You scared me to death." My stomach clenches with the memory of when I saw him right after the accident.

"I know. I'm sorry."

"Don't be sorry, fool."

Mom clears her throat, but Tariq only laughs.

"I mean…"

He pats my hand, then squeezes it. "I know what you mean."

"Well, I'll leave you two to catch up. Just press the button if you need anything."

When Mom leaves, I rotate back to him. "Press the button? Who's hooked up to the button? Not Mom."

He chuckles, then winces. "Definitely not your mom.

There's a nurse and a 'caretaker' as your mother calls him. He keeps me fed, bathed, and, uh, you know."

"Bathroom stuff?"

"Yeah."

"So you're comfortable here, I take it." I can't stop myself from twisting my lips to the side. I'm happy he's got a nice setup, certainly better than anything Joy and I could have come up with, but I still reserve judgement as to why he's even here.

"I'm grateful your parents stepped in."

"We could have probably set you up in your house..." I bite my tongue because I'm not certain what the situation is with his house now that Ashley has made her move.

"The house has already sold." His face crumples, and he turns away.

"Oh, Tariq. I didn't know you were selling it so soon." I have a sudden urge to tear out of here and find Ashley. That probably wouldn't be the best idea in the world.

"Yeah. Everything's moving quickly. I couldn't afford to buy her out so I'll get something else where the kids can be comfortable when I have them. Maybe I'll move near you. They'd love the beach."

My eyes prick, and I take a deep, shuddering breath to keep the dam from breaking. "That would be great."

"Hey, what's your problem?"

"I just... You wouldn't have to sell your house if I hadn't lost all your money." I stand and walk over to the window, the view stretching out over the side of the house where there's a vegetable garden. Mom doesn't garden, but she loves fresh vegetables.

He blows out a loud breath. "If we have to go through this one more time, let it be the last time. Please, Kasi."

"We don't. I know what's up."

"You don't. I made an investment. People do that all the time. It didn't pan out, and that's okay. I took it as a loss on my taxes."

"You and I both know where we live and state taxes are a thing. Don't play."

"Why do you keep doing this, Kasi? You have to let it go. It's not your fault. I begged you to let me invest."

I still stare out the window because I can't quite face him yet. My skin vibrates with anger and my eyes burn with unshed tears all at the same time. "Yeah, because you believed in me. And—"

"I still believe in you."

This time the tears come and I'm helpless to stop them. "How can you? And how can you stay under this roof knowing the man who lives here did us both so dirty?"

Tariq sighs.

I turn around to find some tissue because holding back my emotions is a lost cause right now. Guilt twists my gut over bringing this up at a time like this when it only causes more pain. I swipe at my eyes, then sit in the chair next to his bed, placing my hand back on his shoulder. "I'm sorry. And I won't bring it up anymore, but I promise you, when I sell this show, yours is coming right off the top. And whatever you need in the meantime, you only have to let me know."

He squeezes my hand and closes his eyes.

I watch him for a few minutes until his breathing deepens. I have so many restrictions on my trust fund, but whatever is available to me will be his if he needs it. Even if I have to move in with Joy. More than ever, I need to get this series made.

THE LAPTOP OPEN on my desk displays the completed storyboard for the entire movie. Kristin, our location manager has just contracted for the last locale and I've set my scenes down to the most minuscule shot. All that remains is to finish hiring crew and get all the travel booked. We'll work with Kristin over the next week to get that done. Hopefully Dec will be able to come back as soon as he promised, otherwise he'll have to dial in on our calls. Which is perfectly fine from a business aspect, but I ache for his touch.

The final round of competition is still two weeks away, and they'll have to stay in San Francisco almost a whole week. He's invited me up for it, and a luncheon at his aunt's house over in Berkeley, but I'm not sure I'm ready to meet his extended family. That seems like a big step.

I roll over and stretch across my bed. I really should be doing this work in my office slash guest room, but I've been bone-tired ever since getting back from Scotland. The whole Tariq thing hasn't helped my mood either. Maybe a little beach yoga will help, so I grab my mat from my closet and walk the few paces to set up on the sand.

There are so many people out for a Tuesday morning, but then again, it's full-on summer now so it's not a complete surprise. A cool breeze sweeps off the ocean nulling the sun peeking out from somewhere behind me, the air salty and fresh. Whole families set up chairs and lay out towels, coolers filled with food and drinks nearby. Others roller-skate to outdoor music. Couples walk hand in hand looking in shops, and a little pang shoots through my chest, thinking about how that could be me and Dec, relaxing and enjoying each other. Hopefully someday.

I put earbuds in and play a yoga routine on my phone. I can't see the screen because my phone is secured in a band around my arm, but I've been doing this long enough to not have to watch. The quiet, calming voice coming through my earbuds puts me in a better mindset, and I shape myself into the first pose, balancing my bare feet on my mat. The sand makes it more difficult, but all the more for a better workout.

An hour passes before my phone ringer sounds in my ear. I press the switch on my earbud once the intuitive device tells me who's calling. "Hi, you."

"Hey. Why am I looking at the pier in the near distance?"

"Just a sec." I plop down on my mat and wipe the sweat off my face with a sandy towel, then pull the phone out of the band securing the device to my arm. When I flip the screen around, Dec's gorgeous, but tense face greets me.

"Ah, that's better."

I smile because I miss him, and this is the next best thing to being here. "Much better."

"You're out on the beach, I'm guessing."

"Yeah, I'm done with everything I can do for now, so came outside to soak up some vitamin D and stretch my muscles a bit."

"I got your email. Everything looks perfect. You're really good at this whole movie thing. Even Dad was satisfied with our progress."

I smile soaking up his compliment, even though I couldn't care less about his father's opinion. "It was a team effort. I couldn't have done the food part without you."

He only nods, and stares at me through the phone. His expression has relaxed the smallest bit, but strain creases the corners of his eyes and mouth.

"Is there something wrong?"

"No." He moves his mouth into a smile, but somehow the feeling doesn't come through. "I miss you."

"Me too, Dec." I don't want to nag, so I won't ask him again, but something feels off. My stomach clenches at the thought he's holding back.

"I don't think I'll be able to get off before the final competition in a couple weeks. Do you think you might be able to come my way?"

I purse my lips and think. "I can, but I won't be able to stay the entire time. Just because my parents have Tariq trapped inside their house doesn't mean I can abandon him."

"Of course not. I would never ask that."

I soften my voice and smile into the screen. "I know how that sounded but I promise I didn't mean it that way."

He runs a hand through his hair and sighs hard, then looks at me with soft eyes. "I shouldn't have taken it that way. I know you better than that."

I know I just told myself I wouldn't nag, but clearly something's up, and I've never been great with holding back.

"Just tell me what's wrong. Please."

"There's so much tension here. Even Weston's sunny disposition has been limp. Knox and Dad are becoming impossible to be around when they're together."

"Wow, that bad, huh?"

"Worse. Dad has declared to Knox that if we win the restaurant, it'll become a second location of Everheart Bar and Fine Dining. He even plans to go to the competition with us to protect his investment."

I snort. "He sure does like to keep his eye on his investments, doesn't he?"

He relaxes again and leans back in his chair. From the looks of his surroundings in the background, he's in one of the private rooms at work. The collar of his white jacket is visible now that he's leaned away from the camera a bit. "This is a dick move he's pulling with Knox, but I'm glad he pushed me on you for this particular investment."

"Me too." I make kissy faces at him, and he finally releases a comfortable laugh. "So Knox isn't getting the new job after all?"

"He definitely is."

"Then why does he care about winning the restaurant?"

He leans forward again, lowering his voice. "Can you keep a secret?"

"Not even a little bit." I smile, and shrug. It is what it is.

"At least you're honest."

"I'll always be one hundred with you, Dec."

A shadow passes over his face, and not for the first time today, he gives me the impression he's holding something back. "Hey, I've got to go. Knox is waving at me from the kitchen."

I give him a toothless smile and wave at the screen.

He kisses his fingertips, then disconnects the call.

I immediately text Joy. *Has Declan signed the deal memo yet?*

No.

I stare at her response, then book a flight to Austin. Time to find out what's really going on.

CHAPTER EIGHTEEN

When daddy issues are the order of the day.

I STEP INTO the muggy Austin air, and Declan is sitting in his car at the curb waiting to meet me. I raise the two cups of coffee in my hands when he spots me. The bag weighing down my shoulder threatens to fall, but I'm near enough to the car for Declan to jump out and grab it.

He's dressed in a plain white T-shirt and black pants. Considering the early hour, he'll probably throw on his chef's jacket when it's time to go in a couple hours from now. I took the next thing smoking out of LA a little after midnight, but even though I got to Texas at five thirty local time, there was a long layover in Houston so I'm only here three hours before he has to work. If I don't get to the bottom of things before he leaves, we can always hash it out later.

Dec takes the bag from me, and one of the coffees, then hugs me with his free hand, burying his head in my hair. "Hmmm you smell good."

I'm sure I don't, but he smells like baked goods covering his normal spicy scent. "You do too. Donuts?"

He laughs and takes my hand, leading me to the car. "Close." Once we're secure inside, he reaches behind the seat and opens a pastry box filled with beignets and kolaches. "I went by Weston's on the way and picked these up. He made them special for you."

Tears prick my eyes at his brother's thoughtfulness. "But I just decided to come a few hours ago."

"We were together when you told me." He pulls out into the early morning traffic, taking care to not jostle our coffees sitting between us in the console.

"This is incredibly nice of him. I'll have to thank him."

"If you come to the restaurant for dinner, you can thank him then."

"It's a date." I smile and pick out the biggest beignet and savor it with my coffee. "Do you want one?"

"I'll have a couple kolaches if you don't mind sharing."

"Are they all the same?"

"I believe they're all sausage and cheese, but some have jalapeno. I'll take a couple of those."

I pull out two and put the pastries on a napkin. Weston helpfully baked in a small piece of greenery on the end to distinguish them. They smell divine, and I momentarily pull the napkins back. When I had them from a local donut shop last I was here, they were absolutely delicious, but I have a feeling Weston's are on another level. "I may have changed my mind about sharing."

"That would be your right, but that was quite the tease."

I set them in his lap and brush against his crotch, taking my time pulling my hand back. "Now that's a tease."

He looks over at me briefly, and his eyes darken. "Damn that Houston layover."

"We have plenty of time later."

He places a hand on my thigh and squeezes, nearly knocking over his kolaches with the movement. "Damn it."

I reach over and straighten the napkins, then pick up a pastry, and pinch off the end. "Open."

He opens his mouth, and I place the piece on his tongue, lingering again as I pull my hand back, trailing a finger along his lip.

"You are so bad."

I sit back, satisfied, and pick up my beignet. "You like me bad."

He barks out a quick laugh. "You are so right."

We enjoy our breakfast as Declan speeds toward his house. The GPS says about twenty minutes away with traffic. The coffee I picked up inside the airport from a local coffee shop is rich and full. They had tea, but an extra pick-me-up after all the time spent sitting in the concourse waiting on my connecting plane couldn't hurt. Even though Dec has to work today, I can still get some work done while he's gone. Maybe a little swim this time too since I'm staying at his house, and we didn't have a chance to use that beautiful pool.

"Almost there."

I start, and look over at Dec.

"I think you dozed a little."

"Jeesh. I didn't even notice. I was just dreaming about swimming in your pool."

"I don't suppose I can talk you into waiting for me." He pulls into his driveway and hits the button on the garage door opener.

"Who's to say we can't go again when you get home?" I

close the box on the pastries. I can eat more when we get in the house. Maybe make some fresh coffee too.

Before he opens his car door, Dec leans over the console and runs his thumb near the corner of my mouth. "You have a little something." Powdered sugar falls in a big clump onto the top of the box, and I chuckle, but pull his thumb into my mouth before he can move it away. I suck on it a lot longer than necessary, closing my eyes, savoring the taste of sugar and all man.

"You're trying to kill me." Before I can respond, he pulls his finger out and dips his tongue in my mouth. The spiciness from the jalapeno hits my tongue first, and I taste him more, sucking his tongue until he groans in my mouth. He fists my hair, pulling me even closer, then suddenly pulls back. "What are you doing to me?"

"Me?" I muster up the most innocent face I can. "You're the one with your tongue down my throat."

He smirks, then opens his door, and grabs my bag from the back seat. The boat doesn't appear to have moved since the last time I was here. "You haven't taken it out?"

He pats the hull in passing and we enter the house through the laundry room. "I haven't had time."

The back of my neck prickles at his declaration. For some reason, it doesn't sit well with me. "Because of the movie?"

He turns down the hallway in the opposite direction of the path to the kitchen we took last time and stops at the end where a door stands open. He drops my bag on the floor and turns to me, taking the pastry box from my hands. "No, Kas. Because if I have any free time, I want to spend it with you.

The boat isn't as important." He cups my cheek with his free hand, and the tenderness in his eyes does something to my emotions, making me suddenly weepy.

I lay my head on his chest and wrap my arms around him and allow myself to relish the moment. In the back of my mind, I know I came here for a confrontation, but seeing the way Declan looks at me...really seeing it this time, I only want to think about our future because there's no way in hell, no matter what else is going on, that I will ever let him go.

THE PARKING LOT at Everheart Bar and Fine Dining is packed to the gills. On a Wednesday night. I hop out of the rideshare and gape at the front door, bustling with people going in and out. With so many customers, I probably won't get a chance to even thank Weston, the whole reason I'm here.

I stand in the line at the entrance and wait to give my name.

Ten minutes later, when I reach the front, the woman standing there smiles at me. "Right this way, Ms. Blythewood."

I blink.

She arches her eyebrows, waiting patiently, even though there are a jillion people waiting for her attention.

"Oh, sorry. Do I know you?"

She smiles and turns, beckoning for me to follow. "I remember you from a few months ago. Chef alerted me you'd be coming tonight."

"Ah, that makes sense."

We arrive at a table for two and she gestures with her hand, then sets down the menu. "Can I get you something to drink? Or do you need a little time?"

"Just water for now. Thanks." I glance at the kitchen, trying not to be too obvious, and the only brother I spot is Knox. Then I glance at the chef's table because that has a view of the entire kitchen.

"Sure thing." She leans down and lowers her voice. "Sorry about that. The chef's table has been booked for weeks."

"No, no. It's no problem at all. Please don't apologize. I was just people watching a bit."

She smiles again. "I'm sure Chef will be out as soon as he has a spare moment."

"Thank you."

"Enjoy."

She leaves and a man comes over less than a minute later with a glass filled with ice and water, a carafe also filled with water, and a small bowl of lemons. "Here you are, Ms. Blythewood. Someone will be over shortly to take your drink order."

"Thanks." I smile, but it's beginning to get a little creepy that everyone knows my name. I scan the menu but don't land on anything I want. At least not of the alcohol persuasion. Then I remember the wonderful ginger beer Joy had last time we were here.

A different man comes up, white shirt pressed to within an inch of its life, a black vest, and a crisp white apron tied around his waist over black pants. I guess I didn't notice last time how much the waitstaff looks like penguins.

I cover the smile breaking through with my hand.

"Good evening, Ms. Blythewood. My name is Henry, and I'll be your waiter this evening. May I get you something else to drink?"

"Yes, please, Henry. I'll have the ginger beer." I point to it on the menu just in case there's more than one.

"Of course. Do you have an appetizer in mind or do you need a few more minutes?"

"Definitely need some more time. Thank you, Henry."

He nods then leaves the table, disappearing into the throng of bodies near the bar in the back of the restaurant.

I scan the menu, but I'm not sure what I have a taste for. I'll definitely order the dishes I know for sure Dec added to the menu, but I'm not sure what else.

"You look beautiful. As always."

I look up as Declan leans down to kiss me on the temple. "This old thing." I packed a couple of nice sundresses knowing I was lacking during South by. Tonight I'm wearing blue which happens to take up the majority of my closet. It's always been my favorite color but is growing on me even more after staring into Declan's beautiful eyes.

"Hardly." He chuckles, then gives me another appreciative scan. "I wish I could stay but we're really busy tonight."

"Really? I hadn't noticed."

He grins and shakes his head. "Okay, smarty-pants. I was wondering if you might let me order for you tonight. I have something special in mind."

Ever since Declan tried to pay my bill without asking, he's been wonderful about checking in with me first on even the smallest decision. That's the only way this producing collaboration has worked. "You may. But I at least want the appetizer you mentioned last time that was your idea."

He nods, his expression solemn. "Thanks, Kas."

I squeeze his hand before letting him go and watch him walk in the direction of the kitchen. Who knew such a small request would make him emotional? It just reminds me how much of his father's validation and affection he's yearned for but hasn't received. I glance around for the man himself, but don't see him anywhere. That's probably for the best.

Henry returns with my ginger beer. "Here you are, Ms. Blythewood. Chef informed me you've given him permission to order for you. I'll bring out your appetizers in no time at all."

"Thanks so much, Henry."

I sip my ginger beer and peer around the room. There's such a mix of people here from older couples huddled together at small booths, to families with older children, to younger singles, mixing it up at the several bars. A large group of people occupy one of the private dining areas with balloons and streamers spread around. Looks like a birthday party because there's a tiered cake in the corner. Another private room is full of professionals so I'm guessing an after-work celebration of some sort, especially since it's the middle of the week.

This time when I glance at the sliver of kitchen I can see, Knox is still there, but Flynn has joined him, his face notice-ably red even from the distance. I have no idea what they're saying, but they both have rigid postures. Knox raises a hand and slashes it through the air above him. Flynn balls his fists at the end of stiff arms, then walks out of my line of sight.

Declan hinted there's plenty of stress at the restaurant, but I didn't realize it's this bad. I take another sip of my ginger beer, the bite reminding me how strong it is.

Henry returns with two small plates. "Your appetizers, Ms. Blythewood. Bourbon figs with bacon and chile, and carrot tart. May I get you anything else?"

"Nothing. Thank you, Henry." I want to tell him to call me Kasi, but somehow it would insult him. I'm just picking up that vibe.

"You're welcome. Enjoy."

I've just taken an incredible bite of my carrot tart with the creamy ricotta and crunchy almonds complementing the different-colored carrots when Flynn comes to the table. "Mind if I sit?" A smile is pasted on his handsome face, but his eyes are stormy.

Inviting him to sit is going to bite me in the ass before this night is over, I just know it, but it is his restaurant. Who am I to tell him he can't sit in the chair he owns? "Help yourself."

He sits across from me and smooths his white chef's jacket, not a splash of food or wrinkle to be found. He studies me while I eat, taking in every detail of my face. His gaze isn't lascivious. It's more someone sizing up the enemy.

I savor a fig, and nearly groan at the sweet and salty combination along with the flavorful bourbon finish. "These are delicious."

He nods.

"I'm sure you didn't sit here to watch me eat so go ahead and get whatever it is off your chest."

He smirks and for a hot second, Declan's features are noticeable in his father's.

I shudder.

He misinterprets my shaking. "I'm not here to berate you, Kasi."

"What are you here for, Flynn?"

His eyes tighten just a tad. He probably isn't used to being addressed by anything less than Michelin-star Chef Everheart.

I'm not impressed.

"I took a high-level look at your progress this morning. Commendable."

I incline my head but don't respond because I'm waiting for the huge "but" coming my way.

"However, this venture has taken more time from Declan's schedule than I anticipated."

I narrow my gaze. "Your investment came with plenty of strings, the longest and thickest being your son. You'll recall I didn't ask for a producer."

"Well, good. We're in agreement. You'll continue without him."

A pounding knocks around in my head. "I could handle the remaining producing responsibilities although it's been nice to share that with someone and have time to focus more on directing. It's a little late on the talent front though. Declan has committed to being the face of this show, and I've designed all my shots around a hot guy with chef skills. Those aren't easily replaced."

Flynn's face flushes and a vein on the side of his neck throbs. He clenches his jaw and squints his eyes. "You're mistaken."

I wipe the corner of my mouth with my napkin and place it on the table. "I'm quite certain."

He stands, clearly shaken, and opens his mouth to say something, then slams it shut. He turns on his heels and walks in the direction of the rear of the restaurant.

I place my hands under my armpits to keep them from shaking. I was all bravado and lioness in front of Flynn, but he shook me to the core. This is not going to turn out well for any of us.

THE RUMBLE OF the garage door alerts me to Declan's arrival, and I hop up off the couch. I've rehearsed my speech over and over since I returned from the restaurant. I just hate I didn't get to see him again or thank Weston. As it is, I barely choked down the food he made special for me. I certainly didn't have an appetite after Flynn left the table, but after Dec made such a touching display when I told him I wanted his originals, I didn't have the heart to disappoint him by not eating. It's bad enough I've betrayed him by telling Flynn his plans. That wasn't my place, and I'm sick about it, but damn if Flynn wasn't able to drill under my skin with a quickness.

Dec comes through the door, his jacket undone and the white T-shirt underneath peeking through. His hair is still perfect, and his beard has that sexy amount of growth I love so much, but his gait is slower than usual, and his body slouched.

My eyes prick at the sight of him. Did I do this?

When he spots me, his eyes light up. "You didn't have to wait up." After slipping out of his shoes by the entry, he walks my way through the kitchen, shedding his jacket on the floor. A very un-Declan-like thing to do. "I'm dead tired, but seeing you makes me not care." He wraps me up, nuzzling his face in my neck.

What's happening? Why isn't he angry?

He leans back and looks me in the eyes. "Everything okay? You're so stiff."

"I, uh, no, everything's fine. I'm worried about the way you look."

He shakes his head, ever so slowly, and sits down on the couch, bringing me down with him, settling me in his lap. "Dad was extremely unreasonable today, especially tonight."

I stiffen again and bite my lip. Here it comes.

He rubs my back and kisses me on the shoulder. "I love this dress by the way. I'm sorry I didn't have more time to spend with you tonight."

"Don't apologize. I hate that I didn't get to thank Weston."

"I told him how surprised and appreciative you were. It lit up his face even more than usual. Who knew that was possible?"

"He's such a sweetheart."

"It's really incredible. His spirits stay up even while Dad is yelling and berating him. It's amazing how Weston doesn't let him get to him."

I hold my breath, waiting. For what I don't know because it seems like if there was a problem with my telling

Flynn, Dec would have said something by now.

He rubs his nose across my neck, then kisses the skin behind my ear.

My confused body doesn't know how to react. One minute I'm wound so tight, I almost crumble into tiny pieces. The next, Declan is sending thrills through my bloodstream.

"Thanks for dinner, Dec. It was amazing. You're very talented. Don't ever let anyone tell you differently."

He leans back, and his head lolls against the back cushion of the couch, his eyes barely open. "Thanks, Kas. I love you."

I freeze in place, and stare.

His eyes are closed now, and his breathing light. Just when I think he's asleep, he opens his eyes, barely cracked. "Did you hear me?"

"Do you mean it? Or are you delirious?" I release a nervous laugh. My emotions are jumbled between guilt over outing him to Flynn and those words that have come out of nowhere. If I'm honest, maybe it's not nowhere. I've been feeling the love for a while now.

He cups my cheek with the palm of his hand, his eyes still hooded. "I'm probably delirious, but I know what I'm saying. I love—"

I lean down before he can finish the sentence, and capture the words in my mouth, kissing him deeply. Tenderly. Then I lean back and take a breath. "I love you too." Heat travels over my skin where I thought it would be cold. I want to be scared because I've never said these words to anyone. Not in a romantic way. Yet, it feels so right. There goes that last half-piece of my heart. I kiss him again.

He smiles against my mouth and hugs my closer. "Let's go to bed."

I follow him down the hall, hand in hand, and although I've been in and out of his bedroom all day, between the pool and changing for dinner, this will be the first time I've ever been in Declan Everheart's bed. For some reason, butterflies flood my belly when we cross the threshold.

He drops his pants right by the door and pulls his T-shirt over his head, leaving him in those overpriced underwear he loves so much. "Shower?"

"Sure, meet you in there."

A few minutes later, the water turns on in the bathroom, and I unbutton my sundress, then fold it and put it back in my suitcase. I love the way Declan is so fashion-conscious, but never tries to inflict his will on my casual-clothes attitude. He doesn't even mention my lack of couture interest. My mother tried it, but she gave up years ago.

When I've rid myself of my panties, I make my way into the bathroom. Declan's already under the stream but has stretched his long body and leaned against the tile, balancing on his forearm above his head. He reminds me of a sculpture I've seen. The *Pouring Satyr*, I think. My heart skips a beat when I think about maybe seeing this image from now on. The rest of my life expands before me, and yet I can imagine Dec in it until the end. I shake my head, and open the shower door and step in.

He turns and folds me into his strong arms, laying his head on top of mine. "I can barely keep my eyes open."

"Then let me wash you and put you to bed."

He kisses the top of my head, and slowly rotates.

There's no washcloth to be found, so I pick up a bar of richly milled soap and lather my hands as much as possible. When I run my palms over his shoulders and down his back, Dec sighs. I don't hear it over the pounding of the water, but I feel it under my touch. I make quick work of my task which feels more like a pleasure because obviously Dec is too tired for anything else. At least not right now. Then I wash myself while he stands under the stream to rinse himself.

By the time we snuggle under his covers, intertwining our legs and arms, hearts beating against each other, Dec kisses me once more, then sighs an "I love you," and falls right to sleep.

I lie there for hours, sleep alluding me. My brain is in overdrive replaying the conversation with Flynn. I can't figure out why he wouldn't have confronted his son. But worse than that, I try to figure out why I haven't mentioned it either.

Maybe Dec won't care that I've told his father. He was going to anyway in less than two weeks when the competition's over and Knox has broken his news.

I sigh and close my eyes, hot tears running down my temples into my hair. I may have lied to Declan by omission tonight, but I can't lie to myself. After twenty-eight years on this spinning rock, I've finally fallen in love with someone, and probably ruined it.

CHAPTER NINETEEN

When things were said, and mistakes were made.

T HE NEXT MORNING, I awake to the smell of coffee, and Declan's muffled yelling on the other side of the closed bedroom door. The sun streams in through open curtains, and I sit up and rub my temples. I'm not sure if my headache is from a lack of sleep or the memory of my betrayal.

I sit up and squeeze my eyes closed, then go to the bathroom in search of some sort of medicine to take the pain away. The medicine cabinet only contains what looks like pricey natural remedies, but I finally find something that boasts taking headaches away in minutes. The bottle directs me to take two. I take three and chug some water directly from the tap, then sit back on the bed.

Declan's still using his outside voice inside the house, so I lie back and give the pills time to kick in. My headache dulls but before it leaves completely, the bedroom door flies open and hits the doorjam hard.

"What's wrong with you?" His voice, rough from yelling, bounces around inside my head.

I peek an eye open and see the man I met months ago. An arrogant smirk creases his beautiful mouth. His eyes are ocean-depth grayish blue, and narrowed, his callous gaze pointed my way. This isn't the man I've come to know.

I sigh, and roll into a sitting position, covering my nakedness with a blanket from the bed as I go, and press a palm against my left eye. "My head hurts." I don't ask him what his problem is because I already know. There can be no mistaking what has him in such a tizzy this morning. "I took some medicine from your bathroom cabinet and it's starting to get better."

He nods and walks over to the curtains, raising his hands to open them. He glances at me, then changes his mind, and puts his hands in his pockets. "I just spoke with Dad."

"You don't say."

"I realize your head hurts, but I don't have much time before I need to get to the restaurant. Do you want to discuss it now or later tonight?"

"Can I have the CliffsNotes?"

"No."

"Now it is then."

He leans against one of the posts of his bed, not two feet away from me. It seems like a hundred feet. His posture is as rigid as I've ever seen, and he keeps his hands in his pockets. Maybe to keep from reaching out lovingly to me because he's mad and wants to stay mad. Then again, perhaps it's to keep from strangling me.

I hold my breath to tamp down the nervous laughter bubbling up, and study him from the corner of my eye. We may not be in a great place right this minute, but violence is the last thing Declan would pull out of his hat.

He bites out a quick, "What gives you the right?"

"I get you're mad but watch your tone."

"My tone? My fucking tone? Are you kidding me right now?"

"Careful." I stand up and wrap the sheet from the bed around me, indignation warming my skin.

"You really are something. You screw me over completely, and don't say a single word about it. Then have the nerve to tell me to watch my tone." He doesn't move from his spot but crosses his arms across his naked chest.

"I didn't mean to tell him, Dec. And when you came home so tired, I figured we'd just talk about it this morning." I lean on the other post and fold my arms across my own chest. "And here we are."

"Okay, so it was an accident?" Sarcasm etches every one of those words.

"Yeah, actually. It slipped out. He baited me."

He releases a harsh bark of laughter. "You allowed my father to bait you. I thought you were smarter than that."

My head snaps back, headache forgotten. "Excuse you." My free hand flies to my hip. "Your father manipulates and belittles you your entire life, and you have the nerve to insult my intelligence. That's rich, Dec."

With his olive undertones, I didn't think it possible for Declan's skin to turn beet red, but it makes its best effort. Add in the bulging eyes, and I think we have a full-blown fight on our hands. "Don't put your daddy issues on me."

"You had daddy issues long before you set those pretty eyes on me, baby doll. Matter of fact, the night I met you, you were trailing around behind him like a puppy dog. And the more he kicks you, the more you try to gain his approval.

News flash, Dec, you ain't never gonna get it."

He blows out a gust of air from his nose, then uncrosses his arms. "So that's what you think of me."

My stomach twists in knots from the way I just hurt him. My mouth is forever writing a check my soul can't cover. "I don't mean it that way."

"I'm unsure how else you could mean it, Kas."

"It's your father I'm upset with. It's his fault the way he treats you. Not yours. I'm not sitting here trying to blame you for Flynn's shortcomings."

He nods and thins his lips into a sad frown. "I've got to go to work."

"Um, okay."

He strolls over to his walk-in closet and disappears within. A few minutes later, he returns fully dressed for work including a white chef's jacket. "I'll be back tonight. Maybe we can talk then if it's not too late." He brushes by me, then turns back and gives me a quick kiss on the temple. "I hope your headache goes away."

Before he can make it to the door, I call his name. When he turns his head ever so slightly without actually looking at me, I say, "I love you."

He nods three quick times, then walks down the hallway.

I sit back on the bed hard and listen to his retreating footsteps. The laundry room door makes a quiet click, then he's gone.

THE DAY STRETCHES out ahead of me, there's so much I

could get done. Unfortunately, I can't think of anything other than arguing with Declan. I know I'm wrong on so many levels, but damn he said some hurtful things.

I drag myself to the living room after throwing on some shorts and a tank top. I have zero appetite so I pass the kitchen without a second glance. I probably should get some water to at least keep myself hydrated. That headache this morning was no joke. Maybe in a little while.

I strain my eyes to see the time on the microwave. Wait, that can't be right. Looks like I'm headed for the kitchen after all. When I get closer, it does indeed read ten thirty. I guess I got more sleep than I thought. No wonder Dec had to dip so quickly. He was probably already late. Although it's not like Flynn could say anything to him considering he started the whole mess this morning.

Since I'm already in the kitchen, I look through five of Dec's fancy cabinets before finally finding a glass. Refrigerator number one doesn't have water. Refrigerator number two has ice and water built into the door, but it's like a fucking spaceship, and I can't figure the thing out. I finally find a filtered pitcher sitting next to the sink and pour myself some water. I've certainly earned the drink.

There's a sticky-note on the window above the sink. *Look in the microwave.*

When I open the microwave, there's a plate with a stack of pancakes on it. I shut the door and sit on the floor. The tears flow down my face, and run into my mouth, hot and salty. I cry until my nose is so stuffy, my head hurts again.

Back in Dec's bathroom, I start the day all over again, looking through his cabinet for headache medicine. If only I could start this whole trip over. I wouldn't even go to the restaurant. It's not like I ever got to see Weston anyway.

The tub is looking pretty inviting right about now, so I turn on the spigots and when it gets half full, I flip the switch for the jets. Having a Jacuzzi seems redundant when he has this huge tub making its own bubbles right here. I'm pretty sure it could hold three, maybe even four people. Today it's a party of one of my own making. I slip under the water nonetheless and try to relax my tense body. As I replay our fight—because of course I do—I feel more and more awful. He did say some hurtful words, but I did too. Probably far worse. And that's on top of selling him out to his dad.

I slide farther under the water allowing the jets to really pound my neck. Too bad my hair gets a good soaking too from all the excess spray. This must be a top-of-the-line tub because it's almost like I have my Jet Ski in here. Ugh, thinking about my Jet Ski brings me around to Tariq. What if I've fucked up the investment? I mean, we have signed contracts. Everyone except Dec that is.

The tub's no use because as soon as my limbs even think about loosening, my mind amps them up again. I get out and wrap a towel around me then go in search of my phone. I find it on Dec's nightstand, battery completely dead. Next, I hunt around in my laptop bag and get the cord, and plug in my phone. It's already almost noon here so that means ten in LA. I fire a text off to Mom asking how Tariq is doing.

Then I call Joy.

The phone goes to voicemail and I leave her a message to call me back as soon as she can. I need to find out my options with this whole mess brewing here. You'd think I'd learn my lesson after what my own father did to me, but somehow I let Dec slip through my trust walls, and now I may be screwed.

Before I finish leaving the voicemail, a slew of messages come through from a couple different people related to the movie, but most are from Kristin.

Hi, Kasi. Give me a call when you get this message.

Just making sure you got my text message.

Hi, me again. Don't panic, but New Zealand's trying to pull out of the contract. Really could use your input on how to proceed. It's airtight, but they may not put in their best effort if we hold them to it.

Okay, I've talked with them and we worked something out. Check your email.

This is one of the places I wanted to visit to do some pre-work, but with all of Dec's scheduling conflicts, time ran out. I pull my laptop out and fire it up, scanning my email first. There are several unread from Kristin, but only one with New Zealand in the subject line. I'm satisfied how she handled it, but it's another reminder that this is the worst time for falling in love. I've been distracted and didn't even pay attention to my phone running out of juice. We could have lost one of the main locations I wanted. Thankfully Kristin is really good at her job.

I text her back. *So sorry. Didn't realize my phone died. Your email filled me in so well. Thank you for saving the day!*

Next, I read through my outstanding emails not only from Kristin, but from other people as well. Then return all the text messages. I can't believe I was really going to sit here and sulk all day instead of taking care of business.

My stomach grumbles become so loud, it's impossible to

ignore anymore. Hopefully pancakes that have been sitting out for six hours won't make me sick because I hit reheat on the microwave and search for some honey. I find a cute jar with a dipper on the island. My heart squeezes thinking about Dec moving around this beautiful house alone. Okay, mostly alone. I'm not stupid enough to think he's just been sitting around all his life waiting for me to step into it, but even since we've been long distance, his schedule is basically going to work and coming home late. Rinse and repeat. He has every single creature comfort known to man but didn't seem happy until he spent some extended time in nature.

The ding of the microwave pulls me from my thoughts and while I eat, I continue to check messages and respond. Every bite reminds me where Dec's talents truly lie. These are not regular tasting pancakes. They're special and I'm sure it's some original twist he's put on them. Maybe he does actually love what he does and I'm seeing something that's not really there because I want it to be true. Perhaps his own restaurant would make him happy. Somewhere he could create.

Joy calls me back when I'm washing my dish to load into the dishwasher.

"Finally, heffa."

"Bish, please. I do have a job that doesn't entirely revolve around you. Or have you forgotten?"

Properly chastised, I take a breath before responding. "I haven't forgotten. And I appreciate you because I'm not even making you any money to be acting so high and mighty."

"Yet. Not making me any money yet. It's soon though."

"Is it? I feel like it's falling apart around me." My eyes

prick again. I blink a few times to get myself together.

"Babe, why are you feeling that way?"

"I made a big mistake."

"Are you going to tell me about it? I could guess if that's what you're waiting for."

"I'm just…" I inhale and hold my breath as long as I can. "Things were great with Dec, but I was already feeling like he may back out because he hadn't told his dad yet. Then you confirmed he hasn't signed the deal memo. I told Flynn everything and Declan's super pissed."

Joy snorts. "Can you blame him?"

"Well, no. I didn't mean to say anything, but Flynn lives rent-free in my head even though I'd never said more than five words to him before last night."

"Oh, Kasi."

"I know. It's stupid really because he basically saved me. If he hadn't invested, I'm not sure of my next move. And then what's happened with Tariq… I should probably be kissing his boots, but instead, I really dislike the man. I don't know what's happened to me."

"You're in love with his son."

I suck in a surprised breath, gripping the phone. "Who told you that?"

"I've known you since we were children. Why would someone need to tell me? Have you told him yet?"

"Yeah, last night. That was before he found out about me snitching."

Joy laughs.

"Joy, hush. But what does me being in love with his son have to do with me being sour on the man?"

"You really need to go to therapy. Have I mentioned that lately?"

"Basically every time I speak to you."

"Maybe one day you'll take me up on it. Anyway, as your fake sister-therapist, because Flynn doesn't treat Declan well. You can't stand the man because of how he makes the man you love feel. I would think that would be obvious, Kasi. Jeesh."

I sit down on the living room sofa and lay my head back, then stare at the ceiling. "It is obvious. Maybe Declan had a point this morning."

"Do I even want to know?"

"Probably not. At least not if I plan on keeping a relationship with him. He didn't mean it though. We both said some things we didn't mean."

"I've never known you to be so quick to forgive. I like it."

"Hardee har har. You should take your show on the road."

"Maybe I will. Then where will you be?"

"You right."

"So about Declan and this deal memo…"

I take a deep breath and stare at the ceiling a little longer, hoping the answer will drop down. When it doesn't, I take a deep dive into my heart. Then my brain.

Joy patiently waits because like she said, she's known me a long time.

"He has to sign, or we'll need to move on. We're already too deep into preproduction that if he pulls out, it'll be a major problem. If we wait even longer, and this thing goes sideways…" Another couple breaths. "I don't even want to think about it."

"Sounds like an ultimatum. Is that going to cause problems?"

"Probably. But Tariq needs this more now than ever. I can't let him down again."

"Maybe you can talk to your dad about releasing some money from your trust fund to cover Tariq. It's not like your dad doesn't owe him."

I grind my teeth at the thought of asking my father for anything. Doesn't matter because even if I did ask, he wouldn't do it. "My grandfather set the trust up with very specific old-fashioned rules. I don't get full control until I'm either thirty or married and can only draw a living wage before then. He also gave my father control over releasing additional funds. If I thought him releasing more money was an option, I'd give everything up, and go work for him. Because those would be the strings that would attach to that particular favor. As it is, I'm lucky the rules were set up on the trust when I was a little girl, or he'd cut it off altogether."

Joy's sigh through the phone is audible. "I wish I could say I don't believe he'd be like that, but I totally can believe it."

My phone vibrates with an incoming text. "Hold on a sec, Joy."

I'll be home early. Will bring dinner with me.

I think a moment how I want to respond. My first instinct is to tell him how great it is that's he'll be home early. But then I wonder if maybe it's because he's had it out with Flynn and that's why. In that case, it wouldn't be great.

"Kasi?"

"What? Sorry, I forgot you were on the phone."

"Gee, thanks."

In the end, I keep it simple. *Okay, see you then.*

"Sorry, that was Dec. He said he's coming home early. I'm not sure what that means."

"I guess you'll find out soon."

I fidget with the bottom of my tank top and bite my lip. I guess I will.

CHAPTER TWENTY

When it goes south, and not in a good way.

"IN HERE."

Declan walks into his fancy dining room and surveys the changes I've made.

"I thought it would be fun to use this space. What do you think?" I've unpacked plates from drawers in the nearby buffet. The room is simple and elegant, just like everything else in Declan's house. The table seats ten and looks to be made out of marble or stone. Maybe it's just really shiny wood. I've never paid attention to these types of things before. I've set the table for the two of us, using all the place setting items Declan has. Which is a lot. There are two huge clear vases with plants in water. I thought it odd he would have such a thing, but when I investigated, the plants aren't real even though I had to really test them to figure it out. I couldn't find any tapered candles so improvised with a couple pillar candles from the guest bathroom.

"What's the occasion?"

"You coming home early?"

"You sound like Weston. Is that a question or statement?"

"Statement?"

The look on his face is so close to rolling his eyes, but he turns and walks back into the kitchen. "I'm going to take a quick shower. The food's on the counter."

"Okay." I sift through the takeout containers and move the food onto a large platter, and set it in the dining room. Hopefully Declan really meant a quick shower and the food won't get cold even though it's just steak, broccoli, and baked potatoes. Completely uninspired. None of this bodes well for our future.

I sit at the table and try not to fidget with the hem of my sundress. It's the second fanciest thing I brought so I figured I'd pull out the big guns for tonight. Maybe my sexy body will make Declan forget what an ass I was to him this morning. And last night, really.

As promised, Declan comes into the dining room, looking good enough to eat in what looks like an expensive pair of sweatpants slung low on his hips, and a form-fitting plain white T-shirt tucked into them. The outline of his dick is barely visible, and I have to look away to keep from staring. This is probably not the time even though I was just thinking about trying to distract him with my own body.

Well played, Dec. Well played.

When he sits, I turn back.

His eyes are serious, but he manages a small smile. "This is really nice. I hardly ever use this room."

"Thanks for bringing dinner."

He nods. "We better eat before it gets cold."

I smile and pick up my fork. The steak goes into my mouth, but it's completely tasteless. Or maybe it's flavorful, but my thoughts cloud any chance of relishing this food.

When I first met Dec, he was sort of understated, I guess. Maybe that's not the right word, but he wasn't one to be too animated, almost stern. And I actually liked that about him. As I got to know him, and love him, I've come to understand that's a coping mechanism for him. He's so warm and easy, and open to excitement in his life. And I've come to love that about him too.

"Your shields are back up, and that breaks my heart."

He doesn't even acknowledge me.

I eat a few bites of my steak and maybe a crown of broccoli before I give up and set my fork down. I don't even attempt the heavy potato.

Declan has mostly moved his food around his plate. "Let's just give up."

My heart pounds, and it gets harder to breathe. "What?"

He sets down his fork and stands. "Neither of us are eating much. Let's just give up trying. We should talk."

"I thought you meant something else."

He draws his eyebrows together. After a moment, it obviously dawns on him what I thought. "No, Kas. Not that." He reaches his hand out for mine.

I take a couple of deep breaths to stop my hand from shaking before I put it in his. The breathing doesn't work though.

He kisses the back of the offending hand while we walk to the living room. Only he doesn't stop and pulls me through the door leading into the backyard. We pass the pool and find a bench in the darker depths of the yard. The moon is out in its most full form so I don't miss the sadness crinkling Dec's eyes.

My heart breaks all over again. It's my fault he's sad, and there was no reason for it. "Dec, I'm really sorry about what I said earlier. And especially about telling your father. You were right. That wasn't my place, and I should have taken better care."

He sits on the bench and pulls me down next to him, never letting go of my hand.

I lean on his shoulder and smell his spicy cologne. Underneath, the scents of the restaurant crawl over his skin, intertwine in his hair. His skin is warm and damp, maybe from the shower. Most likely from the extreme humidity plaguing this town.

I can barely breathe, but I'm not certain it's from the oppressive air. Declan is too quiet.

"I appreciate the apology. I do, but you've set some pretty severe consequences in motion."

My heart sinks. Not because of what Flynn may do to me, but because of Declan. I could have avoided causing him harm. "Like what?"

He shrugs and lets go of my hand, then stretches his longs legs out in front of him. "Dad's apoplectic. Not just at me. Ryan had to call in replacement chefs tonight. That's why I'm home early. All we did was snipe at each other all day. Plenty of mistakes were made, and finally Dad got fed up and called me and Knox into his office." He rubs his hand across his face a couple times, and I sit up straight and watch him. He's barely saying anything, but the few words he does relate sinks my heart farther and farther.

I don't have a good feeling about this. None of it. What Declan isn't saying is loud and clear, and I'm pissed off he won't just man up. "Where does all this leave us, Dec?"

"What do you mean us? The movie or me and you?"

I snort and cover my mouth. *Take it down, Kas, before you say something you'll regret again.* "How about both. Anything you'd like to share would be greatly appreciated." I know that sounds snarky, but honestly, it's much calmer than what I really wanted to say. Ha, take that, Joy. Who needs a therapist?

"I still love you. Is that what you mean?"

"No, it's not. If you fell out of love with me in a day, then it wasn't love to begin with."

He stands and walks over to the bushes lining the rear fence and rubs the back of his neck. "I suppose that's true."

"Listen, I've never been in love before, but seems to me like new love is hard."

"It is. Old love can be hard too."

I've never asked Declan about past loves. It's just not something that interests me. But now I wonder. He lives in this huge house with several guest bedrooms where the doors are always shut. A beautiful dining room he doesn't eat in. And a boat he never takes out. Nothing about it signals anyone other than Declan has ever lived here though because it reflects his highbrow tastes so well. Still, he could have changed some things around. Even though I'm a smidge curious, now is definitely not the time to take a detour down that road.

I stand and traverse the small distance between us and stand next to him, and stare at the same bush. "I can't read your mind, Dec. I need you to talk to me."

"I don't know what else to say other than I love you."

"Love is great, and I'm glad, but what does that mean for us?"

He turns to me and pulls me into his body, squeezing me so tight. He moves his mouth next to my ear, his breath tickling the sensitive skin there. The fresh memory of his kisses there. "I want you. Do you still want me?"

"Of course."

He nods. "Okay then."

"Okay then, what though?"

"Okay then, we'll be together. I can't answer for anything else right now. I'm still negotiating with Dad."

I step out of his grasp so I can see his face. "Are you saying there's a chance the movie is in jeopardy?"

A cloud passes over his face, but he shakes his head. "I'll never allow that to happen."

"And what about you as talent?"

He rubs a finger next to his eye, suddenly catching a furious itch. He turns back to the bushes. "I don't know yet."

"You're serious?"

"I'm afraid so. And before you work yourself up, don't forget why we're here."

I open my mouth to really tell him about himself, but his words finally sink in. I caused this. I clamp my mouth together and give thanks he's still looking away from me. "Okay, but when will you know? You know I go back tomorrow, right?"

"Right. Tariq."

"Well, yes. I can't just leave him for days on end right now. Especially with my parents hovering. Plus, there's a lot of work left to do. Just because we're ahead of schedule doesn't change that."

"I understand." His voice is even, devoid of all emotion.

I hug him from behind, wrapping my arms around his firm chest, and lay my head on his back. "Can we forget all the outside stuff? Just for tonight?"

He's still for almost a minute, then turns in my arms, and bends down to kiss me. His mouth is urgent and probing, and I open to him completely.

He breaks the kiss just as suddenly as he started it. "Let's go inside."

AS SOON AS we hit the bed, Dec is on me. Or maybe I'm on him. It's such a rush to come together that I'm moving on instinct rather than thought. I grab the back of his neck and pull him down to me, and our lips crash together. He pushes his tongue into my mouth, and I suck on it so hard, it pulls a sharp grunt from his throat. That only heats my blood higher.

I push him off me and sit up, tearing off my dress, then shimmy out of my panties.

Declan doesn't watch me like he normally would. Instead, he lifts himself from the bed in one smooth motion, shedding his own clothes, then yanking open the bedside table, and reaching in. He tears open the package and sheaths himself with the condom while I lie back and ready myself, rubbing my clit in hard circles. He does watch then, only for a moment, and his pupils enlarge to an unhealthy degree.

I open my legs wider in invitation, and he slides between them, pushing against my opening. After a couple of pumps, he gains complete entry. He buries his head in my hair, and balances on his forearms while pounding into me. I can't get enough. I circle my legs around his back, and grab his tight ass with both hands, pulling him deeper.

There's an itch inside me that's just out of his reach so I push him off me onto his back and straddle him. Only, I don't face him because even though I want him deep inside me, I don't want him in my soul right now. He grabs my butt from behind and holds on while I ride him hard and fast, angling my body just so, balancing my hands on his strong thighs. When he finally scratches at that itch, the relief is immediate and I come hard, a wordless, quiet scream escaping my mouth. I bend forward as I come down, giving him a full view of my pussy grabbing and swallowing his dick. He grunts and holds me against him as he plows deep inside one last time.

I'm worn out. From the physical exertion, but also from the emotional journey that got us here. When Dec gets up to go to the bathroom and dispose of the condom, I'm out before he returns.

When I awake the next morning, I'm on one side of the bed, and Dec on the other, our backs to each other. Declan's pants are on the floor near me, the edge of his phone peeks out from a pocket. I reach for it and check the time. It's early, but less than three hours until my flight leaves.

My instincts drive me this morning too, and I roll over and slide across the bed to settle against Dec's back.

He reaches behind him and pulls me closer, flush against

him.

I wrap my arm around his stomach and trail kisses down the long length of his back, then urge him to turn over with my hand. He rotates and is gentle when he slips his hands into my hair, skating fingernails across my scalp as I take him into my mouth. I draw him in with slow strokes until he hardens completely, then lick up and down his shaft, taking my time to savor the taste of him.

My pulse quickens, and my nipples harden against his thigh as I take him full back into my mouth, swallowing his entire length. He bucks against me and lets go of my hair, falling back against the pillow, grasping the sheets next to me. I repeat the movements and cup his balls, squeezing ever so gently. They tighten against his body right before he pulls out of my mouth and comes all over his stomach. "Fuck, Kas."

He pulls a tissue out of the bedside table and quickly swipes it across his stomach, then pulls me up on top of him. He raises up for a kiss and I happily meet his mouth. It's warm and gentle, and he wraps his arms around me, squeezing me almost reverently, then flips me onto my back. He nips at my chin and kisses that special place behind my ear, taking his time.

I reach for my own breast, circling and tugging the hard nipple. Dec smiles against my throat, then places a soft kiss on the hollow of it before pulling my untouched nipple into his mouth. He circles it with his tongue, and I clench my thighs together, searching for relief from the tug of the string attached from my nipple to my clit. Dec trails his hand down my stomach and my legs pop open again of their own volition. I twine my hand with his and push his fingers through my soaking folds and into my needy pussy.

He groans around my nipple, then releases it and follows the trail of his hand with soft kisses, and licks down my stomach until he reaches my swollen nub. He flattens his tongue against it just as I like and applies delicious pressure while pumping his fingers inside me. It's my turn to grip the sheets and hold on for this exquisite ride as my orgasm tugs at my stomach, then travels to Dec's mouth. He holds my hips as I writhe against him, euphoria flowing through my entire body.

BACK HOME, UNEASE sweeps through my body as I look up to the sun, then lay my yoga mat on the sand. I need this session badly because my stomach is in knots and my muscles are so tight. You'd think the mind-blowing orgasm I had first thing this morning would have relaxed me, and it did for about a minute, but the surface-level conversation on our way to the airport undid any goodwill built up by exchanging a few bodily fluids. Declan's parting kiss was tender, and deep, and felt like goodbye.

I'll visit Tariq next but don't want to go over there all wound up, hence the workout. It's still early-ish here because of the time change, which is another reason I want to wait a bit before I head over. If I go too early, Dad will be there. I've successfully avoided him for nearly a year, and I don't want to break my record now. Although it's tough with Tariq being under his roof.

I shake my head to dislodge some of these thoughts. I've gone from worrying about my relationship with Declan, to worrying about Tariq's health and well-being, to worrying about my relationship with Dad. I put in my earbuds and crank the volume on my phone, the instructor's smooth voice drowning out the unwanted rumination.

A couple of hours later, I pull up to my parents' house and take one last look at my phone before I get out of my car. Still no call or message from Declan. I dawdle near my car and do some breathing exercises. Over an hour of yoga and my nerves are no better off. Matter of fact, since I stepped into the airport this morning, I've been frazzled, and no amount of meditation is going to help as long as both the professional and personal are unsettled between me and Declan. He says he wants to be with me still, but his actions don't exactly match up.

The gate opens before I can hit the button on the intercom, and I frown. Another thing I hate about this house are the cameras everywhere. Even if I wanted to sneak out in high school, I couldn't. So many of my friends, including Joy, partied like it was 1999. Their parents were a lot less restrictive than mine, even those with celebrity moms or dads like my father. Seems like, the higher the profile, the more freedom those kids had. Not at my house though. Tariq was always studious and took football seriously, so we often kept each other company, mostly at my house, but a lot of online gaming took place too.

Speak of the devil, Dad opens the front door wide and steps back with his burly arms crossed over his barrel chest. He's tall and big and blocks the sun. Always has. Unlike

Mom, he doesn't dress to impress. He has on jeans and a wrinkled USC sweatshirt. His influence is pretty much where I got my style.

Because I can't catch a break today, I don't even flinch. My dread was building up for a reason, and the payoff is upon me, standing right before me. "I'm here to see Tariq."

"Obviously."

It takes everything in me to not roll my eyes. I know better. That's why I stay away. Because disrespect will not be tolerated by Reggie Blythewood, and I run hot too fast around Dad to pull it in most times. It's been a peaceful year only because we haven't been around each other. "I didn't come here to fight with you, Dad. Somehow you wrangled my friend here, and now I'm stuck. Congratulations."

He closes the door behind me, and sighs. "We are helping your friend, a man we've known nearly all his life. I didn't expect appreciation from you, but I also didn't realize I'd be on the bad end of your contempt either."

"You're trying to manipulate me, Dad. You didn't expect me to be angry about that? I had Tariq handled."

"According to your mother, you've been distracted so we stepped in to help. I get that you don't want my assistance, but surely you'd want more for Tariq."

My mother will be the end of me. I swear. "I feel like this is an ambush."

"I had no idea you were coming over today."

"Yet, here you are. Waiting by the front door."

"We need to talk, Kasi. This has gone on long enough."

My phone buzzes, and my hand twitches, anxious to snatch it out of my purse. "You will never be able to run my life, Dad. The sooner you accept that, the sooner we can talk. Until then, I need to go see Tariq." I walk across the entryway and race down the hall to Tariq's room, hoping Dad doesn't follow me.

CHAPTER TWENTY-ONE

When it was done.

I DON'T DARE call Declan back until I get home. Hopefully he'll be able to talk since that missed call was two hours ago, and he's so busy between the restaurant and the upcoming final competition soon. I sit on my sofa and press the call icon under the picture I assigned to his contact information. It's a picture of him when he first bit into alpaca jerky, surprised delight brightening his face. It was the first time I realized his incredible talent for being in front of the camera.

I'm too cowardly to video call him, so the phone rings until it goes to voicemail. It's expected but still no less a gut punch.

There's no fancy chef here to cook for me so I heat up a frozen chorizo and egg burrito and pour myself a rather large glass of wine. By the time the buzzer goes off on the microwave, my phone alerts me to an incoming call. This time I snatch the device up before the first ring ends. "Hello?"

"Hey, Kas."

I exhale a sigh of relief because I didn't even take the time to look at the screen before answering. If it hadn't been Declan, I'm not sure if I wouldn't have hung up in the person's face. "Hi. Sorry I missed your call earlier. I was having a confrontation with my father."

"There's a lot of that going on today. How'd it go?"

"About as well as you'd expect. How about you?" I grip the phone harder and hold my breath. Is this going to be fantastic news or terrible news? There's really no in-between.

"Knox told Dad that he submitted his idea for a pasta restaurant to the producers. That didn't go over well. He said it was lucky he was traveling with us."

"You're kidding."

"I wish I were. At least I'll have some time with him where he's not distracted by the restaurant."

"But why does he need to go? How will that change anything?"

"He says it's to protect his investment. If we win, he intends to open a second steakhouse in The Domain."

I remember Declan mentioning that before, but it seems so unbelievable. If he'd screw over his son like that, I know my little production doesn't have a chance. "Will Flynn want to come to LA next to protect his investment here too?" I sort of add a nervous laugh.

But Dec is quiet.

"Declan?"

"I've got to go, but I called to ask you to come up to San Francisco tomorrow. We'll be there really late, but I could let the front desk know that you'll be joining me."

It's my turn to be quiet. I need to think.

"Kas? You there? I'm sorry to rush you, but I really have to go."

"Okay, but I'll get my own room. Text me the hotel info."

"Okay. See you tomorrow."

The phone clicks off before I have a chance to respond. I realize he was in a hurry, but dang.

The text doesn't come through until after I've gone to bed which is super late on his end considering the time difference. I book a room first thing when I wake up, but my fingers skitter over the keyboard when the prices pop up. Maybe I shouldn't have been so prideful and just stayed with him. I also didn't want to be that close to Flynn either if I can help it.

WHEN MY RIDESHARE drops me off in front of the hotel, I look straight up at the towering building, then at the door-man holding the door open for me. I thank him as I walk through, then take in the decor. No wonder it's so expensive. I roll my bag to the check-in counter, but there's a group already checking in together ahead of me. Two women, and a man. One of the women says her name to the man behind the counter and that they're checking in for the competition, and I realize it's Rowan, the women who's had Knox turned completely upside down. My mouth drops open. She's fucking gorgeous. Why is she here though? I'm certain Dec said they didn't make it past the semifinals.

When it's my turn, I check in easily and head up to my room on the sixth floor. It's cramped with a full-size bed and tiny bathroom which isn't a complete surprise considering I booked the cheapest they had. And when I walk over to the window and glance out, there's a bustle of people below, but

I can't see a whole lot of anything else because I'm not very high up. It's not my first time in San Francisco but I think today would be a great time to sightsee and keep my mind off bad ideation until Dec gets here later tonight.

I stay out until dark and when I get back to the hotel, Rowan comes off the elevator headed to the restaurant. I want to stop her so badly and introduce myself, but I'm not sure where Knox is in his pursuit of her. She'll probably think I'm just as creepy as he is. Instead, I head up to my room, full on chowder and sourdough bread, and throw myself across my bed.

I receive a text message from Dec. *Landed.* That's it. The whole message.

Not for the first time, I wonder what I'm doing here. I'm confident he wouldn't bring me all the way up here to sink the deal with Flynn as a witness. Even if he were still upset with me, Dec isn't cruel.

I don't bother to text back. He didn't text me back when I told him I'd checked in and saw Rowan. He wasn't on the plane yet so there's no excuse.

I grab my head and squeeze. Then text him back. *See you soon.* I can't start this tit-for-tat mess with Dec. I'm sure he had his reasons for not responding.

Over an hour passes before he finally sends another message. *What room are you in?*

I text him the room number then run to the bathroom to freshen up. Before I can wash my face good, there's a soft knock.

When I open the door, Declan stands on the other side, looking a little haggard. Not his normal put-together self.

Even his pants aren't as crisp as usual. Not exactly wrinkled, but not cared for either. His eyes are tired. "Hi."

"Hi. Come in."

He brushes my arm as he passes, and that bit of touch sends an electric current straight through me. It must affect him too because he grabs me up in his arms and buries his face in my neck. His arms shake ever so slightly, and my heart breaks in two.

He kisses my neck, then my cheek, then angles to my mouth, heat in his eyes.

I put a stilling hand on his chest. It kills me to stop him because I want his touch terribly, but we need to put some stuff out there first. "As much as I enjoy sex with you, we've done enough communicating that way. It's time to use your words."

He nods and lets me go, then runs a hand across his face. "You're right. Of course you're right."

"What's going on, Dec?" I walk the couple steps to the bed, plop down, and cross my legs.

He falls down beside me, lying back with a hand over his eyes. "My family's falling apart."

I want to ask, "Is that it?" But that sounds harsh even bouncing around in my brain. Not to mention selfish. I guess I'm used to family drama so it doesn't seem like this should affect him so hard. "With Knox?"

"All of us. Even Weston has expressed some discomfort with how we're interacting. In his Weston-way."

I rub his thigh. "Tell me about it, Dec."

"You texted that you saw Rowan earlier. I'm not sure if I mentioned the other family dropped out so that's why her family is here."

"Oh, wow. I wondered why she was here."

"Yeah. Well, Knox plans to drop out for sure now that she's back in. He's prepared to tell Dad to sub in for him, but he wants to compete head-to-head with her on the cooking. For some reason he thinks her confidence is lacking. Personally, I don't see it."

"She looked pretty darn confident the five minutes I saw her while checking in. Then I saw her later stepping off the elevator. She's absolutely drop-dead gorgeous."

"So are you."

"I'm aware. This isn't a competition. We can both be showstoppers."

He sighs and shakes his head. "Of course you can. And she has Knox completely whipped and doesn't even know it."

"Wow."

"Yeah. I saw her right before I texted you. She was in the hallway, and you should have seen how both of them were so flustered. It's only a matter of time before they finally get together. Knox always gets what he wants."

I don't miss the edge to his voice. "Where's the drama though?"

"Dad, as always. When he finds out Knox is dropping out of the competition, he won't be happy. When he realizes Knox is quitting being a chef, all hell will break loose. I feel like I'm in the middle, keeping this from Dad. But I can't betray my brother either."

"Ah, I see why you're so stressed."

"No, that's not why."

My heart pounds so hard, I can hear it in my ears. I should have known this was too good to be true.

"I can't be your talent, Kas. I'm sorry."

I move my shaky hand from his leg. He moves to catch it, but I'm up off the bed before he can touch me. "You're sorry?"

"Yes, I'm sorry. It's unavoidable."

"That's it? That's the only explanation I get?" My heart is beating so hard I can hardly hear my own angry voice.

"It's the only one I have. I'll still produce and keep Dad out of it, but that's all I can offer."

I release a harsh gale of breath, somewhere between a laugh and a strangled cry. "When I met you, I knew you didn't have anything to offer. I knew it in my bones, but I fell for you anyway. Your confidence was surface, but I didn't know that until I dug deeper. Then it was too late. I told myself it was because you weren't doing what you really loved. And then when you found it..." I shake my head. "Man, when you found it right in front of my eyes, I was blown away. I believed in you, but you never believed in yourself. You never will."

He sits up during my speech, and a frown creases his beautiful face, his eyes guarded. "You have no idea what I've been through for you. And then you just spit in my face?" He stands and scrubs his hands across his face and into his hair. "You really have no middle ground, do you? It's fire or ice with you. Every single time."

"What's that supposed to mean?"

"Well, there's Tariq. You've gone all in when a measured response would do. It's not make this series or Tariq will live in the gutter the rest of his life, but that's how you treat it."

I try to speak, but he holds up his hand. "I'm not finished. Let's talk about your own father, shall we? You haven't spoken to the man in a year because of something that happened years ago. You won't even listen to him on what really went down. Because you're so fucking stubborn."

"What really went down? Oh, you're an expert on parent-child relationships now? You're standing at thirty thousand feet and have no idea what went down between me and my father. How could you?"

"You forget I've spent some time with Tariq myself. I know you haven't given your father a chance."

"Get out." My voice is low, but my tone icy.

"Gladly." He marches to the door, and practically swings it off its hinges.

"Hey, don't let the door hit you where the good Lord split you."

He doesn't even turn around.

I slide the bolt in place and sit in the middle of bed, then grab the pillow where Declan just laid his head and smother the crying scream that escapes my throat. His spicy smell is right there in my nose, and I throw the pillow across the room which isn't very far.

I'm nearly thirty years old and felt love for the first time in my life. And I'm glad because if this is what someone can do to you who says they love you, I don't want any part of it ever again.

CHAPTER TWENTY-TWO

When there's no coming back. For real, for real.

I OPEN THE gate to my place just as my phone buzzes. Again. I'm back in my element now, so I answer because I obviously wasn't clear enough before. "You need to stop calling me."

"Kasi."

"Keep my name out your mouth. We're done." When I end the call, I block his phone number. If I had Knox's and Weston's phone numbers, I'd block them too. Then I go inside and pull out my laptop and go to my email, and block him there too, and anywhere else I can think of. I mean this. For real, for real. I am done forever with Declan Everheart.

I text Joy instead of calling because I've lost track of time. I'm not even certain what day it is. *Can I get out of my deal with Flynn?*

She texts me back. *On my way over.*

My hand trembles as I set the phone on the kitchen table. There's some tequila somewhere, and I finally find it in one of the cabinets. I pull it down and take a shot. Joy comes in as I'm pouring my third shot, my hands finally calm.

"Whoa, there. It's nine in the morning." She takes the

shot glass out of my hand and sets it near the sink. "What in the world?"

"Is that it? I could have sworn it was later. It feels like I've been up for hours." Considering I didn't sleep last night, technically that's true.

"Yeah, very true. And while I'm not against a little day drinking once in a while, this is straight tequila, girl. Why are you self-medicating?"

I lay my head on the table and watch the ceiling fan rotate. It's surprisingly relaxing.

"Kasi?"

Oh, right. Real life is calling. "Declan pulled out from talent."

"I know. He emailed me very early this morning."

"Hmmph."

She sits down across from me at the table. "Is that why you want to cancel the whole deal with Flynn?"

"I can't work with Declan. He's still a producer."

"Seems a little rash."

I widen my eyes as much as my tequila-impaired motor skills will allow. Then flip her off.

"Okay, that's one way to take care of business, I suppose. Fuck you too, heffa."

"It's not rash, Joy. I love him, and he broke my heart. How can you expect me to work with him?"

"He broke your heart because he dropped out?"

"Yes. I mean no. Because he chose his father over me. Over his own happiness." I snort and stumble to my feet, reaching for the shot glass. "He called me stubborn."

A wheezing noise comes from behind me, and when I

turn around, Joy is lying out on the bench, holding her stomach. Her pencil skirt has ridden up her thighs and she's kicked off her pumps.

"I'm glad my misery entertains you." I down the shot, and wince.

"Girl. Your picture is next to the word stubborn in the dictionary."

"You're corny as fuck." I hold on to the sink because the floor moves suddenly.

"Sit your ass down before you fall."

I do as she says because I just may fall. I prolly should have eaten something before I started shooting tequila.

Joy stands and gets me a glass of water. "At least drink this before you get a headache. You know better."

I drink the whole glass, then slam it on the table.

"Kasi."

"It was an accident." It was because those aforementioned motor skills have abandoned me.

"Come on." She hauls me to my feet.

"You just told me to sit down."

"I know, honey." She holds on to my waist and walks me to my bedroom. "When's the last time you ate?"

I reach for a coherent memory but come up empty. I shrug and lie down in my comfortable, familiar bed, wishing I'd never gone to stupid San Francisco in the first place.

"HERE, EAT THIS."

I blink. "I was asleep."

"I know, but you need to get something in your stomach. Then take this." She shows me a pill but doesn't give it to me. She knows me so well. I would have downed that thing and turned right over.

"Fine, give me the damn toast." When I'm done, she hands me the pill and another tall glass of water.

When I wake, Joy's nowhere to be found, but my phone is on my nightstand, and she's texted me a message. *I had to go back to work. Lots of meetings today. I'll be back this afternoon.*

I sit up and steady myself before standing and walking to the bathroom where I pee like a racehorse. When I slide back under my covers, I check the time. Then fall back asleep.

The next time I wake, Joy is standing over me and the smell of a hamburger fills my nose. I croak, "I'm not hungry."

"Maybe not, but a nice greasy hamburger will help you."

"I'm not sure I want to take food advice from you. Yanno, your track record and all."

She shrugs and sets the carton on the nightstand.

I close my eyes and roll over.

"My feelings aren't hurt. I definitely would not know. The advice came from someone who would."

I groan and open my eyes, then turn to face her. "I blocked him from my life. That means you too."

"Kas. I'm your friend, but I'm also your agent and lawyer. You can block him from your personal life all you want, but professionally is a different story."

"I don't want to talk about him today."

"Okay, but you're the one who texted me this morning

trying to get out of the deal."

I swing my feet out of the bed and stare at the carton. My stomach grumbles when the smell hits me again. I open the box and take a bite of the hamburger, feeling less thick-headed after I swallow. "I know, but can we talk about him tomorrow?"

"Sure, doll." She kicks off her shoes and hops in the bed, fancy skirt and all. Then turns the television on with the remote. "What shall we watch?"

"Anything but food-related shows. I never want to see another chef again." I take another big bite of my burger, and chew. "No documentaries either." A piece of food flies out of my full mouth. "Sorry."

"Gross."

"I know."

We watch *Pride and Prejudice* and I drift off to sleep when Darcy professes his love in the most egregious way possible. Reminds me of someone I know. Only I can't decide if it's Declan or me.

JOY'S OFFICE IS not my happy place. I don't know what it is, but every time I walk through those glass doors and profes-sional entry, I get hives. Having to dress like a grown-up doesn't help either. I look down at my tan trousers and blue blouse, and frown. Blue used to be my favorite color. Now every time I see anything of the livid blue variety...I shud-der. Turquoise, sure. Navy, no problem. But that blue gray or anything close to it makes me want to cut somebody.

Turns out even though your best friend is your agent and lawyer, that doesn't mean she gets to be at your beck-and-call and meet you wherever you want. Sometimes you have to go into the office, so here we are.

I slump into the seat across from her cherrywood desk. Joy is old school when it comes to her decor, and this desk is shined to within an inch of its life. I don't put my folder on the desktop for fear of all the papers within sliding across it. Instead, I hold the sleeve close to my chest.

Joy clicks on her computer, then turns to me. "I don't know why you brought those documents. I have all the originals, plus they're scanned on my system."

"Because I've been doing some research, and I've made some notations I want you to look at."

She stretches her eyes and bucks them my way. "Okay, Miss Director, let me, your lawyer, see what you have there."

I bite my lip before handing the folder over. She's right. I don't know what the fuck I'm doing. I only know I can't work with Declan.

She reads through, patiently scanning each handwritten note.

I interrupt her concentration, pointing at the comment she's already reviewing. "You see there, that's an out clause, right?"

"Right."

My heart skitters because I can't believe I found something. "Really?"

"Yes. Declan is able to get out if he chooses. Or really if Flynn chooses. He can replace Declan with another producer of his choosing."

I deflate, sinking back in the chair. "I don't want Declan or a producer of Flynn's choosing at all. I have no say so?"

"No. And I explained that to you both last time you were here." She continues turning pages and reading.

When she gets to another section I think will get me out, I point again. "What about that one? I can pull out if there's a material breach, right?"

"Sure. Do you know what a material breach is?"

I worry my lip, trying to remember what I researched on it. "Ummm, something something if he does something something."

Joy releases a heavy breath from her nose. Not quite a snort, but pretty close. A white-collar razz I suppose.

"I guess that means he hasn't done the material breach thing, huh?"

"He has not."

"What if I do the material breach thing?"

"Obviously. He doesn't even need that much to get out of the investment. You'll recall I explained that to you as well. And if you breach the contract, he can certainly pull out, but also sue you."

"Gah."

"This is why I should never take on friends as clients. I've learned twice now that neither you nor Tariq value my advice. You only want me to handle the transactions." Her lips bend into a heavy frown.

"Way to kick me when I'm down."

"Listen, doll, I love you to pieces, but time to put your big-girl panties on and do what you contracted to do. I get that the whole Declan thing is an issue for you, but I'm all out of advice. It's not like I'm doing anything in that department at all."

I mumble because it takes too much energy to open my mouth. "You could have a man if you wanted one."

"Anyway. What are you going to do?"

I raise a confused brow. "Do?"

She looks at the ceiling then closes her eyes. After taking a deep breath, she levels her gaze my way. "Did you not just hear my big-girl panties speech like two seconds ago? I want to know how you're going to fulfill this contract with the Everhearts."

I worry my bottom lip and look anywhere but her. "Can't you just pass instructions between us?"

"You can't be serious."

No, I'm not really. I want to be serious and have Joy pick up my load, but also if I want to be taken seriously in this industry, I can't drop my responsibilities as soon as my feelings are hurt. I'm not sure if I have any big-girl panties, but if not, looks like I'll need to purchase some. "I suppose I'll have to call Declan so we can get this film made."

"Okay, now that's settled, anything else?"

I reach for a thought that's been niggling me ever since Declan spoke it. *You forget I've spent some time with Tariq myself. I know you haven't given your father a chance.* "Declan mentioned something about Tariq and Dad. Basically saying I haven't given him a chance to explain what went on with the investment money. Do you know what Declan was talking about?"

She frowns and draws her brows together in thought. "Not at all. You could always ask him."

I kick her desk with my low-heel sandal, then squeeze my face in pain. Fucking open-toe shoe.

She shrugs and stands. "My eleven o'clock will be here soon. Do you need anything else?" She passes the folder full of papers back to me, and as I suspected, they glide to me easily.

"No." I stand too, shoulders heavy.

"Okay. See you later for dinner. Where you headed? Back home?"

"No. Going to see Tariq."

"Okay, give him a kiss for me." She opens the door to her office.

"I will not. Gross."

Her soft laughter follows me down the hall.

CHAPTER TWENTY-THREE

When her eyes are opened.

T HE LIGHT IN Tariq's eyes has returned, and I grin like a possum eating grapes. Then I frown because that's a saying I heard while visiting Austin.

Tariq sniggers. "I thought you were happy to see me, but now you look mad."

I shake myself and walk over to the bed, laying Joy's kiss on his forehead. "That's from Joy. And I am happy to see you. I can't believe how great you look."

"I suppose it's all relative." He looks at his leg, not in traction anymore, but still in a cast.

"I suppose. And I'm thinking how you look today relative to about a month ago. How do you feel?"

He chuckles, then sets down the Kindle book he was reading. "I feel so much better, honestly. I don't think I'll ever get on a Jet Ski again, but other than that, good."

I sit in a chair next to him and pat his hand.

He laughs, a big one with teeth showing. "What's that for?"

"What? I'm comforting you."

"As long as your face is, I think I need to be patting your hand. What's up?"

"I don't want to talk about it. I came over here for you, not me."

He looks around, then picks up his Kindle and turns it over in his hand. "This will be a short visit then. Unless you want to talk about the book I'm reading, I don't have much else going on."

"That's not true."

"We've already spoken about my health. I mean, I guess I can throw in that I should be up and about in another two weeks." He shrugs. "That's it. I'm out."

"Two weeks. That's outstanding. Sounds like Joy and I need to get busy decorating your new apartment. So far, we've only ordered the bedroom furniture. It should be there next week."

"It's temporary, so don't go overboard."

I hold my hands up in mock surrender. "Wouldn't dream of it."

"If I haven't told you lately, I appreciate you."

I try to smile, but my lips don't want to cooperate. They tremble instead, and a tear suddenly appears in the corner of my eye. Gosh, why am I so emotional these days? "Sorry. I have no idea what's wrong with me. Helping you is the least I can do, Tariq."

"The least you can do?"

"Even if I didn't owe you a shit-ton of money, you're my best friend. Of course I would buy furniture for your stupid apartment." I take a few quivering breaths until they come out smooth. "Fucking Ashley."

"Hey, she's still the mother of my children."

"You're so generous. You always were."

He pulls himself up in the bed so he's sitting higher. "Kasi. I don't know what's going on with you, but I can say that for me, I wouldn't change a thing."

"But…" I wipe at the several other tears that have joined the first one, and now stream down the side of my face. "She hurt you."

"She did, but it was great while it lasted. I know what you and Joy think of her." He huffs, his shoulders shaking. "How could I not?"

"We just didn't want you taken advantage of."

"I get that. And I love you both for it, but neither of you have ever been in a serious relationship. Sure, you had Gregory, but you barely tolerated him. I don't even know how you stayed with him so long."

"He had a huge—"

Tariq sticks his fingers in his ears and commences acting childish. "Da da da da da."

"Boy, stop."

"As I was saying. I wasn't looking to you two for relationship advice. And I don't regret a thing. We had so much fun, and we clicked. She's a great mother."

"You sound like you still love her. Even after everything she's done."

He shrugs. "Like I said, I have no regrets. I don't know Ashley's motivations, but I know how I felt when we were together. I had a great love, and it was perfect while it lasted. Plus, how could I ever regret my kids?"

Good point, I suppose. "Of course you shouldn't regret your children, but I'm struggling to understand how you could just sorta shrug off all the bad stuff that's happened.

You may not know her motivations, but you do know how it all turned out. You gave her everything but got hardly anything in return."

"Wow, you are seriously messed up. Love isn't transactional, Kasi."

My face heats, really burns. Mostly because Tariq has hit a nerve. An idea that's been bouncing around my head since I spoke with Joy. "That's not fair."

"Then why do you look like you're going to spontaneously combust at any moment? I heard about what happened with Declan."

"Of course you did. I would expect nothing less from Joy. If she told you, why did you pretend you didn't know why I was upset when I came through the door?"

He sighs and twists his mouth to the side in thought. "I was hoping you'd tell me about it without me asking. My marriage is over, and I had a hard time with the realization." He waves his hand over his body, proof of his difficulties. "But I had a real relationship for quite some time. I could help you."

I rub my eyes, willing tears to stay firmly inside their ducts. "You've already helped me by telling me your perspective on Ashley."

He smiles, eyes twinkling.

I hit at his leg but pull back before I connect. "You're not slick."

He shrugs, then smooths his smile into a more serious expression. "I'm glad my story helped. What are you going to do?"

What am I going to do? I've mistreated Dec past the

point of forgiveness, I'm sure. I never intended to tie my feelings for him to getting the financing from his father—that's the entire reason I didn't want to get involved—but here we are. "I'm not sure I can fix it."

"Is Declan not worth it?"

I want to scream of course he is. He's worth everything, but thinking it on the inside, and putting it out there on the outside are two different things. "I…um. But what about my project?"

"What about your project? We're talking about Declan, Kas. How do you feel about Declan?"

I suck in a deep breath and blink back the tears threatening to fall again. On the exhale, the words whisper on my breath. "I love him."

Tariq cups a hand to his ear. "Pardon?"

Before I can answer, there's a knock on the door, then it opens. I pull myself together with a quickness. There's been too many emotions spilled in this room today, and I don't want anyone else to be a witness.

Dad's bald head comes through first, then the rest follows. "I saw your car out front when I pulled into the garage."

There's really nothing for me to say. Yes, my car's out front.

He clears his throat. "Anyway, I wanted to stop in and say hello."

My mouth gapes open, and I stare at him with wide eyes. Reggie Blythewood doesn't do casual drive-bys. "Um, hi."

He steps farther into the room, then wraps a knuckle on Tariq's cast. "You're looking better since even when I saw you this morning."

"Doing real good. You coming from golf?"

Dad chuckles. "What gave me away?" He looks down at his breezy gray pants and plaid shirt. Definitely a golfing outfit. "Never mind. I plead the Fifth."

They laugh easily with each other, and my head's on a swivel, following their conversation.

Dad turns his big body my way. "I hear you've been doing quite a bit of travel. I'd love to hear about it."

I just bet he would. "Not a big deal."

The corners of his eyes tighten just enough to give away his anger. Most people wouldn't even notice, but I'm not most people. And just as quickly, his skin smooths out again. "Well, you know where to find me if you want to talk." He walks to the door and before he closes it, he steps just inside the threshold. "It's good to see you, Kasi. I hope you start coming around again even after Tariq leaves." He doesn't wait for an answer. He closes the door with a small snick.

I sit there and study the closed door. I try to check in with my feelings, but they're all jumbled up. Between Dad and Tariq, and of course Declan, I'm not sure what's going on with my emotions.

"Hey, I need to tell you something."

Tariq's tone conveys he's about to tell me something that'll pull that wrong Jenga block. I turn to him and his eyes are weary. "You're about to fuck me up, aren't you?"

He nods. "Pretty much."

"Declan hinted at something the other day. Something about you and Dad. Is this about that?"

"Yep."

I glare at him, then soften my gaze because he's still injured. Still immobile and that's the worst thing a man like Tariq can be. I remind myself what he's been through the past couple months and extend him grace preemptively. Joy would call that growth. "Okay, let's have it."

"What I'm about to tell you can't go outside this room. I signed an NDA and I'm not supposed to say anything."

I blow out a harsh breath, then breathe in a cleansing one. "Okay."

"Your father returned most of my money years ago. I couldn't tell you because that was a condition."

I'm not stunned, because I figured that's what it was. I'm not feeling great either though. "Why?"

"Why did he give me the money? Or why did he swear me to secrecy?"

"Sure, all that, but mostly, why did you tell Declan?"

"Good question. I'm not sure. We were just talking. The whole reason he was there was because the investment, and I guess I just wanted him to know so he wouldn't think you were desperate."

"Why tell me now?"

"You know why."

I glance at the door again and shake my head. This is just like when I was a little girl and Dad broke my favorite bracelet accidentally. He could have easily replaced it but was trying to teach me a lesson. Unconditional love or some shit. I don't think I ever forgave him for that either. He should have learned a lesson of his own back then.

"My father is so dumb."

Tariq raises his brows. "You don't seem mad."

"I am, but I know him. This has gone on for years, but he's so fucking stubborn, he thought he'd teach me a lesson. Stupid man."

The snort that comes out of Tariq is almost comical.

This time I give him my best glare and hold it. I know what he's getting at. I am stubborn and I recognize that more than ever now. Between losing the deal with Melissa and blocking Declan from my life, I've become acutely aware of how my tenaciousness works against me sometimes. I just don't want Tariq to say it.

He withers under the pressure of my judgmental eyes, then frowns. "You are stubborn."

Ugh. "So Dad has you sign an NDA and gives you your investment back—"

"Most of it. He deducted fees."

It's my turn to snort. That's typical. "Okay, most of your money back, and he doesn't want me to know because he wants me to love him anyway. I guess he showed me."

"He maybe didn't get what he wanted, but in his defense, I don't think even those of us who know you so well would have thought you'd carry this grudge so long."

A thought pops into my head, and my skin suddenly pricks with panic. "Did Joy know this whole time?"

"What part of NDA did you not understand?"

Relief is instant, and I slump back in my chair.

"What are you going to do?"

"About Dad? What can I do? You weren't supposed to tell me."

"Are you going to start coming around again?"

"Oh that. I'd already made up my mind that I would

when I saw the two of you together just now. He genuinely cares about you." I put up a finger before Tariq asks his next question. "No, I will not be joining him in his business. That's a hard boundary. He's my father and I love him, but I don't want to work for him again. He's always teaching the wrong lessons and doesn't even realize it. I don't need that kind of strife in my life. Plus, I want to make it in this business without his clout giving me the leg up. I have the talent for it. I need to prove it to him more than anyone."

"Yeah, cause everything's going so well for you."

For the second time this week, I flip off a best friend.

THE DARK PANELING and brass fixtures of the restaurant remind me of Everheart Bar and Fine Dining. I try with everything I have to keep an open mind that Dad's choice of dining establishment isn't a sign of how this tête-à-tête will go. I reached out to him. And as usual, he took over and ran with it, selecting a high-end eatery I wouldn't normally choose. But I'm trying to better understand him, and myself, so I'm gonna let slide a little thing like picking where we eat lunch.

Before the hostess has a chance to open her mouth in greeting, I spot Dad seated at a prime table chatting with the waiter. His face is open and friendly, and I watch their interchange a moment before stepping back from the host stand, into the corner of the entry vestibule, mouth dropped open. Dad doesn't do friendly chatting with waiters. What's happening?

After leaving Tariq's bedside, I had plenty to think over. Not just the stuff about Declan and how incredibly inexperienced I am in real love, but my life in general. The choices I've made to shield my heart where everyone's concerned, including my own parents. I've always recognized some of the traits I inherited from Mom—her no-nonsense, take-no-stuff bluntness. And from Dad with his drive and stubbornness. I'm only now understanding when I attempt to control my life, I end up trying to control everyone around me. Exactly the treatment that makes me run from Dad.

I take a couple of deep breaths, then make my way back to the hostess and smile at her, then point Dad's way.

He spots me on my trek over and offers a toothless smile, but his wariness broadcasts through his eyes. I fix my face hoping to not reflect the same back to him. He stands when I reach the table and leans ever so slightly before pulling himself back and offering a small wave in greeting.

My heart sinks when I realize that the way I've treated him has him acting like he can't even offer his daughter a hug. Not that he hasn't done a bunch of stuff to deserve my cold treatment, but maybe not as much as I thought now that Tariq has clued me in. I pat him on the shoulder, my touch a bit awkward, then sit down across the square table that usually seats four. "Hi, Dad. Thanks for meeting me for lunch."

"You're my daughter, Kasi. Why wouldn't I meet you?"

Okay, so we're delving right in I see. "Well—"

The waiter comes over with two glasses of lavender lemonade, freshly squeezed. "Are you ready to order or do you need some more time?"

My skin heats and I take a sip of the cool drink, then speak under my breath enough for Dad to hear me but not the waiter. I do have some home training. "I'm surprised you haven't already ordered for me."

He doesn't address me. Instead, he turns to the waiter. "We'll need a couple of minutes. Thank you."

That puts a damper on my rising anger. "Did you just thank the waiter?"

He releases an exasperated breath. "Good God, Kasi. I thought the teenage years were over."

"I just. What?"

"I'm happy you're ready to speak to me again. To work out our differences, but I was expecting to have a mature conversation."

Anger flairs deep in my soul, but I refuse to rise to the bait. Lashing out will only prove his point. "You're right. I'm not a teenager anymore. I do want to address our differences. Hopefully we can work them out, but my major complaint is you trying to control my grown life." I take another pull of the lemonade and eye him over the glass. "Maybe I overreacted about the drink, but don't you see how ordering for me is a symbol of the bigger things you want to run?"

He throws up his hands in surrender. "Excuse me for ordering you something cold to drink. Since you were running late, I figured you'd be overheated rushing here."

"Late?" I check my cell phone again just to confirm. "I was right on time."

His shoulders tighten. I imagine he's holding back a casual shrug. "Fifteen minutes before the appointment is on time, on time—"

"Is late. Yes, I recall you saying that." He only said it a bajillion times my entire life. "Look, Dad, let's start over. We have plenty of other mess to talk about. More important things, don't you think?"

He nods, then glances at his menu. "Do you know what you're having? The waiter will probably be back in a moment."

Defeated, I scan the menu. "I'll have the chef's salad."

"That's it? What about a side of steak?"

I have to smile then as the memory of my last parental lunch invades my thoughts. Mom wanted me to have the chef's salad like her, but I was too stubborn even though I wanted it too. Mostly because she was hinting I needed to watch my weight. Here Dad is encouraging me to pile it on.

"Yeah, that's it. It really looks good, and I've been wanting one for a minute."

Once Dad has ordered, he turns his gaze on me. His eyes are serious, but kind. "You have something to say?"

"Why are you trying to ruin me?"

He blinks.

"Don't look so surprised, Dad. You sabotage me at every turn. I got financing for my documentary series in spite of you. Who treats their child that way?"

"Listen, Kasi. There's no reason for you to be out there running around begging people for money. Blythewood Productions has a development deal with a major streaming service. That's all you need."

"That's all you need, Dad. It would be different if you allowed me my own space to make moves within Blythewood, but you don't. Everything has to be under your supervision, and you make all the decisions."

He huffs and crosses his arms across his barrel chest. "Because my name is on the door. Ultimately I'm on the hook to get projects greenlit."

"I get that. That's why I left to do my own thing. You'd think someone like you would get it."

He flinches at my mention of his humble beginnings. Mom brought a ton of family money into their marriage, but he's done well without relying on it. "What I get is that you have a leg up. Why not take advantage of it?"

"I'd happily plunge face first into Blythewood Productions and take advantage of all that means, but I need to have some control over what I do. I can't be smothered. That's why it's better I go it alone."

"Do you have complete control now?"

And therein lies the rub. All roads lead back to Declan Everheart. "No, not completely. Everheart's son is coproducer."

"I believe I heard something about that. How's that going?"

Oh, fuck me. How's it going? I've made a total and complete mess out of everything. That's how it's going. "We've had some bumps, but the footage has been incredible."

"Some bumps, huh? So you'd rather have bumps with a stranger than continue to learn and grow with me?"

I take a deep breath and hold it for a moment. "I've learned and grown with you, Dad. And I appreciate everything you've done for me including paying for all my film education then allowing me to work my way up through the system. I have a ton of experience and that's all thanks to you. It's time for me to use it though." He opens his mouth, but I shake my head. "I'm not saying that I've learned all there is, but I've learned enough to rely on my own mastery now." And on Declan's talent and experience. Dad's right; I don't have to go it alone. Especially when I have someone like Declan willing to prop me up if I only bend a little and accept what he's giving me.

"I wish you would reconsider."

I shrug and take a sip of my lemonade. "Maybe someday. You never know. But in the meantime, I'd love to be able to ask you for advice."

"Well, first I think you should—"

"When asked, Dad. I want to be able to get your council without you trying to take completely over."

He nods and grunts but doesn't exactly agree in words. That'll have to do for now.

CHAPTER TWENTY-FOUR

When he takes a new path.

I TAKE A breath and call Declan's number. After two rings, it goes to voicemail, and I press the end icon so hard, my phone flies out of my hand and lands on my sofa. I have no idea why, but there's a pricking in the back of my eyes. I've promised I'll stop lying to myself. I know why my eyes are pricking. He just sent me to voicemail. Maybe he never wants to hear from me again.

I retrieve my phone and call him again, leaving a voice message. "Hi, Declan. We need to talk about the talent. We probably need to make some decisions this week or we'll already be behind schedule. Everything's booked and making changes will cost money. Okay, call me back." I hesitate before ending the call then put the phone back to my ear. "I'm sure you're completely done with me and I can hardly blame you."

I lay my head on the back of the sofa and stare up at the ceiling. Then I pop back up, grabbing up my phone and unblocking his phone numbers. He can't call me back if he can't get through.

When a return phone call doesn't come in a reasonable amount of time which I deem as about five minutes, I drag myself to the guest room slash office, and power up my laptop. I unblock Declan there too and when I'm done, I sit back in my office chair and smile. A real smile with teeth and everything. Suddenly I feel lighter.

When an hour passes without a return phone call, I pace my living room. Declan better not have torn a page from Dad's playbook and is trying to teach me a lesson. This is business.

There's a tickling at the back of my neck. Who am I to talk? I blocked his number, and we couldn't conduct business for over a week.

My phone buzzes, and I dive for the coffee table. "Hello." The damn thing is upside down. "Hello?"

There's no reply, then a breath travels through the phone and straight to my heart. "Kasi?" His tone is lyrical and thrumming. Or maybe I've missed it so much, his voice is music to my ears.

"Yes, hi. I dropped the phone."

"Oh okay. I was, uh, in a meeting when you called."

A meeting? Since when does Declan have meetings? It's none of my business, but I sorely want to ask him. "Thanks for calling me back."

"Thanks for unblocking my phone number so I could."

Ouch, I deserved that though. "I apologize for that. We have a movie to make and that was immature."

His end is quiet.

"Are you still there?"

"Yes." His voice is low, almost a whisper.

I grip the phone and close my eyes. Tears slide down my face, but I don't make a move to wipe them. I only sit there and listen to Declan's light breaths and my own pounding heart. When I realize neither of us is going to speak, I clear my throat. "We should probably get together on next steps."

"I'll be there tonight."

"You will?" My heart takes flight, and my smile is way too wide, stretching my face to a painful degree.

"Yes. I'm staying at the Georgian. I'll text you when I get there." His voice has turned cold and businesslike.

I clutch my chest as my heart dives back into my body, deflating into its former self. I muster a smile so he won't notice my disappointment. "Okay."

He disconnects the call without a parting goodbye.

I sit there in my misery, gaping at the background picture on my phone screen. It turns black, and I stare at my darkened reflection. I'm not sure what I expected when Declan called me back. But the coldness when he told me he was staying at a nearby hotel definitely wasn't it. And now I have to face him in the flesh after confessing a small hope to him on his voicemail and him ignoring it completely. I'm not sure how I'll manage, but for the good of this movie, it's time for me to get it together.

I SIT ON a bench on the sandy strip of land between the PCH and Ocean Avenue, and stare across the street at the Georgian. The boutique hotel has been a mainstay here for nearly a hundred years. And it's blue because of course it is. I squeeze my eyes shut but the color is singed on my soul.

Even though the hotel is a five- or ten-minute walk from

my little place, I hardly ever notice it. Well, I'm noticing it plenty now. I have no idea which room Declan's in or even what floor but there are only a few to choose from. I gawk at one of the windows as though I know that's where he is. That window is pulling me, but I dig my shoes firmly in the sand. If he wanted me in his room, he wouldn't have asked me to meet him in the veranda restaurant. Before I go, I survey my outfit and shoes, ensuring I haven't made myself all wrinkly and unpolished on the walk over. Then I backtrack to the crosswalk and hold back for the light to turn. There's already a family with two little kids waiting. On the other side, there's an older couple doing the same. When the lit-up red hand turns green, we exchange sides of the street.

I stroll down the sidewalk like I don't have a care in the world. Fake it till you make it, right? There's a driveway in between me and the blue-and-white-striped awning covering the veranda. And under that awning sits Declan, looking finer than any man has a right to. He's shaved completely and let the top of his hair grow out just a bit to reveal lush curls. He's wearing royal-blue trousers, and a sky-blue shirt, and my heart clenches hard enough that I stop in my tracks. He's wearing my favorite color. Does that mean something? Please let that mean something.

He raises a tumbler of clear liquid to his lips, and I have to close my eyes to break the image before I sprint to him, and vault over the iron fencing bordering the restaurant. Before I can think of doing anything remotely close to that, I need to come clean and admit my bad behavior. It doesn't matter if he forgives me or not—well I hope he forgives me—but I owe him a huge apology for my behavior. I won't even begin to wish he might take me back. Not after this last blowup, culminating after a series of blowups.

A horn blares, and I turn to face a delivery truck trying to move from the driveway to the street, but I'm standing in the way. I hurry across, but when I find Declan again, he's standing. And looking at me. I'm still not close enough to gauge his mood, especially with the darkening sky.

I get my feet moving again and make it to the few steps leading up to the door of the hotel. I watch Declan the entire time.

He's still standing, watching me.

When I make my way through the hotel and back outside to the veranda, he's still standing. "Hey." His eyes are unreadable and that unnerves me because I usually can read him.

I grip my hands tight because the adrenaline has me shaking. "Hi."

We both sort of lean in at the same time, hesitant, and he pecks me on the cheek, then moves quickly away.

I could certainly be imagining it, or maybe it's wishful thinking, but there's so much heat in that kiss, my insides light on fire.

He waves his hand at the chair opposite him. "Have a seat." His tablet sits on the table open to our budget. He's all business when he folds himself into the chair, his back facing the beach and the setting sun.

The last time we were here, in Santa Monica, having dinner together, we watched the sun set into the Pacific side by side. He marveled at the beauty. I watch it now because it never gets old to me even though I've witnessed it my entire life. "Do you want to trade so you can see the sunset?"

He thins his lips, then shakes his head, a pained look in his eye.

Water wells in my eyes, and before I can do anything about it, a tear slips down my face.

"Don't."

I release a quick gust of air, then take some breaths and blink back the rest of tears. I'm truly not good at this love mess.

The waitress comes before I can reply and thank goodness she does, because I have zero idea what to say. Theoretically knowing you need to apologize is one thing. Getting the deed done is entirely different.

Declan picks up the menu, then looks over it at me. "Do you know what you want?"

I paste a smile on my face and look up to the woman. I've been here before, although it's been years, but they probably still have the basics. "I'll have the grilled salmon, please.

She smiles back, and nods.

Declan orders the seared ahi salad, and the waitress takes our menus and leaves.

He turns the tablet around to me and points at the first line item, but never looks up, speaking but I'm not listening.

I observe the top of his beautiful head, bent in review. I stare at his smooth jaw, square and free from the beard I'd grown so used to, moving as he talks. I study his long fingers, tapering at the tips, moving around the keyboard.

"Kasi?"

"Sorry, what?"

"Which part?"

I shrug. "All of it, I guess."

"You didn't hear anything I said?"

I shake my head.

The waitress returns with more water, and Declan asks her to send the food up to his room.

He stands and reaches for my hand. "We need to talk."

WE RIDE THE elevator in silence. My conviction turns to nervousness. I scan my memories for a time I've ever felt so vulnerable and come up short. When we step off, there's a placard above the room number—Clark Gable. I shake my head because Declan is true to form. Of course he booked the best suite in the hotel.

By the time we step into the room, I've regained my confidence. "Declan, I'm really sorry."

He raises a brow, recently manicured, and bends his head forward ever so slightly.

I look around the suite and decide on the love seat in the farthest room. I'm not sure how to qualify this suite. Second living room? The room with all the views? The room on the opposite end of the bedroom? That's the one. I want my head clear while we hash this out and definitely don't want thoughts of rolling around with Declan in that king-size bed. He's right. We need to talk.

He follows me but stretches his length on the chaise lounge in the corner. All of the furnishings, the carpet, even the drapes, are in shades of blue and gray.

I'm sitting in my own personal fun house right now, distorting all my thoughts. I squeeze my eyes shut and try to form a cohesive idea, rubbing my temples. "Listen, I realize things have sucked between us."

He snorts.

I open my eyes and glance at him. He's more relaxed now, his expression smooth. The sky is almost completely dark behind him, but the street below is so well-lit, his features are clear.

"Yes, that's probably understating it. But the thing is, I'm not sure what to say. I am sorry that I was so upset and hurt about you pulling out from the film, but I realize now that I shouldn't take your decisions so personally. For me, it was a rejection."

He sits up, places his feet on the floor, and leans forward, his forearms resting on his thighs. "I'm listening."

I look away from the hurt in his eyes and my stomach clenches. It's killing me I put that feeling there. But I turn back and meet his gaze. It's the least I can do. "I thought I was helping you, but what I was really trying to do was control you."

The look in his eyes changes from hurt to surprise. He doesn't say anything though, expectation creasing his expression.

"Yes, I realize how ironic that is. I mean, I do now. I didn't then. Then, I only saw us as kindred spirits. I was fighting against a father who wanted to order my steps. And I saw that for you too. To me, your father was stifling your real talent, and I hated it."

He nods and shifts on the chaise. "But we aren't the

same, Kas. I loved working for Dad. My only regret was not being his right hand. I never blamed him for that though."

"I get that now, Dec. Honestly, I do. I was lost in a haze of wanting you to be happy which I thought meant railing against your father. That first day, when we were in the Sacred Valley, and you'd climbed that mountain then savored the alpaca jerky, it was so clear to me what you should be doing with your life. I made it my mission for you to see it too, no matter if it might cost you your family."

He nods. "Because you bulldozed straight ahead in your own relationships."

"Exactly, but that's not even what I needed to do with my own father." I stand, intending to move closer to him, but thinking better of it, I walk over to the window and look down at the traffic below, the beach and water beyond hidden in the darkness. "My relationship with my father was different than yours. But even with Dad, I should have talked to him. I'm not sure we'll ever agree completely on the path I want to take, but when I stopped communicating with him, he took matters in his own hands to get me back in the fold. It was misguided, but I understand a little better now that we've talked."

"I suppose a lot has happened since we last spoke." He rubs his clean-shaven jaw. "A shame I missed it."

"That's for sure. Tell me what happened in San Francisco."

"If you hadn't broken up with me and completely blocked me from getting in touch with you, we could have talked about it."

I sigh. "I know, Dec. I said I was sorry."

"You do realize that sorry doesn't erase everything, right? This was… I don't have words, but I know I don't want to ever feel it again."

Those words are a gut punch. It's not like I don't deserve this rejection, but fuck. "I understand. It hasn't been fun for me either. I was wrong for not communicating, but I was deeply hurt. And why have me fly all the way up there just to stomp all over my heart? You could have done that over the phone."

"I didn't know until you got there. My father—"

"Yeah, I already know about your father. His opinion means more to you than I did. I get it."

"That's not what happened."

"Tell me what happened then."

"I will. But first tell me how you're feeling right now."

I study him because I'm not sure what he's asking.

He leans forward even more, his brows furrowed. Waiting.

"About us?"

He still doesn't respond, only stares, almost willing an answer from me with his eyes.

"I…I'm sorry for how I responded."

"You already said that. I accept your apology. Anything else?"

I check in on my feelings and beg the tears to stay banked. I understand what he wants now, but I'm afraid to give it to him. I've hurt him so much that I couldn't blame him for another rejection now, but damn if I want that in my life. My heart races, pounding in my ears. I close my eyes and concentrate on my breathing. When I open them, he's patiently waiting. "I love you, Dec."

"Don't say it if you don't mean it."

"I love you, Declan Everheart."

He smirks and stands. Then smiles.

I launch off the couch and stumble into his open arms. His spicy cologne smells like home, and I nuzzle my face into his chest, inhaling as much of it as I can. "I've missed you so much."

"Me too, Kas. And I'm sorry too for the hurtful things I said. You almost killed me this time though." He kisses the top of my head.

I squeeze him tighter, and my body finally relaxes. "I know. I'm working on trying not to regulate everything and everyone around me. Maybe attempt to be a little less stubborn too."

His chest vibrates, and I pull my head back, and look up. "What's funny?"

He sits down on the chaise lounge and pulls me down with him, wedging me against his length. "What work have you been doing?"

"Well, for one, I had lunch with Dad a couple days ago."

His eyebrows shoot up. "Is that right?"

"Yes, it is. And for two, I just made this huge grand gesture of apologizing and accepting you for who you are because that's who I fell in love with. Jeesh."

"You want a cookie?"

I slap his chest but snuggle closer. The hard planes of his chest and strong arms have been missing in my life for too long. "No. Just you."

"Well, good thing because looks like you're going to be

stuck with me for quite a while."

I sit up as best I can on this narrow piece of furniture, but enough to peer at his face. "What do you mean?"

He releases a long breath. "About my father. What I was going to tell you a minute ago." He bites his lip and creases his forward. "I'm trying to figure out how to tell you this without causing you immense guilt or scaring you to death before I can explain."

"Okay, you're already scaring me. What did Flynn do?"

"When you came to San Francisco, all the stuff was going down with Knox. Dad is always on edge, but I've never seen him like that. But he was also upset about what happened with you. What you told him. So he said if I went through with it, he'd pull the money from your project."

I gasp and nearly fall off the chair.

Dec's there to stop me from falling, pulling me back into his arms. "You know what I chose. If I'd told you why I was turning down the talent part, it would have been a big thing. I had no idea not telling you would be an even bigger thing. I couldn't even walk it back because you blocked me from your life. Then I was just pissed."

I barely mumble, "Rightfully so."

"Yeah. So I stewed for a little while. Finished the competition, with Dad by the way, not Knox. He dropped out right in the middle as planned. We lost which was fine with me, but Dad was furious. He blames Knox for everything, but he'll forgive him some day."

"Wow. That's a lot. I'm so sorry, Dec."

He kisses my forehead and pulls me close again, wrapping his arms tightly around me. "Yeah, so anyway, I quit too. Knox inspired me."

That last sentence should have me over here panicking, but just because Flynn has pulled out from my project, I'm proud of Dec for making his own decisions. "That's okay. I'll find the money somewhere else." Maybe I'll ask my father. A week ago, that wouldn't have even crossed my mind.

"I've already replaced his money, Kas. We're still a go."

I blink, but he can't see my stunned expression because my face is still firmly pressed in his chest. "How?"

"I have investments and savings. When you called earlier today, and I said I was in a meeting, I was at a closing. I sold my house."

I elbow him to let me up. My voice raises before I can help myself. "You did what? I would never ask you to do that for me."

He shrugs. "I didn't do it for you. Well, not just for you. I did it for me. I'm unburdened to follow the dreams I didn't even know I had. You helped me with that." He strokes a thumb across my chin and looks at me with so much love.

I let the tears fall. This time they're tears of happiness. We're going to have such a wonderful life.

CHAPTER TWENTY-FIVE

When the mountain's call is too strong.

I WATCH THE video feed as Dec climbs the tree with Nina. She's local here in New Zealand and is really giving Dec a run for his money. I switch to looking with my own eyes, but they've disappeared into the foliage. Thank goodness for Neal. He knows how to get the perfect shot.

Dec complains to Nina that the tree is really up there and starting to get more flimsy the higher they go. I listen to him through the feed. "Are you sure they're up here?"

"I'm sure, Chef. Wait until you have these berries."

Neal zooms in on Dec's face and skepticism is written all over it. He mumbles, "These better be some transcendent berries."

"What's that, Chef?"

He doesn't speak again but keeps climbing. And grunting. Thankfully the temperature is so nice down here in December so at least he doesn't have that to contend with like when we were in Norway last month. What a clusterfuck. I shake my head at the memory of Dec falling off that snow mobile. I nearly had a heart attack.

"These are the sweetest berries I've ever eaten." Declan is hanging from a limb, no ropes or harness for his safety, marveling at fucking berries. I want to yell up to him to pay attention, but I've learned the hard way, those types of outbursts aren't welcome. He gathers plenty, placing them in a bag hanging over his neck and shoulder, then follows Nina down.

I don't release a breath until he's safely back on the ground. Then I suck in another to give the direction. "Cut. Check the gate." This is wholly unnecessary because Neal is the best cinematographer I've ever worked with and that'll be the first thing he does. It's routine though.

Declan fist-bumps me. "That was incredible." His eyes are alight and a huge smile spreads across his face.

It's my turn to smirk. I rarely see it from him anymore so now I've adopted his signature facial expression. "You need to be more careful."

"I was. That's a lot harder than you think."

"No, it looks hard."

He laughs and pulls me into a tight hug, then kisses me fully on the lips. We gave up being professional and hiding our relationship after the first official shoot in Hawaii.

I step back and scan the crew. Nobody's paying us any attention. "Okay, everyone. Next setup is on the beach. See you in the morning." They all have their call sheets so I've stopped reminding them what time too after I was on the receiving end of a few harsh stares.

Dec slings an arm over my shoulder, and we walk to the hired car. We share an assistant so she drives us both.

Sarah jumps out of the car as soon as we come over the hill. "How was it?"

"First things first. You feeling better?"

"So much better. I can't believe I got that sick."

It was good that she vomited up whatever she ate right away, even if the rest of us didn't enjoy watching. "I'm happy you're okay."

She shrugs and pops the trunk. "Did you get everything you wanted?"

I glance at a smiling Dec, then back at Sarah. "Oh yeah. A little more than we wanted to. Declan's pants came all the way down after getting stuck on a branch."

Sarah gasps, then slaps her hand over her mouth. "I can't believe I missed that." She's always quick with the quips where Declan is concerned. She's had plenty of material for her entertainment since we started this project in earnest.

Declan puts his backpack in the trunk. "In my defense, I was so pumped up on adrenaline, I didn't even feel the tug. I wondered why everyone was yelling all of a sudden, then the breeze hit my ass."

Sarah squeals in delight. "Oh em gee. It got your underwear too?"

I've been trying to hold it together, but this has got to be one of the funnier bloopers Dec's pulled. "Too bad it won't make the outtake reel because, honey," I bend over, holding my stomach, "whew, he was ass out, beans and frank all over the place."

Dec laughs too, then pulls me close. "Let's get back to the hotel because my beans and frank want a little compensation."

Dec's breath caressing my face never gets old. As soon as the heat from his words hit my ear, I'm ready to knock Sarah out of the way, and speed back to the hotel. "Okay, Sarah, we're ready."

Looks like Dec still has a few smirks left in him.

WHEN WE GET to the hotel, we slog our stuff upstairs, and my phone buzzes in my pants pocket. My hands are too full to fish it out, so I wait until we enter our room.

"Who is it?"

"You sure are nosy."

Dec shrugs and pulls the soft shirt that hugs his muscles right over his head in one motion.

I contemplate ignoring the phone altogether, but of course it could be someone from the crew. "It's my father."

"Oh, okay."

I text Dad back. *Just finished shooting for today. About to take a shower and get some food.*

Okay, let's touch base tomorrow.

Sounds good.

I put the phone on the table and unbutton my own shirt. "He just wanted to run something by me for his movie." I still refuse to join Dad's company, but I don't mind consulting here and there. We think so much alike that it ends up me confirming whatever he wanted to do anyway. He's still full of shit, but none of that bothers me anymore.

"You coming?"

I bite back a laugh. "Not yet, but I hope to soon."

Dec can't do anything but shake his head at my corniness.

"Whatever. You love me."

He walks over, his eyes serious but soft, and presses his bare chest against my naked breasts, then dips his head down to capture my mouth, kissing me deep and slow. He tastes of sweet berry juice, and smells of the sun and the island breeze. "I do love you. So much."

I bite my lip because sometimes when he expresses himself like this, I want to cry from so much excess emotion and pure joy. I take a breath. "I love you so much too."

He takes my hand and walks through the bedroom to the bathroom.

I gladly follow.

Dec eyes the shower then the tub. "Which one do you want?"

I think for a moment of how I want him right now. My blood heats just thinking of the various scenarios. "Quick shower now, make love in the bed, wash up, go eat, then a nice long bath."

He nods and flips on the faucet in the shower, then drops his pants and underwear.

Another thing that never gets old? Gaping at Dec's hot body. His muscles have lengthened and strengthened even more since we've been going around the world on our adventures. I run my hands over his tattooed chest and stomach, dipping over and in the ridges of strong muscle. "Okay, maybe not a quick shower. I need you now."

While I'm preoccupied with feeling him up, Declan reaches for the buttons on my pants and the fabric drops to the floor. He reaches for my breasts, and my breath catches from his tender touch.

I hurriedly snag a finger in the side of my panties and tug

them off.

Dec circles a finger around one nipple and bends to take the other in his mouth.

I put a hand on his chest. "Let's at least get in the shower first." We've been filming all day, and I'm sure my body is stained with sweat and whatever else I brushed up against out in the thick underbrush of the forest we were in today.

He grins, but his eyes are glowing, his pupils wide.

When Dec opens the door to the shower, I dip in and allow the warm spray to pound my skin. The harsh water relaxes my muscles, tired from today's exertion. If I'm this tight, I can imagine how Dec might be.

I move over and share the stream with him although I'm getting a bit of a cold breeze from the backside. "Let's just wash real quick. My ass is cold."

That brings a chuckle from his throat. "Then we better face away from each other and wash ourselves."

I know exactly what he means. If he touches me or even looks at me too hard with desire in his eyes, I lose all my sense. I soap up my washcloth and rub and scrub as quickly as I can, but Dec beats me as usual. Even though he's taller, I have more body to cover. Plus, he doesn't have the washcloth step.

When I dry off and make it to the bedroom, he's sitting in the middle, his back against the high wooden headboard. His dick is already standing straight up, condom on, and my mouth actually waters. Fuck, I have it so bad for this man. I do my best sexy walk, then basically hop, skip, and jump onto the bed, and straddle him. Then bend my head to put my mouth on his.

His skin is still warm and damp from the shower, and my hands glide easily over his shoulders and down his chest. He nips at my bottom lip, then draws it into his mouth, with a delicious suck. I grind against his erection, careful not to let it slip inside yet. I want to work myself into a frenzy and devour him until I can't remember my own name. Dec must feel the same because he maneuvers his hips just so, until we're not lined up, then grasps my waist in strong hands, holding me in place while he goes to work on my neck. When he nibbles the place right behind my ear, I squirm, but he's got me, secured to the tops of his thighs.

I smile, a wicked grin, because he may know how to drive me wild, but I've had time to study his body, and I know where to lick and suck to make him lose his carefully cultivated control. I kiss down his neck in turn, then lower until I reach a nipple, and flick it with my tongue just so.

Dec bucks against me, sliding his hands down to my hips again, grabbing big handfuls. "Kasi." A warning, but it's too late. I lick circles around the hard nub then blow cool air. He flips me on my back before I know what happens and kisses me urgently, settling between my legs. I reach between us and guide him to my entrance, urging him in. He pushes ever so slightly, and the feel of the pressure sends heat down the walls of my pussy to greet him. He groans, "Kas," and pushes farther until he's seated all the way in. I wrap my legs around his waist, giving him better access, and he buries his head in my neck with another groan before sliding back out, then in again, but with greater force this time.

Then we're moving against each other, our bodies melding. He grabs my shoulders for leverage, and I put my hands on his ass, pulling him deeper, hitting my clit just right. "Oh my God, Dec, I'm coming." I slam against him and grind, my orgasm vibrating around his dick, my luscious relief succulent. He stills and lets me rub it out, but when I've come down, he moves again with renewed energy. He sits back on his knees and lifts my legs over his shoulders, pounding into me while staring into my eyes. "You are so fucking beautiful." The roughness of his voice and casualness of his cussing has me breathing heavy again, arousal heightening. I grab his forearms and stare right back. "Yeah, you too." He turns his head and kisses the inside of my knee so tenderly, you'd never know he was driving his dick into me below. My blood rushes in my ears, and I reach for my own nipples. It's not enough though, so I move my hand down farther, between my thighs, and rub circles around my clit, applying the perfect amount of pressure. It only takes a couple more strokes from Dec, and I'm coming apart again, but this time when I slam into him, he meets me, and we ride out our release together.

Dec lowers my legs as though moving them through molasses, his motion slow and languid. Then he relaxes into my side, rests an arm across my chest, and lays his head on my shoulder. "I could do this for the rest of our lives." He blinks lush lashes against my neck. "That's right, we can do whatever we want for the rest of our lives."

I snort, but there's no effort behind the action. "Isn't it beautiful?"

Sometimes Dec has to remind himself that he isn't under his father's thumb anymore. That his life isn't planned out by someone else. But the time between comes quicker now.

The more time he spends creating something he loves, the less time he spends worrying he may have disappointed his father too much.

Sometimes I have to remind myself that it's okay to trust and depend on someone else once in a while, even my father with his warped sense of education and enlightenment. Dec makes it so much easier to remember.

I turn to him and pull him close, and we hold each other like our lives depend on it. They don't, but we got this if they did.

Want more? Check out Rowan and Knox's story in
An Acquired Taste!

Join Tule Publishing's newsletter for more great reads and weekly deals!

If you've read book one of The Everheart Brothers of Texas, *An Acquired Taste*, you should know you wouldn't get out of here without a recipe or two. Enjoy!

Farofa ala Chef Declan

4 cloves garlic, diced

Kosher salt

6 ounces smoked pork belly aka slab bacon, chopped

2 tbsp cold butter, separated

2 cups manioc flour aka cassava flour aka yuca flour, coarsely ground

Place bacon in a large cold skillet over medium heat, stirring until fully rendered and lightly browned. Add 1 tbsp of the butter.

Mash the garlic and a few pinches of salt into a paste. Reduce heat to medium-low and cook garlic about a minute. Add flour and stir continuously, 6 to 8 minutes. Turn off heat and stir in remaining butter. Salt to taste.

Yield: 8 servings.

Chef Flynn's Bourbon Figs with Bacon and Chile

5 ounces smoked pork belly aka slab bacon, sliced into ½-inch squares

3 tbsp pure maple syrup

8 ripe fresh figs, halved lengthwise

4 ounces goat cheese

2 tbsp sherry vinegar

½ tsp crushed red pepper flakes

Place bacon in a large cold skillet over medium heat, stirring until fully rendered and lightly browned. Remove bacon and save for later. Pour all but 2 tbsp fat from skillet into a container and save for later. Add maple syrup to skillet and heat over medium-high. Arrange figs in skillet in a single layer, cut side down. Cook about 5 minutes, circulating liquid, until figs are slightly softened. Arrange figs cut side up and place pieces of bacon on the surface of each fig along with a small dollop of goat cheese. Place under the broiler a few minutes until cheese melts. Remove from skillet onto a platter.

Set the skillet over medium heat, add vinegar, and stir into juices. Bring to a simmer and cook, stirring constantly, about 1 minute. Drizzle syrup over figs, then sprinkle with red pepper flakes.

Yield: 8 servings.

Everheart Carrot Tart

Enough flour to roll out pastry

1 (14-ounce) package frozen puff pastry, thawed

½ cup sliced almonds

1 pound multicolored carrots, cleaned and sliced into ¼-inch-thick pieces

1 yellow onion, peeled and thinly sliced

2 tbsp butter

Extra-virgin olive oil, separated

Kosher salt and black pepper

8 ounces ricotta cheese

4 ounces feta cheese, crumbled

Fresh thyme

2 garlic cloves, minced

Chopped fresh parsley and chives

Preheat oven to 400°F. Spread almonds on a rimmed baking sheet and bake until lightly toasted, about 5 minutes. Let cool.

Increase oven to 425°F. On a lightly floured surface, roll pastry into a 10-by-14-inch rectangle. Lightly score a border around the perimeter of the puff pastry about a 1/4-inch away from the edges. Place puff pastry on a parchment-lined baking sheet and prick the pastry inside the border using a fork to prevent puffing in the center. Bake on top rack of oven until puff pastry is lightly golden, about 20 minutes.

Toss carrots with 1 tablespoon of the oil, and season generously with salt and pepper. Place on a baking sheet in a single layer. Roast carrots on the bottom rack of the oven until the edges are golden brown and carrots are still crisp-tender, 15 to 20 minutes.

While puff pastry and carrots are in the oven, use a large pan to melt butter over medium heat and add onions. Cook, stirring, until onions are soft and starting to turn translucent, 1–2 minutes. Reduce heat to medium-low and continue to cook, stirring every few minutes until golden brown.

Blend ricotta, feta, thyme, and garlic in a food processor until smooth. Season with salt and pepper.

Remove pastry and carrots from oven. Spread the cheese mixture onto the puff pastry up to the border and arrange the carrots in a single layer on top, then spread caramelized onions throughout. Bake until the carrots are tender, and the edges of the cheese mixture are golden brown, 15 to 20 minutes.

Drizzle with olive oil and sprinkle with herbs and almonds before serving.

Yield: 8 servings.

Weston's Canelés de Bordeaux

⅔ cup whole milk

4 tbsp butter, separated

1 vanilla bean, split horizontal

1 ounce beeswax

1 egg yolk

¼ cup white granulated sugar

⅓ cup bread flour, sifted

1 small pinch salt

⅛ cup cognac

Preheat the oven to at 450°F. Place a pan on the lower rack to catch any overflow.

Heat the milk, 2 tbsp butter, and vanilla bean to a rolling boil then turn off the heat. Set aside and allow the vanilla to steep.

Melt the remaining butter and beeswax together. Brush the insides of copper canelés molds with the beeswax and butter mixture.

Whisk the yolk with the sugar, salt, and flour. Temper the egg yolk mixture by whisking in 1/3 of the milk mixture, then mixing egg mixture back into the remaining milk mixture. Whisk in the cognac. Chill batter overnight if possible, but not necessary. Pour the batter into the mold up to about a 1/3 of an inch from the top. Bake the canelés for 10 minutes at 450°F then lower the temperature to 375°F and continue to bake for about an hour until they are a very deep, dark brown color.

Unmold the canelés while they are still hot from the oven.

Yield: 6 servings.

If you enjoyed *A Tasty Dish*, you'll love the next book in…

The Everheart Brothers of Texas series

Book 1: *An Acquired Taste*

Book 2: *A Tasty Dish*

Book 3: *Tastes So Sweet*
Coming in August 2022!

About the Author

Kelly Cain is a native Californian but has spent the last couple of decades in Texas, currently residing in the live music capital of the world, Austin. Consequently, most of her books are set somewhere between those two locations.

Kelly writes multicultural romance with determined women directing their own fates, and the swoon-worthy men who adore them. She loves reading most genres but please don't ask her to pick just one. However, she can pick her favorite book boyfriend – Will Herondale.

When she isn't reading or writing, Kelly is most likely using a genealogy site to research her extended family, both old and new. Or cooking/baking something delightful.

She has two adult daughters, and a new granddaughter. Visit her website kellycainauthor.com for more info.

Thank you for reading

A Tasty Dish

If you enjoyed this book, you can find more from all our great authors at TulePublishing.com, or from your favorite online retailer.

TULE
PUBLISHING

9 781956 387254